On the bed lay a woman, her long, loose auburn hair spreading across the pillow.

Walker's body gave a jolt of surprise. Or maybe of primal recognition. *There was something about that hair....*

His mind was still working in slow motion when her face turned toward him.

He froze, his entire being shocked to the core.

It was *her.*

There on the sterile hospital bed lay his delectable Lady Sarah. No longer a young ingénue, but all grown up and sexier than ever, her mouthwateringly curvy body ill concealed under the thin white sheet, her beautiful face pale and fragile, her sensual eyes wide with apprehension.

She gazed right at him.

Without an ounce of recognition.

Dear Reader,

The warm sun, a cool drink and a sizzling hot hero to fall in love with. What could be better summer fun than that? I can't think of a thing I'd rather be doing on a lazy July day than relaxing and indulging all my senses with a sexy Intimate Moments adventure.

Royal Betrayal is a bit of a departure from my usual edgy stories, but one that I thoroughly enjoyed writing. I'll bet you never guessed that I'm a closet historical writer.... But it's true. I've always loved reading historical romances, with their lords and ladies and luxurious aristocratic settings. Finally I got to write a book with all that, and a dynamite mystery, too! What more could a lady...er, author, ask for?

It was such fun working with the other talented IM authors on these contemporary fairy tales! It's not every day you get to invent a whole new country, complete with princes and dukes, lords and ladies, and a dastardly villain or two thrown in for some spine-tingling action.

So get ready to be swept away once again to the Kingdom of Silvershire as my hero, Dr. Walker Shaw, and heroine, Lady Zara Smith, continue the quest to find the true royal prince, and along the way find something even better—true love.

Nina (who dedicates this book to my wonderful editors, Julie Barrett, Melissa Endlich, Patience Smith and Jessica Alvarez. You are a true joy to work with, ladies!)

NINA BRUHNS
ROYAL
BETRAYAL

Silhouette®

INTIMATE MOMENTS™

Published by Silhouette Books

America's Publisher of Contemporary Romance

Special thanks and acknowledgment are given to
Nina Bruhns for her contribution to the
CAPTURING THE CROWN miniseries.

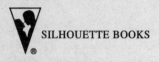 SILHOUETTE BOOKS

RECYCLED PAPER

ISBN-13: 978-0-373-27494-9
ISBN-10: 0-373-27494-7

ROYAL BETRAYAL

This edition published by arrangement with Harlequin Books S.A.

® and TM are trademarks of Harlequin Books S.A., used under license.
Trademarks indicated with ® are registered in the United States Patent
and Trademark Office, the Canadian Trade Marks Office and in other
countries.

Visit Silhouette Books at www.eHarlequin.com

Printed in U.S.A.

Books by Nina Bruhns

Silhouette Intimate Moments

NINA BRUHNS

credits her Gypsy great-grandfather for her great love of adventure. She has lived and traveled all over the world, including a six-year stint in Sweden. She has been on scientific expeditions from California to Spain to Egypt and the Sudan, and has two graduate degrees in archaeology (with a specialty in Egyptology). She speaks four languages and writes a mean hieroglyphics!

But Nina's first love has always been writing. For her, writing for Silhouette Books is the ultimate adventure. Drawing on her many experiences gives her stories a colorful dimension and allows her to create settings and characters out of the ordinary. She has won numerous awards for her previous titles, including the prestigious National Readers Choice Award, two Daphne Du Maurier Awards of Excellence for Overall Best Romantic Suspense of the year, five Dorothy Parker Awards and two Golden Heart Awards, among many others.

A native of Canada, Nina grew up in California and currently resides in Charleston, South Carolina, with her husband and three children. She loves to hear from her readers, and can be reached at P.O. Box 2216, Summerville, SC 29484-2216 or by e-mail via her Web site at www.NinaBruhns.com or via the Harlequin Web site at www.eHarlequin.com.

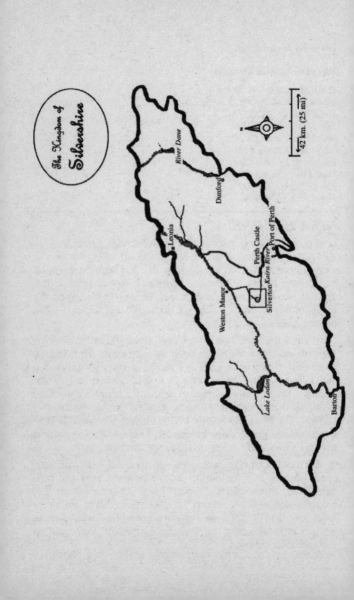

The Kingdom of
Silvershire

Prologue

The Royal Palace, Silverton
In the country of Silvershire
July

The king was dying.

And there was nothing she could do about it.

Panic crawled deep within Dr. Zara Smith. Gently grasping the old man's hand, Zara willed King Weston to regain consciousness and once again shine his wise, kind smile upon her. The smile she'd worked so hard over the past month to put back on his face.

All for nothing.

Why wouldn't he wake up? She'd removed the tumor ravaging his brain days ago. The surgery had gone perfectly. There was no reason the king should still be in a coma.

Not again, she prayed. *Please, not again.*

"Any change?" asked Emily, the day nurse, sending both of them a worried glance.

Zara shook her head, turning away from the trace of pity she saw in the other woman's eyes. She knew exactly what the nurse was thinking. If King Weston died, the country would lose a much-beloved monarch…and Zara would lose her future. Between this and the child's death last year, no amount of medical brilliance or even Lady Zara's aristocratic title would be able to save her career as a doctor. The tabloids would have a field day—again. She'd be forced to go crawling back to her father's estate in disgrace, her plans shattered, her goals crushed. Lord Daneby would never forgive her for besmirching the family name by allowing the king to die on his daughter's watch.

God, Zara would never forgive herself.

Maybe if she—

Suddenly, a deafening roar ripped through the room like the boom of thunder. Glass and wood and metal exploded all around her, sending deadly shards in every direction. Screaming for help, she instinctively launched herself over the old king, shielding his body as a wall of flaming instruments from behind his bed collapsed over them.

Again she screamed, this time from the pain stabbing through her shoulder and side. Something hard and sharp cracked over her skull, and a red-hot shower of pain detonated through her head.

Then all went black.

Chapter 1

Late afternoon, one week later

Dr. Walker Shaw tried to look somber and professional while accompanying His Grace, Russell, Duke of Carrington, the acting regent of the tiny country of Silvershire, as they strolled through the imposing halls of the palace toward the medical wing. After all, he was here on official business. Walker's appearance might be a tad disreputable, and his accent slow and lazy as molasses, but his credentials as a consultant with the elite Lazlo Group were sterling enough to allow him regular admittance to places mere mortals rarely visited. Places such as this.

It was not appropriate to be wearing the roguish grin of a man with nothin' but romance on his mind.

But he simply couldn't help himself. He'd been fantasizing about coming to the quaint island kingdom for seven years now, to track down and charm the exquisitely sexy and mysterious Lady Sarah—with any luck right into his bed—as he'd done so memorably all those years ago at that medical conference in Italy.

Lord willing, she was still living in her native land. And single.

"I understand your specialty is memory loss," Lord Carrington said, yanking Walker from a particularly vivid memory of Lady Sarah's delicious behind bending over a breakfast tray.

"That's right," Walker answered, shifting smoothly into his professional persona. "Mainly as it relates to advancing age and dementia."

As a doctor of psychiatry, Walker had spent the better part of his adult life researching the affliction in the elderly. In his flourishing practice, he had treated patients with all kinds of memory loss resulting from everything from psychological trauma to physical accident to Alzheimer's. Medical research hadn't been his job, it had been his calling.

Well. Until the ugly scandal that had tanked his meteoric career three years earlier put an end to all that.

"I trust it won't matter," Lord Carrington said, "if your patient here is all of thirty-four?"

Walker hardly registered the quick churl of regret at the word patient. He certainly didn't bother to correct it. What the hell. He had moved on. And the life he had now was far more relaxed than the one he'd had as an overworked doctor. He was even doing much of the same kind of work—minus the research, of course. With the Lazlo Group, he consulted on fascinating cases by day and had lots of free time by night. He'd be a fool to miss his old life.

"Not at all," Walker said, turning his attention to his newest assignment. "I understand she was injured in the assassination attempt on King Weston."

"The palace bombing, yes."

"A terrible thing. She's a doctor, isn't she?"

Lord Carrington nodded. "Dr. Zara Smith."

"The renowned neurosurgeon?" Walker asked, vaguely surprised. Though they'd never met, he'd read a couple of her papers in the journals. Intelligent woman.

"She's been treating the king's brain tumor. She sustained her head injury saving his life during the blast."

"How did it happen, exactly?"

"Under the plaster, the palace walls are made of stone," Carrington said. "Several dislodged in the explosion, and one of them caught her in the temple. She remembers nothing. Not even her own name."

Walker thought about the relative merits of being able to forget one's past so completely. There had been days over the past three years he'd have gladly traded places with her. But no more. He'd made peace with his demons.

Besides, not for anything would he give up the memory of a certain auburn-haired young lady stretching across an elaborately carved feather bed, bathed in the glow of the magical Italian dawn. If he couldn't remember her, how could he find her?

"Has Dr. Smith regained consciousness?" he asked, getting back to the point. The sooner he dealt with this, the sooner he could start looking. And hopefully fill some of those free nights he had…

"She woke the next day. Her physical injuries are nearly healed now. It's just her memory that is lacking." The duke's long-legged stride slowed. "That's why we need your help. We're anxious to have her remember as quickly as possible, so she'll be able to tell us more about the bombing. We're

hoping she saw something. Perhaps even the perpetrators."
The future king's eyes sought his. The weight of grave
concern and heavy responsibility were clearly etched in his
young face. "We need to catch these traitors. Silvershire is
already in an uproar over the death of Prince Reginald. And
now this vile attempt on the life of our king. The stability of
my country could very well depend upon the information Dr.
Smith might give us."

Walker returned his gaze steadily. "I understand."

Corbett Lazlo, Walker's boss, had given him a bit of background on the situation before sending him in. Crown Prince
Reginald had been found murdered at his lavish country estate—poisoned by cocaine spiked with digitalis—and there
had been all sorts of speculation in the press about who might
have killed Reginald, and why. At the moment the leading
contenders were the Union for Democracy, a radical anti-
monarchy group that had been steadily gaining political clout
over the past decades, and Lord Carrington himself.

In addition to clout, the UD had also been increasingly accepting of violence as a vehicle for political change. On the
other hand, before the murder, Lord Carrington, although un-
related to the present king, had been second in line for the
monarchy. Now he'd not only moved up to number one, he'd
also hastily married the crown prince's fiancée and then
become acting regent when King Weston collapsed. Two
months from now, due to an ancient, quirky law that mandated
the ascension of the heir to the throne upon his thirtieth
birthday, Carrington would be crowned King of Silvershire.

It all seemed a little too convenient to the country's rumor-
mongers and particularly the local weekly tabloid, *The Inquis-
itor*, popularly dubbed the *Quiz*.

Still, the Lazlo Group's money was on the UD and not the

duke, who seemed sincerely reluctant to become king. It was he who'd hired them to investigate both the prince's murder and the attempt on King Weston's life. But it would be nice to have proof of his innocence in the tangled intrigue. Walker could see why Carrington was anxious for Dr. Smith to recover her memory if he was indeed innocent.

"How long has it been since the bombing?" he asked.

"Just over a week."

Walker pursed his lips consideringly as they passed through a magnificent gilded hall filled with mirrors and tapestries, huge paintings and windows overlooking a formal courtyard garden. A week wasn't all that long. He'd seen cases where it took a year or more for the memories to return. "She's remembered nothing at all?"

"Nothing."

"And your physicians have ruled out any lingering physical injury?"

"Their examinations have been meticulous. Can you help her, Dr. Shaw?"

"I'll certainly try," he said, knowing better than to promise anything. The mind was as unpredictable as the weather in a South Carolina springtime. As they approached the palace medical wing, Walker added, "But there's one thing I need to insist on."

"Anything. Just name it."

"The way I work requires that the subject not be told anything about their former life other than what's strictly necessary. Has anyone talked to Dr. Smith about her background?"

Carrington shook his head. "Just her name, nothing else. Corbett Lazlo already made that recommendation. She hasn't been allowed to watch the news or read the papers, since she has been all over both since the blast. I even managed to dissuade her family from visiting her yet, though it wasn't easy. Her father is the Marquis of Daneby, one of the most influential men and highest ranking nobles in the country."

"I appreciate his cooperation. The reason for the precaution is to prevent false memories. It can be hard for amnesia victims to distinguish between something they are told and a true memory. We don't want to influence Dr. Smith's recollections in any way."

"No, of course not."

They'd arrived in the medical wing, and Walker glanced around at the compact facility, modern and crisply white. The nurses' station was manned by a rosy-cheeked matron named Emily, whose smile lines indicated she was usually a lot more cheerful than she appeared today. There was a short bank of blinking monitors, cozy furniture and a couple of framed paintings of flowers. No signs of fire or debris.

"You've already made repairs from the explosion?" he asked, surprised Corbett would have allowed that.

"Good God, no," Carrington said, indicating a hallway to their right. "The room where the bomb went off is down at the end. We haven't touched anything, since the investigation is ongoing." He swept a hand in an all-encompassing gesture. "Damage was pretty much confined to King Weston's recovery room and Dr. Smith's connecting office and lab. The stone walls are over three feet thick."

"Is that a fact?" Walker hid a smile, recalling a similar comment by the nubile Lady Sarah concerning the walls of the Florence palazzo where they had been staying. And they'd been grateful for every sound-dampening inch. "I'm surprised anyone even heard the explosion."

They arrived at a closed door and Carrington halted. "This is Dr. Smith's room. Would you like me to go in with you?"

"I'm sure your schedule is more than full, Your Grace, so I won't keep you any longer. Thank you for meeting with me."

With a formal nod and an offer of any further assistance, Carrington strode purposefully back down the hall.

Walker watched him round the corner, then he turned to the door in front of him and took a deep breath. After a quick knock, he entered the room and stood in the doorway, his eyes adjusting to the dimness. The lace curtains were drawn, but the sun was setting on the other side of the palace, throwing the interior of the room into a misty sort of soft focus.

On the tidy bed lay a woman, her long, loose auburn hair spreading across the pillow.

His body gave a jolt of surprise. Or maybe of primal recognition. There was something about that hair….

His mind was still working in slow motion when she turned her face toward him.

He froze, welded to the spot, his entire being shocked to the core.

Sweet merciful heaven.

It was *her*.

There on the sterile hospital bed lay his delectable Lady Sarah. No longer a young ingenue, but all grown up and sexier than ever, her mouthwateringly curvy body ill-concealed under the thin white sheet, her beautiful face pale and fragile, her sensual eyes wide with apprehension.

She gazed right at him.

Without an ounce of recognition.

Another stranger.

Lord, who was she kidding? *Everyone* was a stranger to her. Including herself.

She stared back at the handsome man standing in the

doorway watching her with an appalled expression. As though he'd seen a ghost.

Did she really look that awful?

"Sarah?" he whispered. Or rather, croaked.

She swallowed, resisting the urge to pull her unruly hair back in a twist at her nape. "They tell me my name is Zara. Zara Smith. And you are…?"

His startlingly blue eyes skittered up from her body. "You don't remember?"

Something in the way he said it made her think she should. She clutched at the sheet covering her and pulled it a smidgen higher, to the base of her throat. Then shook her head.

"No," she said through a trickle of panic that was beginning to seep through her veins. "Not a thing."

Panic? Or was it embarrassment, over the sudden sexual awareness that engulfed her…?

"Who are you?" she repeated. Then a startling thought occurred. "Are you my…gentleman friend, or—" *surely they would have told her!* "—or my husband?"

The stranger's square jaw dropped. It was *definitely* panic that flew across his face, accompanied by a low curse. "No. I'm not— I'm your— That is, I'm a—" He clamped his teeth together, said, "Excuse me," through them, then turned on a toe and disappeared back through the door. It closed behind him with a soft whoosh.

"Well," she whispered aloud, feeling uncomfortably like Alice at the Mad Hatter's tea party. "That was very curious. But then, everything's curious these days."

Not the least of which was that she could quote passages from Lewis Carroll but not remember her own name.

She squeezed her eyes shut, wondering who the stranger

was. And why he'd seemed so upset. Was he the consultant Dr. Landon had mentioned? She was certain he'd recognized her. Why hadn't he said anything? And why had he called her Sarah, when everyone insisted her name was Zara? What was this all about?

Her nerves hummed with tension. She wasn't afraid, exactly. Not for her safety. Everyone had been very kind, especially Dr. Landon and Emily. But nobody would tell her a flipping thing. She wasn't even allowed the morning papers.

She despaired of ever knowing who she was.

Fighting the hot tears she felt just below the surface, she focused her mind instead on the stranger. He was American. He hadn't said much, but she'd recognized his accent, slow and smooth, like spun honey. *Southern*. How did she know that? Had she been to the US? She tried to think, but nothing came to her. Except the face of the man.

He even looked American. Though very nicely tailored, his gray wool suit had a rebellious cut to it and his white shirt was defiantly cotton, rather than silk. And despite his too-long wheaten hair, his shadowed, angular jaw and those piercing blue eyes that looked like they'd seen more than most men cared to, his face had an open, sincere quality to it that European men's lacked, especially the blasé, sophisticated men with whom she came in contact.

Her eyes sprang open at that little insight. It was the very first personal revelation she'd had since waking up a week ago with bandages wrapped around her head. She smiled. A small triumph, but huge nonetheless. Could this be the beginning of remembering?

Suddenly, there was another knock and the door swung open. It was the American again. He stood there in his James Dean suit, hands on lean hips, a muscle popping in his jaw.

"I'm Dr. Walker Shaw," he said, almost angrily. "I'll be treating your amnesia."

She sucked in a breath. "You?" The word just jumped out. She hadn't meant to sound so incredulous. Or so disconcerted.

"Yes, ma'am," he responded. "And there're going to be a few rules." He raised his hand to tick off fingers. "First—"

"You're a doctor?" she interrupted, sitting up on the bed. She tried for authority, but it wasn't easy with her hair falling down about her shoulders and the rest of her covered only by a lace dressing gown.

To which his eyes immediately dropped. His mouth worked for a second before he jerked them up again.

"I'm a psychiatrist," he said. "Specializing in memory loss. You should know I'm not licensed to practice in Silvershire, so I'm here only as a consultant, at the request of…your government. If you have any objections to working with me, please say so now and I'll—"

"Can you get my memory back?" she cut in, filing away his hesitation over who'd requested his services, to think about later.

"I don't know," he said, and glanced away. The muscle in his jaw popped again. "There are a lot of factors—"

"Yes, yes, I know all about the factors." She waved away his speech irritably. She'd heard it at least a dozen times a day for the past week. At least he'd been honest. All of the others had bent over backwards to reassure her the memories would return. Sooner or later…

She sank back on the bed, pressing her temples between her fingers, rubbing at the beginnings of a headache. The pain in her head had been ferocious for the first several days, but had slowly receded as her wound healed. She'd barely felt it today. Until now.

"What's your methodology?" she asked through the throbbing.

His brow raised slightly. "I was about to get to that when you questioned my credentials."

"I'm sorry," she murmured. "I didn't mean to—"

"Don't apologize. You have every right. The fact is I'm not allowed to practice medicine here, and you should run anything you're uncomfortable with by your regular physician, Dr. Landon. I'm only here to suggest a possible course of treatment. Anytime you want out, just say the word and I'm gone."

"I appreciate your candor," she assured him. "But what I want is to remember my life. If you can help, I'm willing to do whatever you ask."

His bald gaze held hers, and for some unfathomable reason she felt herself blush.

He cleared his throat and looked away. "Yes, well, as to how I work…I'd say fairly casually. The only thing I'm adamant about is that you must remember everything on your own. You'll get no help, or hints, that could just as easily throw you off."

She closed her eyes and rubbed her throbbing forehead. "Ah. That explains it." Why no one would tell her anything.

"Do yourself a favor and don't try to cheat. It'll only hurt your recovery in the long run. And you'll never know if those memories are real or fantasy."

"I understand."

"Meanwhile, if you feel well enough, in the morning we'll walk around a little and hope that something clicks. Oftentimes you'll see something, or hear something, or smell something, that triggers your mind and suddenly all your memories come flooding back."

"Smell?" she asked, her lip quirking.

"The sense of smell is the most powerful one we have. A particular smell can bring back things you've forgotten for years, or even decades. A long-ago holiday, the scent of your mother, a different country you've visited…" his deep voice paused infinitesimally "…a favorite lover."

Her fingers stilled on her temples as the word hung in the air between them like one of the evocative scents he'd described. The hairs on the back of her neck prickled, and she reached deep into her mind, searching, searching. For a favorite lover, for his unique scent, for the brush of his hand over her skin. A shiver traced through her body. But the memory eluded her.

She turned to him and his gaze lingered on her, questioning, encouraging. He remained silent, though, until she gave a nervous laugh.

"You've quite a bedside manner, Dr. Shaw."

After a second of surprise his eyes suddenly shuttered, and the spell was broken. "Whatever works," he said gruffly. He reached for the door handle. "I'd like to start tomorrow. You up for it?"

"Absolutely," she said.

"Get as much sleep as possible. If this is your first time out of bed, it'll be a tiring day."

"I'll look forward to a breakthrough," she said with a weak smile, letting her eyes drift closed against the throbbing in her head. When she heard the whisper of the door opening she added, "Thank you, Dr. Shaw."

"See you tomorrow, Zara," he murmured before it closed again.

Or had he said Sarah? Darn, she thought as sleep wafted

over her, she'd meant to ask him about that. Never mind. She'd see him in the morning. She could ask then.

She sighed happily. And for the first time in a week, felt real anticipation for waking up to a new day.

Pounding.

Her head was pounding, pounding. Like a heavy hammer on metal. Great shifting sheets of metal. She was screaming. Screaming and screaming from the pain in her head and the loud screeching of metal sheets grinding and snapping together.

No. It was not her screaming. It was a baby! No. Two babies! Screaming at the tops of their lungs. Hungry. Wet. Confused. Where was their mother? Gone.

Was she their mother? Desperately, she searched her memory. Why couldn't she remember? She felt warm tears on her cheeks, long muddy grass beneath her bare feet. She was running. Running toward the babies.

They disappeared in a blinding flash of purple. Purple and red, with swirling gold symbols spinning down at her from every direction. Crazy symbols. Meaningless. A kaleidoscope? Purple with gold. Red with Gold. Spinning, spinning. Crashing into her. Crushing her. Pounding.

Smothering her. Suffocating.

Suddenly, everything went black.

She screamed again, desperate, clawing at the darkness, and this time she knew it was her own screams. The babies were gone. Gone.

It was just her, screaming in the dark.

Calling out. For someone. Someone… Who?

And where were the babies?

"Help us!" someone screamed, and she bolted awake.

* * *

Zara sat panting on the disheveled bed, sweat beading on her aching brow. "Good lord," she whispered into the silence of the black night. What was happening to her? She'd never had a dream like that before. Haunting. Terrifying.

She gave a strangled laugh. At least she didn't think she had. Who knew? Talk about falling down the rabbit hole.

She slid out of bed and padded to the porcelain sink in the compact but well-appointed WC attached to her room, then changed her mind. Slipping off her uncomfortable night-dress—she hated wearing anything to bed, it made her feel hot and confined—she stepped into the shower.

The pulsing stream of warm water felt heavenly on her ragged body; it soothed her nerves, easing the residual tension in her muscles and the trembling in her limbs. Soon, even the strange throbbing in her head disappeared.

What an odd dream.

She thought about the babies in it, and what it could have meant. Were they hers?

Could she have children? That was something she'd never even considered before now. Surely, if she had children the doctors would not have kept her from them. That would be too cruel.

As she dried herself, she tried to plumb the depths of her mind, searching for a hint. She didn't feel as though she had children. She glanced in the mirror. Her body didn't look like she'd had them. Her breasts were still high and firm, her waist narrow, her stomach flat. Fairly flat. She frowned. She didn't even know how old she was.

With a huff of frustration, she debated for a moment, then gave up and pulled on a fresh nightdress. The nurses wouldn't care if she left it off, but the new guy might.

Speaking of whom, tomorrow she wanted answers. Lots of answers. She'd tell Dr. Dreamy American exactly what she thought of his ridiculous methods. Keeping her ignorant would not improve her memory. It would only make her more irritable.

And frankly, there were other emotions she'd far rather explore around a man like that. She didn't need to know who she was to know how attracted she was to the good doctor. Bad temper and all. The man was a stunner, if a bit of rough.

But first things first. In the morning she'd confront him. Demand to know some basics about herself. So she could stop worrying about whether or not she had children. Or a husband. So she could move on to more important things. Such as strolling around with Dr. Shaw, dredging up her old memories.

And maybe, maybe even making some new ones.

Chapter 2

"Corbett, listen to me. I'm serious. You've got to take me off this case."

"Wish I could, lad. But you know that's impossible."

Walker held his cell phone and listened impatiently as his boss expounded on all the reasons why Walker Shaw was the only person on earth for this job.

"Corbett, that's bull and you know it. There are a dozen or more legitimate doctors who could do this just as well as I can."

"But they don't work for me. That's really the only reason that counts, isn't it? Besides, you're being too modest. You are still a legitimate doctor, even if presently unlicensed. You're also one of the world's leading authorities on memory loss."

Walker snorted. "Yeah. And that and a five-dollar bill will buy me a cup of coffee."

"Do I detect a trace of bitterness?" Corbett's voice was laced with humor. His boss knew damn well Walker was more than happy with his present employment, but that it irked the hell out of him how he'd been unfairly dismissed from his former one.

"What do you think?" he asked dryly. Then sighed. "Boss, please, have pity on me. I'm telling you, this woman and I have a history. A hot and steamy history. For crying out loud, ninety-five percent of the time we spent with each other we were naked."

"Spare me the sordid details, my boy," Corbett interrupted, laughing. "I'm sorry about that. Honestly I am. But—"

"I'm begging, here, Corbett. Don't do this to me. I won't be able to keep my hands off her. You know what happened to my medical career because of a woman. Except this time it'll all be true." He groaned.

"Does Dr. Smith remember you?"

"No," he admitted. Undecided whether to be relieved or offended. That weekend he'd been—

"Brilliant. My advice is to keep your hands in your bloody pockets and concentrate on getting her memory back. Once she does, you're off the case. And I might even be persuaded to give you some time off for good behavior. Or whatever."

Walker could see he was getting nowhere. An unholy stubbornness was one of the many traits that had helped Corbett Lazlo build the most exclusive, sought-after investigative agency in the world. Once he had his mind set on something, God help the man who disagreed.

Up until now Walker hadn't. He'd also never, ever gotten personally involved in a case in any way, shape or form. Because of his past, he'd been scrupulous about that. Hell, he'd never even been tempted. If anything, the opposite. Once burned, and all.

But Zara Smith was…different.

There was something about her that appealed to him deep inside, in a primal, carnal way. It had knocked the air from

his lungs the first time he'd seen her sitting eagerly in the front
row at the paper he was giving at the World Medical Conference in Florence. It had given him the balls to approach her
afterward and boldly ask her back to his hotel room, and had
kept him hard and lusting after her the entire weekend. Then
it had kept the memory of her alive and smoldering within him
for all this time, waiting for a chance to break away from his
hectic schedule and track her down, drag her back with him
to the States, if necessary, and continue where they'd left off.

He let out a long breath. "All right. Fine. It's not like my
reputation can get any more blackened than it is."

"Walker—" Corbett began.

"No, it's okay," he cut him off. "Frustration is good, my
mama always tells me. Builds character in a man."

Corbett laughed. "Call me if you need to talk."

"In a pig's eye," he said, and hung up.

Damn, damn, good goddamn.

Walker strode down the medical wing's stark white
hallway, heading for Zara's room. Preparing himself to see her
again. He'd put it off as long as he could. It was almost eleven,
and he had said he'd be by in the morning, not the afternoon.

He would be cool and distant, he told himself. Ultra professional. Not a single personal thing would pass his lips. And
his lips would stay firmly on his own mouth. Not hers.

He almost groaned aloud at that particular image.

No.

Distance.

No lips. No hands.

Doctor-patient, he reminded himself. He wasn't about to
fall into that trap. Not even for the luscious Lady Sa—Zara.
He had more self-respect than that. Despite Ramona Bur-

dette's accusations. Despite what the tabloid headlines back home had blared.

"Dr. Shaw." A soft female voice sounded from off to the side. He jerked around to see Zara hailing him from a small round table in a sunny room behind the nurse's station.

"Dr. Smith," he responded, scrabbling for neutral professionalism in his nodded greeting.

Her brows shot up and her mouth curved. "*Doctor* Smith?"

He closed his eyes briefly at his unwitting mistake and growled a low curse.

"I should have known that's why I've felt so at home here. I'm a doctor!"

Good job, Shaw. No point trying to put that horse back into the barn. "You can't always trust your feelings," he said, "but sometimes they do turn out to be right."

"Thank you," she said with a grin. "This is starting out considerably better than I expected. Coffee, Dr. Shaw?"

"No, thanks," he gritted out. "Let's get going."

"By all means." Zara rose and trailed him out of the room. "Don't feel too bad. I was going to make you tell me anyway. This just saves us time and probably a lot of arguing."

"I wouldn't have told you," he groused, then stalked down the hall toward her room. But he realized that was the last place he wanted to be with her. He turned abruptly. She almost ran into his chest, and he barely resisted grabbing her. To steady her.

"Yes, you would have," she said quietly. She was wearing some soft, silky thing the color of ripe peaches, which made her amber eyes mellow, like leaves in a Shiloh autumn. She reached for him. Almost had her hand on his arm.

He stepped back.

Her chin went up. "And there's one other question you'll answer for me," she continued.

"Oh?"

"Family. I want to know if I have any. A husband. Children… It's just not fair to keep that kind of information from a person." She narrowed her eyes mutinously. "And I don't care about your damned methodology."

At the moment, he didn't, either. He was tempted to tell her everything she wanted to know, and more that she probably didn't. He told himself she wasn't asking about a husband because of him…because, however unconsciously, she still wanted him.

"Very well," he said, making a decision that went against all his own firm rules. And told himself he wasn't doing it because he desperately wanted her to still want him, any way he could get it. "No husband. No children." *Talk about being in denial.* "You do have other family. But they've agreed to stay away for the time being."

"What's the time being?"

He held up his hands. "Enough, now. That's all you'll get from me. No more questions."

"Grump," she huffed.

"I'm not a grump. I'm doing what's best for you." He glanced at her but she didn't look annoyed. She actually looked pleased.

His chest squeezed, remembering the comfortable banter they'd shared in bed. From the start it had been like they'd known each other, been lovers forever. It was one of the things that had kept him thinking about her for so long afterward. How comfortable they'd been together, even as they'd gotten to know each other's bodies.

Hell. He had to stop torturing himself. She didn't remember him, and even if she did, she probably wouldn't want anything to do with him. A professional with her reputation wouldn't associate with a dishonored doctor. And no, she wasn't married, but she undoubtedly had a boyfriend. Carrington hadn't mentioned anyone, but it would be strange if a woman like her didn't have men swarming after her.

She hadn't come looking for him after their lost weekend in Florence, had she? Though she knew very well who he was and where to find him.

"Are you all right?"

He jerked back to the present and found her regarding him with concern.

"Just a bit tired. Jet lag," he lied.

"Mmm. I didn't get much sleep last night, either."

He peered at her face, seeing for the first time the taut lines around her pretty eyes and the corners of her luscious mouth. "Why not? Is there something I should know about?"

She seemed to hesitate for a split second, then shook her head. "No. Just excited to start. I want so badly to remember. It's truly awful not knowing anything about myself."

"In that case, we better get going."

The next hour or so Zara and Walker spent talking to the resident and two nurses on duty, and the medical student who took care of the minimalist but ultra-modern lab. Then they went down and checked out the large, basement-level emergency room, which was also used, albeit rarely, as a private morgue.

She recognized nothing and no one from before this week. Every minute that went by, she got more and more discouraged.

By the way Walker directed the casual conversations, it dawned on her she must be one of the doctors in charge of this facility, working regularly with these people. And yet, they appeared awkward speaking with her. It was obvious what Walker was doing. Showing her familiar places and faces, drawing out facts and bits of personal information from everyone, hoping something would trigger a specific memory in her.

But the only thing it succeeded in doing was convincing her she seldom spoke to her staff about anything other than work. For some reason that depressed her.

"What did I do here? What kind of a doctor was I?" she asked him. Realizing, belatedly, that she'd used the past tense. That depressed her even more.

He shook his head. "Sorry. No dice."

They were standing at a window, gazing out over a gorgeous lawn and garden. An endless expanse of lush green flowed out from the butterscotch-yellow building they were in, canted and bordered in a riot of yellow and white roses, dollops of purple violets and mounds of white carnations. She could almost smell the old-rose and sweet-spicy clove scents.

A memory hovered, so close she could almost taste it. Then it vanished.

With a sigh she pressed her forehead to the pane and glanced sideways at the ornate facade of the building.

She turned to him, puzzled. "Is this the Royal Palace?"

She could see the cogs turning in his head, but he nodded. "Yeah. Do you remember, or is that a guess?"

"A deduction," she said.

A wry smile lifted his mouth. "You're one smart lady. But be careful not to make any assumptions about anything. They could land you in trouble."

"Would I get into trouble if I assumed you'd rather be somewhere else?"

During their time together she couldn't help noticing everything about him. The way his raffish trousers hugged his killer backside and athletic thighs, the way he'd casually rolled up the sleeves on his collarless dress shirt to show off his tanned forearms—and the way he avoided looking at her whenever possible, and always kept a good distance between them.

He cleared his throat and for once met her gaze head-on. "I can say without reservation there's nowhere I'd rather be than with you."

Once again, she found herself blushing like a schoolgirl without exactly knowing why. Except maybe that the intensity in his glittering blue eyes made her weak in the knees. And perhaps that he knew it...

"You *are* my boyfriend," she whispered before she could stop herself. Which made her blush even more furiously.

That muscle in his jaw popped. "No. I'm not."

"We know each other well, though, don't we?" she demanded in a hushed voice. "Close colleagues, or—lovers." She slapped a hand over her mouth, mortified. What if they weren't? If there was any doubt about her attraction to him before, there was none now.

The muscle popped twice more. "Of course we're colleagues. I'm aware of your work, and I imagine you've heard of mine. But you live in Silvershire and up until recently I was in the States. Those distances would hardly be conducive to...a relationship. As appealing as the thought might be."

The hand on her mouth shook slightly as she stared at him, sifting through the wealth of information contained in his denial. Except, it wasn't a denial at all. And she didn't believe him anyway.

They'd been lovers. She was sure of it.

If only she could remember.

She turned away. "I'm sorry. I didn't mean to make you uncomfortable."

"Zara." His hands gripped her shoulders. Turned her back

to face him. She caught a whiff of something in the air…musky and masculine. He dropped his hands and took a step backward. "You're my patient."

"You said you were only a consultant," she reasoned.

"And you're splitting hairs. We'll talk about it again when you have your memory back. If you still want to." With that he walked away, glancing over his shoulder. "Coming?"

"Do I have a choice?" This was too frustrating. "Isn't it lunchtime soon?"

"Almost. There's one more stop I want to make first."

Reluctantly, she tagged along after him until they came to a room with two guards at the entrance. They seemed to know who she and Walker were, and one knocked on the door. They entered a room occupied by a phalanx of beeping instruments that surrounded a single large bed upon which an old man was lying. Next to the bed sat Emily, one of the nurses they'd spoken to earlier. She rose as they came in.

"Any change?" Walker asked.

"I'm afraid not." She tucked the book she'd been reading under her arm, checked the monitors, and stepped aside.

Walker silently motioned Zara to the bedside.

She came closer, looking curiously at the man attached to the wires and tubes. "The king!" she exclaimed softly. "My God, it's King Weston!"

Walker's face wreathed in a smile. "You recognized him."

"Yes!" Joy surged through her, followed quickly by distress. "What has happened to him? Why is the king here in the medical wing?"

Some of the brilliance went out of Walker's smile. "I can't tell you that. Well, at least you recognized him. That's something. Why don't you sit down for a moment and talk to him."

She shot him a troubled glance. "He looks unconscious."

"He is. But he might well be able to hear you. You know that. Right?"

She nodded uncertainly. "Yes. I do. But…do I know him? Personally, I mean?"

"Yes. Go on. Tell him what's happened to you. It may do you both some good."

It dawned on her that perhaps the king had been injured at the same time she had. Only he hadn't woken up yet. A wretched thought.

"All right." She took a seat, and unconsciously reached for the old king's hand. It felt frail and cool as it lay in hers. Lifeless, except for a thready pulse barely discernible in his wrist. Inexplicably, tears filled her eyes.

She blew out a steadying breath and started talking. Awkwardly at first. But soon all the terror, the fears and the hopes she hadn't dared let herself feel for the past week came pouring out.

How she'd awakened to a world she couldn't remember and been frightened out of her wits, how she couldn't hear for two days, and how her whole body had ached but especially her head. How she'd fought the despair, feeling instinctively she was among good people. And how, now, she had someone taking special care of her, helping her to remember. That she was certain everything would come back to her soon.

Then she whispered to the king that he must try very hard to get better now, too. His subjects needed him. The country needed him.

When she finally fell silent, she glanced around, a little embarrassed at everything that had come out of her mouth. The nurse stood off to one side, dabbing her reddened eyes. Zara realized her own cheeks were moist, too. Walker handed her a tissue and came to stand next to her, squeezing her shoulder as she composed herself.

"I don't know about you," he said after a few moments, "but I'm starving. Let's go find some lunch."

Zara smiled as she popped the last French fry from her plate into her mouth. "If nothing else, my appetite has returned."

Walker chuckled, recalling the endless room service she'd insisted on during their weekend together. "Hunger is always a good sign. Feeling better?"

"Immensely."

At the time, he'd been surprised she didn't weigh a ton, the way she packed it in. Then again, despite the rounds of heaping plates, they'd probably burned three times the calories they'd taken in during those forty-eight glorious hours.

Besides, he liked her soft curves. A lot.

"Feel like a nap? Or do you want to continue the tour?" he asked, mindful of her tiredness. His own had miraculously vanished.

"Continue, please."

With his cell phone, he called Lord Carrington's secretary, who had promised to send a docent when Walker was ready to show Zara around the rest of the palace, since he was unfamiliar with it.

The place was gigantic. And like something right out of a fairy tale. Naturally he'd been in many castles and palaces in the course of his work with the Lazlo Group. Two of the group's specialties were locating and rescuing kidnapped royals and investigating high-level political deaths, such as that of Prince Reginald. But this place was incredible, even by royal standards.

Room after room was filled with the finest antiques, the

most beautiful tapestries and oriental rugs, the most intricate inlaid floors and plaster reliefs he'd ever seen. The docent droned on about the history of each room, the paintings and the architecture.

Zara listened politely, and he watched her face and her reactions. Interested, but no recognition.

Patience, he told himself. He better than anyone knew you couldn't rush these things. The brutal fact was, she might never regain her memory.

God, what would he do if she didn't? Carrington would have a cow, and Walker— Walker would be right back to square one with her.

"This leads to the oldest section of the palace," the docent said as they came to a dark stone archway that had been roped off. "Originally, the palace was built on the site of an old abbey. Parts of the abbey still remain, integrated into the architecture."

"Looks spooky," Zara said, peering into the dimness.

"I don't recommend going in there. The rooms are in a terrible state of disrepair and it is very easy to get lost. It's like an ancient honeycomb, twisting and full of false doors. There's nothing much to see, either, except for the old Bourbon rose garden located in the abbey courtyard tucked into the east side of the wing. But you can get there by walking around the outside. It is worth seeing if you get a chance. No one tends them any more, but the antique roses are still incredible."

"Sounds nice," Walker said. "Do you like roses?" he asked Zara.

"I love them," she said without hesitation, then grinned and poked him in the arm. "You tricked me."

He shrugged unrepentantly. "Like I said, whatever works."

Of course he knew she liked roses. There'd been a cascade of musky-scented ochre-yellow roses surrounding his tiny balcony in Florence, and she'd been enchanted with them. She'd picked an armful, then plucked the petals off and strewn them artfully over the bed that first afternoon as he opened the champagne.

He hadn't smelled a rose since that didn't remind him of sliding into her, surrounded by that sweet-musky scent.

"We should go see the rose garden," she urged, giving him a smile that told him she had no idea. "Maybe I'll remember something."

He smiled back, doing his best to hide the direction of his thoughts. "Maybe. Maybe tomorrow. I think you've had enough for today."

She took his arm and they accompanied the docent back through the stately rooms and regal halls. He kept his free hand firmly in his pocket and did his damnedest to hide the arousal the erotic memory had given him. He wanted nothing more than to sweep her into his arms and kiss her to within an inch of her life. Instead, he endured her warm hands on his arm and made small talk with the docent until they were deposited back at the medical wing.

"Will you have dinner with me?" she asked as he walked her to her room. "The food's actually not bad. For a hospital," she said wryly.

"Sounds tempting," he said. *Way too tempting.* "But Lord Carrington has invited me to dine with him. No doubt he wants an update."

"No doubt," she agreed, sounding disappointed. "Well—" Suddenly, she stepped close and gave him a hug. "Thank you. For trying."

"No prob—" The banality died and he swallowed heavily when she didn't let go.

Her body was warm and soft and the scent of her hair

filled his nostrils. She'd changed shampoos, but he could still smell her own rare scent under the flowery drift.

"Zara…"

"I know," she whispered. "But I had to see. If I'd remember your body."

He slammed his eyes shut, using every ounce of willpower not to hug her back. Not to respond to the feel of her. "I can't do this. You know I can't."

"Yes," she said, and stepped away. "But you didn't. *I* did."

He turned his head so she wouldn't see the hunger in his eyes. "Good night," he said. "I'll see you tomorrow."

With that he strode straight out the door without looking back. He couldn't. Because if he did and saw a matching hunger in her eyes, he wouldn't be responsible for his actions.

Or rather, he *would* be responsible.

And that was the one thing the world would never excuse.

"Did she remember anything?" Nurse Emily asked as he walked past her station at the hub of the medical wing.

He shook his head. "Nothing meaningful. Just some general stuff."

"Such a shame. She really is a very talented surgeon. I hope she recovers."

"Yeah," he said, and leaned a hip against the reception desk. "Tell me about her."

Emily considered. "I don't really know her all that well. None of us do. I think she's what you'd call…driven…in her work. Doesn't socialize much."

"No, huh? Any close friends? Or…someone special in her life, romantically?"

"She occasionally had lunch with some doctors from the Royal Medical University. No gentleman friend that I know of."

Walker tried not to feel too pleased about that as he strolled down the hall. But failed. He wanted her all to himself.

Why the hell had he waited so long to come look for her? That was the biggest mystery of all.

Okay, not really. She was in her last year of residency in Cambridge, Massachusetts, when they'd met, and had made it clear she had no time for a long-distance relationship. He'd been nearly six years her senior, teaching at Duke, in North Carolina. He'd taken her at her word, but when he'd tried to get in touch after the academic year she'd already moved back home to Silvershire. His schedule was insane, with no time for a European vacation. One year turned into two, then three, and so on, and then— Well, then he lost interest in pretty much everything…especially women.

Until this assignment reminded him how much he missed having a woman in his bed. And maybe even his life.

He glanced around and realized he must have taken a wrong turn somewhere. The corridor he found himself in was cold and deserted, the walls coated with a filmy black substance. With a start he recognized the place Carrington had indicated as the site of the bombing—the assassination attempt on King Weston during which Zara had been injured.

Since he was here, he might as well take a look around. There might be some pictures or some other personal effects left that he could show Zara.

Careful to avoid touching anything, Walker entered the bombed-out suite and frowned in shock. It was a total wreck. Burned husks of monitors and instruments littered the floor, along with bent, upended furniture and giant pieces of stone block. Black, sodden bits of drywall and fabric dangled from everything.

With growing anger, he made his way to the double doors

that led to the room where Zara'd had her office and lab. It was in even worse shape. There was nothing at all recognizable in the space, just a jumble of metal, stone and shredded books in various shades of greasy black and gray.

Holy hell. No one had told him it was *this* bad!

It hit him like a two-by-four in the gut that Zara would surely have died in this room if she hadn't been with the King next door.

With a clenched jaw he turned back through the adjoining door and sought out the bed where Weston had been lying at the time of the blast, where Zara had flung herself over the old king. The explosion had hurled it to the far end of the room, flipping it over in the process, possibly saving both their lives. It'd been a miracle either had survived. If the bed had been just a few yards closer to the origin of the blast—

Suddenly, Walker stood stock still. A gnawing, horrible certainty slowly crawled through him like a pack of rodents.

The blast origin was plain as day, even to someone whose only training was a weekend course in explosives required by Corbett for all Lazlo Group members. The origin of the blast was in Zara's office. That placement made no sense at all. Not if King Weston was meant to be killed by it. And the amount of explosives made no sense if it had not been meant as a killing blast. It was meant to be fatal. But… Oh, God.

The target of this assassination was not King Weston.

The target had been Zara Smith.

Chapter 3

Lord Carrington's eyes flared with incredulity. "You can't be serious. Who would want to harm Dr. Smith?"

Walker kept a tight rein on his emotions and sipped the excellent burgundy being served with supper. "I have no idea. But it makes no sense to plant a bomb in Dr. Smith's office if the intended target is unconscious in the next room and unable to move. Why not plant it right under the king's bed?"

Carrington didn't have an answer. "The National Police are investigating. Surely, they would have checked that possibility."

Walker forced himself to take another bite of the five-star lamb in tarragon, but didn't taste it. "How many bombings have there been in Silvershire in the past year? Or two? Or even five?"

"Well," Carrington hedged. "None, actually."

"Does your National Police even have a bomb expert?"

"No," he admitted. "They've sent the recovered pieces of the device to New Scotland Yard in London for analysis."

"So they're just assuming the king was the intended victim?"

"*Everyone* assumed so."

"Until now. Your Grace, may I suggest you call Corbett Lazlo and have him send someone immediately? I know there are at least two bomb specialists on the group's payroll. I am certainly not one of them. But if even I can spot a discrepancy…"

"I see your point." Carrington sat back in his slender Heppelwhite chair. "I can't imagine you are correct in your theory, but absolutely, it must be investigated."

"Thank you, Your Grace. In the meantime, I recommend Dr. Smith be moved somewhere else. Somewhere safe. I saw signs today that she is beginning to remember things. Her memory should return any minute. There's really no need for me to continue—"

Carrington held up a hand to halt Walker's stab at extricating himself from this damnable situation. "Out of the question. I don't want assurances. I want her memory back completely. Your job is not finished until that happens. Understood?"

He was going to make one hell of a king, Walker thought sardonically. He definitely had that whole ring-of-royal-authority thing down cold. "Yes, Your Grace," he said.

"Please continue your treatment as planned. But if you think it prudent, I could assign her a bodyguard…."

"That won't be necessary. The Lazlo Group puts all of its agents through rigorous arms and defense training. I believe I'm capable of keeping her safe. However…I'm planning to take her around town tomorrow. It's necessary for her treatment, so I can't cancel. But I'll call Corbett and have someone assigned to tail us. Just in case."

"Good Lord!" Zara exclaimed.

It was midmorning and she and Walker had just ambled past the twin telephone-box-sized guard posts at the end of the footpath leading from the back of the palace out onto the main thoroughfare. Walker had recommended a leisurely stroll around town, hoping to jog something loose from her memory. They'd taken the rear footpath in order to avoid the herd of paparazzi that always hung about the official front drive. The press was a constant presence, most often a menace, even if at the moment they wrote about Zara as though she were a hero, having saved the life of Silvershire's beloved king in the bombing.

The colorfully dressed guards saluted them smartly with a snap to attention, gripping their upturned rifles.

Zara gasped. She recognized them! Not the men themselves, but their uniforms and ritual. The whole setting.

"What?"

She spun around and took in the busy street, looking left to the Royal Medical University located two blocks south, and right to the Ministry Complex, several blocks to the north.

"I recognize it! Everything! I know exactly where I am!" She spun back and launched herself at Walker in a big hug, whirling them around in pure joy. "I can't believe it! I remember!"

He laughed with her, his smile lighting up his face. "That's great!" His arms tightened around her. "I'm so glad." Then he pulled away a little, looking down at her, a shadow of uncertainty in his eyes. "Everything?" he asked. And waited for her answer.

She'd been so busy celebrating the overwhelming sense of knowing *where* she was that she'd missed the more important point. She still didn't remember *who* she was.

Her happiness took a crash dive. "Damn. No," she said cheerlessly. "*Not* everything." She shook her head. "Nothing about me. Just the city."

"Ah." Walker released her, leaving her feeling oddly abandoned. "But that's good. Definitely progress," he said, his voice filled with an optimism that sounded slightly forced. He smiled again. "I predict very soon it'll all come back."

She let out a long sigh. "God, I hope so. I can't tell you how strange this is, remembering just bits and pieces of one's life. Like my brain is made of Swiss cheese."

He chuckled, looking at her with sympathy and understanding. "Try and use that. You're a doctor. Store up those feelings of frustration so you can relate better to what your patients go through. When you get back to work."

She felt her own smile return, if weakly. "I appreciate your confidence."

"You'll get there. It's already started. Just relax and give it time."

Something at the edge of her vision caught her attention, and she turned. But nothing was there. Just the traffic and the chin-up guards. Wonderful. Now she was seeing things.

Walker looked at her expectantly, but she shook her head. "Just a shadow."

"Maybe not. I arranged for an agent to tail us today. In case anyone shows undue interest."

"Is that really necessary?"

"Just a precaution. Everyone closely involved with the royal family is getting extra security."

"I understand." She rubbed a shiver that went through her arms.

As they started walking again, her shoulder brushed against him and she felt a jolt of pleasure. At his powerful presence next to her, at the nearness of his body. She could feel his steady strength in the fleeting contact before he moved away.

How she wanted him to pull her back in his arms and hold her! Somehow she knew she hadn't had that in her life—a strong, comforting presence. From what she'd learned yesterday she had few friends, and no man. What a dull and lonely life she must lead!

At least she had family.

Somewhere.

But what about Walker? What was their relationship? Had they once been lovers, as she suspected? What had happened to them? Had they parted friends, or had one of them dumped the other? That would explain the distance he always kept between them, both physically and emotionally. Especially physically. While she longed to pull him close, he avoided touching her.

And yet, his eyes… When they sought her out, she felt the heat of his regard radiate from them like a furnace.

Did he still want her?

"Where would you like to go?" Walker asked, drawing her from her *outré* thoughts.

She gathered herself. "Why not the historic district, Silverton-upon-Kairn, across the river? Have you seen it yet?"

"By historic," he drawled, "you mean older than the two-hundred-fifty years the Palace has been around?"

"Oh, that's right." She grinned. "You're a Yank. Anything built before the last century is ancient to you."

He wrinkled his nose at her. "Very funny. And for your information," he said, feigning indignation, "I'm *not* a Yank. I'm a Reb. Born and bred in South Carolina."

"I thought you sounded Southern. Tell me about your home."

He held up a hand. "Another time. Right now we're concentrating on you. So, what about this old town you're taking us to?"

"It's a bit touristy, but wonderfully quaint and quirky. Full of small boutiques and antique shops and scrumptious tea rooms with sinful pastries."

He gave her a teasing smile. "Sinful's good."

Lord, how she loved his smile. It brightened the whole morning. With his deep blue eyes and his bad-boy hair, the combination was simply deadly.

"We could stop for lunch," she said, looping her arm through his so she wouldn't reach up to touch that dazzling smile. Or worse, kiss it. "I know a place that serves the best pasta this side of Florence."

Abruptly, he halted on the sidewalk so she was forced to stop, too. "You've been to Florence?" he asked, peering down at her intently.

She licked her lips, sensing a sudden tension in the air. "Um…" She wracked her brain. Why had she said that? Did Florence mean something to him? To them…? Her heart took off at a gallop. "Have we been there? Together?"

His gaze didn't waver. "You tell me. *Have* we?"

"I—" She gave her head a frustrated shake and looked away. "I don't know. Please, Walker, can't you tell me? This is driving me mad."

Indecision tortured his expression, but he finally said, "No. I can't do that. Aside from possibly hindering your recovery, it would be a major breach of ethics."

"But how?" she protested. "It's not like you're trying to seduce me! You've been nothing but professional!"

"Think about it. I'm your doctor, and you trust me, right?"

"Of course I do."

"So I could tell you anything, and you'd believe me."

Her mouth opened, but she couldn't truthfully deny it. "I suppose."

"I could lie and say we were lovers, even if we'd never met before yesterday. You'd be vulnerable to me."

"You wouldn't do that."

"How do you know?"

"I just do. Lord Carrington would never have hired you—"

"What if I wanted you so much I was willing to lie about the past to have you now?"

Her mouth dropped further. "Do you?" she whispered. "Want me that much?"

He grasped her shoulders in his powerful hands. "Zara, what if we were lovers in the past," he said, ignoring her question, "but you'd left me for some reason? Maybe I was cruel to you, or had cheated on you, or been accused of doing something awful so you didn't want anything to do with me. But you don't remember. I could be telling the truth, but it could still be a terrible lie, to lead you on."

"You wouldn't," she repeated.

His eyes softened, and he dropped his hands from her shoulders with a gentle sigh. "But you don't *know* that. Not for sure. And until you remember for yourself, I can't talk about us. Not in the present, not in the past."

She stared up at him in sublime frustration. He was right, of course. He was doing exactly what he should be doing to protect both of them. So why did that just make her want to scream?

Apparently patience was not among her virtues.

She took a deep breath. "Fine. But if I still haven't remembered in a week, you're telling me whether you want to or not."

"A year," he countered. She looked up at him aghast. "Okay, six months," he conceded.

"One month," she said firmly. "Non-negotiable. If you refuse, I'll get Lord Carrington to order you." His brow rose, and she lifted her chin. "Don't think he won't. He likes me, you know. The duke is an old family friend." Walker's brow rose even higher. Her head wobbled. "At least I'm pretty sure he is."

He chuckled. "Whatever you say, sugar."

She stared up at him. His words echoed in her mind, low

and sweet, filled with laughter, like the tinkling of a bell from far, far away. *Whatever you say, sugar.*

She tried to latch on to it, but it was already gone.

Behind her, a woman passing them on the sidewalk bumped her, then muttered under her breath. An apology, but it sounded harsh and ugly compared to the sweet wisps of memory.

"Something wrong?" Walker asked.

She forced a smile. "No. But if that's our tail she wasn't very polite," she said as a shudder went through her.

Walker let her set the pace as they threaded their way through the impatient morning crowd of the modern glass-and-concrete business district toward the bridge over the Kairn that would take them to the old town. To be honest, she felt strangely at home in the hurry-up hustle and bustle of the designer-dressed throng. But today she wanted to escape it. Lemon-polished antiques and spice-scented tea houses called to her.

"Wow." Walker whistled as they approached the ornate Golden Bridge over the Kairn River. "That is something else."

The bridge spanned the sparkling blue water in graceful arches, each gilded loop topped by a flickering crystal gaslight crowning a fancy golden lamppost. Iron lace scrollwork, painted gold, made up the railings. At either end of the bridge, two sphinx-like red porphyry lions sat regally on the low granite walls guarding the entrance, their once-golden patina worn away by two centuries of weather. The whole thing was incredibly elegant.

"More than one guidebook calls it the prettiest bridge in the world," she said, the information coming out of nowhere as they strolled to the other side. "It was built by King Theodore in the seventeen-hundreds at the same time as the new palace was constructed. The lions are from the Temple of Luxor, in Egypt. A gift from Napoleon."

Walker winked at her. "Nothing wrong with that part of your memory."

She rolled her eyes. "Yes, a veritable font of trivia about everything save myself."

"Some men would consider that an advantage in a woman."

She punched him in the arm, smothering a smile. "Cheeky git."

He jumped out of range, laughing. "So, was there an old palace? What happened to it?"

"An old castle. It's a museum now. A dark and spooky-looking bit of work, full of hidden rooms and secret tunnels. Very gothic. You can just see the towers, there on the hill, poking above the rooftops."

She pointed to a rise in the jumble of ancient buildings and verdigris copper roofs spreading out in a confusion at the other end of the bridge. Three conical turrets ringed by crenellated parapets were clearly visible.

"Towers, hidden rooms and secret tunnels, eh? Sounds fun."

She gave a shiver. "Until you get lost in one of them. No thanks. I've always been terrified of close, dark places."

He swung a glance at her. "Yeah?"

"The house where I grew up had secret rooms."

"Where was that?" he prompted casually.

She gasped in realization. Another personal memory!

Where had she grown up? Think! But the heavy feeling of moldering darkness evaporated like mist. The creeping unease, however, lingered. She glanced around and rubbed her arms, feeling as though…as though she were being watched. *Good Lord.* She really must get hold of herself.

"Can't remember." She sighed. "Damn, I hate this."

"Never mind," he said. "Don't think about it. You seem to do much better just talking about whatever pops into your head."

At least they'd started trickling in, the memories. As elusive as they were. "I suppose you're right."

So she did her best to put the reason for their excursion right out of her mind and simply enjoy the scenery, the glorious morning and Walker's company. The warm summer sun felt wonderful on her face after being cooped up in her antiseptic hospital bed all week, and Walker's warm smile heated her insides even more. His easy banter made her laugh, and the admiring glances of the women they passed made her proud to be the only one he looked at.

They explored the narrow, winding cobblestone streets, pausing at every curiosity shop and bohemian art gallery on the way, bought sweet-salty pretzels and taffy to snack on and fed cracked corn from converted gumball machines to the swans floating in postage-stamp ponds in envelope parks squashed between quaint timbered town houses dripping with geranium-filled window boxes.

When the sun was high in the cloudless sky and they finally ambled into the square in front of the old castle, she said, "Thank you for helping me like this." For three hours she'd actually forgotten all about wanting her past back, and only thought about the present. "This morning has been so fun. I can't remember when I've enjoyed myself so much." She darted him a wide-eyed look, then burst out laughing. "Oh, my God. I'm so pathetic."

He laughed, and swept her into his arms. "No. You're adorable."

Surprise cascaded through her body, followed closely by a shiver of pleasure. In his embrace, surrounded by the warmth and strength of his arms, at last she was where she wanted to be. Where it felt so very right to be. She wrapped her arms around him and held him close.

And felt exactly when he realized what he was doing. His body stiffened, just a little, and he murmured a soft curse.

"Please," she whispered before he could move away, "don't leave yet. Just hold me for a moment."

She felt him take in a deep breath and let it out slowly. "This is so wrong in every way," he whispered back. "I shouldn't. We shouldn't."

"I know. It's just…"

What could she say? That he made her feel safe and secure for the first time since she'd woken up from the accident? That she was so attracted to him her limbs nearly melted just looking at him? That she felt a connection with him far beyond doctor-patient, beyond friendship even, to a down-to-the-very-core intimacy—despite the fact they'd barely touched each other—that would have scared her if he weren't so honorable, so above reproach in his principles and conduct.

She had a feeling none of those insights would help her case one bit. He would say all of that was due to her vulner-ability. Misplaced feelings of gratitude, and sublimated fear and dependency. She knew all the medical arguments against getting involved. But they were all wrong. She just…really liked him.

And judging by the silent battle waging in his muscles as he held her, he liked her, too.

Unable to help herself, she moved her hand up, slid her fingers into his long, thick hair. And pulled him down for a kiss.

Their lips met with a low moan. Hers. And his. Harmoniz-ing in a soft exhale of longing.

He opened his mouth, teased her tongue with his. The taste

of him flowed through her, spiced with pretzel, sweetened with taffy. And under it, achingly sensual, the warm, rich flavor of desire. *He wanted her*.

All too quickly, he retreated.

"Zara," he breathed. "We can't do this. We're being watched."

He was aroused. Small consolation when he took her arms and peeled her from his chest.

Thank God he didn't let her go completely. She would have dissolved onto the cobbles at his feet.

"I know," she said. "But it's so unfair."

"There'll be plenty of time for kisses after you remember. If you still want to."

Something in the way he said the last part sent a prickle over her scalp. "Of course I'll want to. Will you?"

His gaze filled with a slow certainty, overlaid by another emotion…something…wistful? "Sugar, that's a guarantee."

She took a cleansing breath and shook off her disappointment and yearning. "All right. I can wait. But when I get my memory back, better watch out."

His mouth curved up as he let her go. "I'll look forward to that."

She had to fight not to launch herself back into his arms. Instead, she turned purposefully away and set her attention on the shops and cafés lining the square. The old castle loomed above their heads, dark and menacing like a storm cloud against the pristine blue sky. She ignored the creeps it gave her and took Walker's hand, leading him to the closest shop window, threading through a crowd of tourists.

"The restaurant where I want to take you to lunch is just ahead. The Dog and Fiddle. But let's check out these antique dealers along the way first. Okay?"

"Sure," he agreed. She'd noticed he enjoyed poking around

old things as much as she did. That was good. Something they could do in the future. In between kissing…

If they were still together, a little voice in her head whispered. The way he kept doubting whether she'd want him made her uneasy. Like maybe there was something he was hiding. Something big.

She told the voice to go jump in the lake.

"Oh, look at that!" She pressed a hand to the window they were strolling past. "An old dental cabinet."

It was gorgeous. Dark, rich solid wood, with a zillion little narrow drawers marching down the front in two rows.

"Let's go in." Bells on the door tinkled as Walker opened it and held it for her.

They oohed and aahed over the cabinet and several other outstanding pieces, then wandered through the rest of the shop, which was filled to the rafters with beautiful, curious and odd things. Each wall overflowed with paintings of all kinds. Oils and pastels, watercolors and lithos.

Walker stopped to admire one particularly large oil as she ran her fingers over a damask silk love seat in front of it.

"Man, can you imagine living in a place like that?" he murmured, his voice tinged with amazement. "There's got to be a hundred rooms in it."

"Hmm?" She glanced up at the painting.

And froze.

Her heart stopped. Then zoomed into hyperspeed.

"One hundred and thirty-seven," she whispered hoarsely.

"Huh?"

She clutched at the damask of the love seat she suddenly found herself sitting on. Memories flooded through her in a blinding flash of colors and shapes. "A hundred and thirty-seven rooms. Not counting the secret ones…"

He was sitting next to her in an instant, grasping her hand. "Zara. Baby, are you all right?"

Just then, the store proprietor came over, smiling. "Aye, that's quite the estate. Up in the north country, it is. As ancient and noble a house as ye'll find in all Silvershire. They call it—"

"Danehus," Zara said, making the three-syllable name rhyme with noose. "Danehus Hall."

"Ah! I see the lady's familiar with it," the man said, obviously pleased he had a knowledgeable customer.

"I should be," she said, shock and wonder fueling her words with the breathiness of momentary disbelief. "I grew up there." She met Walker's wary gaze. "My God, Walker. I'm Lady Zara. Daughter of the twelfth Marquis of Daneby."

Chapter 4

Walker swallowed, keeping his excitement at bay, doing his best to maintain a professional facade while inside he was doing cartwheels.

"Good. You remember," he said. Praying this wasn't just another false alarm.

She nodded.

"How much?"

"I—I'm not sure."

He stood, putting his hand on the antique dealer's shoulder. "We'll take the painting. Wrap it up for us, if you will? We'll come back for it after lunch." With that, he pulled Zara to her feet, banded an arm around her waist and hustled her out of the shop. They needed to talk. In depth. "Where's that restaurant?" he asked, scanning up the street.

She pointed. "Half a block that way."

"Let's get something to eat. We could both use it."

She looked pale, like she'd seen a ghost. Hell, she probably had. No doubt more than one. People's pasts usually contained as many unpleasant memories as good ones. Something that was easy to forget while in the panic mode of amnesia.

"I could definitely use a drink," she said.

"That bad, eh?"

Her lips twisted sardonically. "You might have warned me."

He leaned over and placed a kiss on her hair as they walked. "I honestly don't know a thing about your background, other than your father's title."

She looped her arm around his elbow. "Walker?"

"Yeah?"

"I still don't remember about you. Should I?"

A vise of disappointment squeezed his chest. She wasn't the only one who hated this. He evaded her question by asking, "Do you remember your job? Where you went to school?"

Several tense seconds passed. Then she shook her head. "No."

He pressed his mouth into a thin line. *Damn.* "But your family? Your childhood?"

"Yes. All of that."

She didn't sound overly pleased to have discovered she was a titled, presumably rich, aristocrat. He wondered what that was all about. But they'd arrived at the restaurant, so he banked his curiosity until they'd been seated, gotten their drinks and ordered. Pasta, of course.

She took a deep sip of her red wine and gave him a long, wry look. "So is this memory thing reversible? I mean, can I go back to not remembering?"

She looked so pained as she said it, he laughed out loud. "Come on, it can't be that terrible."

"Says you."

"All right, tell me about Lady Zara. Everything you remember."

She groaned and held her head in her hands. "Where to begin. I am the oldest child of the Marquis of Daneby. Our lands lie on a bay just under the northernmost tip of Silvershire. My ancestors were marauding Viking warriors who were given the most remote region of the island as a bribe to leave the rest alone."

He chuckled. "A very sensible arrangement."

"I've apparently inherited most of my blood from those marauding warriors. Or so my father keeps telling me. I've been a fighter from day one."

"That I can believe."

"Because I'm a woman, I cannot inherit his title, even though I'm the oldest. I always thought that was unfair."

"Well, it is," he agreed. He leaned more toward an equal split himself, but he could see how that might get messy when a title and family lands were involved. The American founding fathers had been smart to avoid that whole can of worms.

"At the ripe old age of seven, I made it my life's ambition to change that old-fashioned arrangement. I fought to be better at everything than my little brother, who is in line for the title, thinking I could change my father's mind. But, of course, it's not my father's choice, it's set out in the entailment. Been that way for a thousand years. The oldest boy inherits, regardless of which child is better suited."

Walker could see the veiled pain of a lifetime of disappointment in her eyes, the impossible dreams of an outraged little girl who has been cheated out of that which she holds dearest.

"Life sucks," he muttered. He knew all about being cheated out of one's dreams. He clicked his glass to hers in tacit commiseration. "Go on."

She let out a long sigh. "The men in my family are all doctors. From way back. Kind and nurturing men—at least to their people, the villagers and farmers who work their lands. The Lord-Physician. Healing his flock. Everyone loves my father."

Walker could see just where this was going. *Christ.* "So you decided to become a doctor, too."

"Brilliant idea, yes? Around that time, the king made a proclamation saying the royal succession could pass to any royal child, regardless of gender. Naturally I thought it should apply to all of Silvershire's nobility." She shrugged. "It didn't. But I thought I could change that, too. In the meantime, I'd gotten the bug to become a doctor. So I announced my intentions to the family."

"What happened?"

"Relations have been a bit strained ever since."

"Surely, they couldn't object to that. I mean, what's wrong with becoming a doctor?"

She tilted her head. "Have you known many aristocrats?"

"Well, yeah. The Lazlo Group works with royalty and noble families all the time."

"And what is the preferred occupation of the women?"

He considered. "Charity work. And…well…"

She nodded. "Shopping. Parties. Society functions. Anything but a real job. That's how my sisters live. Why spend years pursuing a career you don't need?"

"I see your point. But if you *wanted* to do it…?"

"As the oldest girl, I was supposed to make a brilliant match and settle down to care for my husband's estates. Solidify political ties. Strengthen the family coffers. That sort of thing."

"But you were a fighter."

A smile, if self-deprecating, finally broke through. "That,

and the fact that the noblemen I've met are either inbred idiots, gay or already married."

Though he grinned, his pulse kicked up slightly at the thought of her marrying. "So... You went off to the university and became a brilliant doctor instead."

She lifted a shoulder. "So you say. But that's where the memories stop."

Damn.

Disappointment tumbled through Walker once again. Would she *ever* remember him? The feel of their brief kiss still sizzled on his tongue and lips. He didn't know how much longer he could resist dragging her to him and kissing her until she recalled every vivid detail of their affair.

Their food came and he dug in, grateful for something to do with his hands besides reach for her. Luckily, the pasta was superb, as promised.

"I'm tired of talking about me," she said between mouthfuls. "Tell me about South Carolina and your family."

He smiled, always cheered by thoughts of his parents and siblings. "Typical middle class. My dad's a teacher, my mom runs a garden center. I have a baby sister and two brothers, all younger. One's married with a kid. The other's a flake."

She chuckled. "Are you close?"

His insides warmed with love. Followed quickly by a flash of anger that he'd been forced to leave them because of the threats of a lying psychotic female sicko. He shut down the anger and concentrated on the love. "Yeah. We are. I miss them, living over here."

Surprise widened Zara's eyes. "You live over here? In Silvershire?"

"On the continent. France. That's where the Lazlo Group is headquartered."

"Oh." She studied him, and he wished like hell he knew what was going through her head. Then her brow beetled slightly and her gaze dropped to her plate.

"Zara?" he asked.

"Yeah?" She didn't look up. *What was she thinking?*

"Do you still want to become the Marchioness of Daneby?"

Her eyes raised back to his and her face took on a proud, serene mien. "Yes," she said with a certainty that pierced his heart. "I do."

And in that instant, he knew why she'd never tried to find him again after their affair. Why he'd never stood a chance with her, even as they'd spent the most incredible weekend of his life together.

He wasn't good enough for her.

A commoner, a middle-class American man with a school-teacher dad would never fit into her glitzy, aristocratic world. Especially not a man who'd been kicked out of his profession for ethical misconduct.

No matter how great their chemistry, a future marchioness didn't marry a lowborn man in disgrace.

Walker had suddenly gotten quiet.

Zara was worried. So worried, her stomach started a slow roil. What had happened to his smiles and his quips, his heated sidelong looks? As they finished up their lunch, he seemed to withdraw, once again becoming the impassive doctor who had first greeted her in her hospital room.

She wanted her friend back.

"Is something wrong?" she finally asked as he opened the door for her after picking up the oil painting of Danehus from the antique dealer down the block. He'd insisted on paying for the painting, but hadn't met her gaze during the transaction.

In answer, a smile appeared on his lips, but the crinkles around his eyes didn't shift. "Nothing's wrong. Shall we take a cab back to the palace?"

He was keeping something from her. But what?

A pain shot from her stomach to her chest thinking about what it might be. She grasped his arm to steady herself. "I am feeling a bit knackered," she admitted.

His brow creased. "You look a little pinched. Didn't the pasta agree with you?"

"No, I—" A wave of nausea hit her square in the gut. Okay, she was concerned about his sudden chilliness, but this was ridiculous. She rubbed her chest, which burned like the devil. "I'm not sure. I—"

"Come on, let's find somewhere to sit down. You're really not looking so good."

"No, I'm fine, really. I just—" Suddenly, her whole body clenched so violently she cried out. "Oh, God! Walker, my stomach! I think I'm—"

And for the second time in a week, the blackness reached out to grab her with sharp, ugly talons, dragging her down into the spinning depths of nothingness.

"I don't *know* what's wrong with her," Walker snapped into the cell phone as he paced the Royal Medical University Hospital emergency room floor. "I'm a freaking psychiatrist, not a—"

"Walker, calm down." Corbett's order was sharp and direct. "Take a breath."

Fighting panic, Walker tried his best to do so. "Okay. Okay. I'm sorry, boss."

"Start at the beginning."

There wasn't much to tell, and what there was took about

three seconds to relate. "And then she collapsed. Thank God I caught her."

"Could it be food poisoning?"

He forced himself to think, dredging symptoms from his med school days and comparing them to Zara's attack. Seemed too violent for that. Unless it was something really nasty. But we ate the same thing. I should be sick, too."

"Heart attack? Stroke?"

"Maybe. She did grab her chest. But she said it was her stomach."

There was a long silence. He knew they were both thinking the same thing. The unthinkable.

"Sounds like she's been poisoned," Corbett said at last.

Just like the crown prince two months earlier.

Walker swore a violent oath. "This is my fault. I should never have taken her out of the palace."

"Don't be absurd. None of us foresaw this development."

"Hey. It was *my* theory she was the real target of the bombing, remember?"

"Yes, but—"

"I should have *protected* her. Instead I led her right out into the open where anyone could get to her. And they did." He swore again. The weight of guilt was crushing. *If she died…*

"Have the hospital overnight a sample of her stomach contents to our lab. Meanwhile—"

"Why the hell would anyone want to poison her?" Walker demanded. "Or plant a bomb in her office? I don't understand. Corbett, is there something going on here I don't know about?"

"I assure you, we're as much in the dark as you are." Walker could plainly hear the anger in Lazlo's voice. His boss hated being blindsided. "We need to find out what's happening. Quickly."

The call to action made him pull himself together "Right. I'll—"

"No." Corbett cut him off. "You already have a job. It' more important than ever that Dr. Smith regain her memor now. *All* of it. I'll send von Kreus to investigate the attempt on her life. He just came off another job."

"But—"

"No buts. You're too close to this. Stay with Zara. Finish what you started. Let me know when she comes round."

The phone clicked off just as the admitting doctor strode around the corner looking for Walker.

He hurried over. "Is she all right?"

The doctor nodded. "Thanks to your quick work. Getting her here in record time made all the difference. We pumped her stomach and stabilized her heartbeat."

"Was she poisoned?"

The doctor's brows shot into his scalp. "*Poisoned?* Well in a matter of speaking. It looked to me like an overdose o some sort. Her heart rate was through the roof."

"Not food poisoning?"

"Definitely ingested, but not the food. It was something chemical."

"Such as?"

"Impossible to say for sure until the tox screen come back. But my guess would be some kind of heart medication."

Walker could feel the blood drain from his face. "Like digitalis?"

"A definite possibility."

The same drug used to poison Prince Reginald.

His head was spinning as he thanked the doctor and asked when he could see Zara. The answer was not what he wanted to hear. She'd be sleeping for a few hours and wasn't to b disturbed. On the other hand, it did give him some badly needed time to think.

What the hell was going on?

Someone really was trying to kill her. But why?

What had his little fighter gotten herself into—or seen—that she shouldn't have?

Pounding.

Something was pounding, pounding on her chest. Like a hammer on her heart. Ripping into her stomach. She was screaming. Screaming and screaming from the pain in her chest and stomach, and the weight of metal sheets grinding into her body.

She tried to turn, but something held her down. She heard voices. Arguing voices. Life and death voices. You won't get away with this. The hell I won't! Then laughter. Laughter fading into a baby's cry.

And suddenly the darkness. The long, eerie darkness. Clawing at her. Suffocating her. Panic. Panic! Wait... There's a light! A pinprick of yellow light, morphing into a symbol. A strange, exotic symbol. Writing? More lines and symbols and weird drawings, dozens, all swirling around her crazily, as though caught in the vortex of a tornado. So dizzy! Her stomach hurt so much, and her chest.

Someone was coming. She had to get away! Away!

She struggled. Fighting to move. Fighting to escape.

Strong arms held her firmly. Held her down, calling...

Zara. Zara!

She opened her eyes and gasped.

Walker saw the terror in Zara's eyes and fury roared over him. Whoever had done this to her was a dead man.

"It's me, honey. Shhh. You're all right."

Her wild eyes focused on him and slowly the fear fled "Walker?"

Thank God. "I'm here, sugar. Wake up. You're having bad dream."

Her breath soughed out. "Just a dream," she whispere hoarsely. Then her eyes darted around the hospital roon "Where am I? What happened?"

Walker made a snap decision. She had enough stress ju trying to remember who she was. She didn't need to kno someone might be trying to kill her. "Must have been some thing bad in the pasta," he said evasively. "Don't worry, the pumped your stomach and the doc says you'll be just fine."

Her hand went to her throat. "No wonder it feels lik sandpaper. What the hell, Walker. Bad pasta? Has anyon heard of that?"

Smiling, he smoothed a lock of hair from her face. "Wh knows? The important thing is you're okay."

She sighed. "At least I didn't lose my memory again."

"You'll have to stay here overnight, I'm afraid." He glance around the stark room. "Not exactly as glamorous as th Royal Palace."

Her lips curved. "I'll live. I hope."

He scowled. "Jeezus, Zara. Don't even joke. You scare me to death."

"Did I? Really?" She looked at him balefully. "Last remember, you were hardly speaking to me."

He sat on the edge of her bed and took her hand. "Yeal sorry about that. Just got hit by a dose of reality, I guess." H said it lightly, attempting to disguise the acute disappointmer ripping through him at the reminder of today's depressin insight. "Nothing to worry about. I'll get over it."

"What kind of reality?" she persisted.

"Zara, now is not the time to go into all that."

"All what?"

He closed his eyes for a moment, then opened them. "Okay, fine. After we talked I realized it didn't really matter whether or not we'd met before yesterday. With your background and ambitions, I'm not the kind of man you could ever get seriously involved with, anyway. I'm not…suitable for you."

Her jaw dropped. "Don't be ridiculous. What could be more suitable than a doctor?"

"A duke. A prince. An earl. Not a poor Carolina boy."

She let out a soft laugh. "Honestly, Walker. The ideas you have. Obviously, you've never read Cinderella. As if any of that mattered. Besides, you're hardly poor. You wear Dries van Noten, for crying out loud."

He glanced down at his open-necked, sleeve-ruched shirt and rumpled pants, amazed she didn't think they came from a thrift store. "You can dress the boy up…" he said with a shrug.

"Is that why you broke up with me before? Because of some outdated bourgeois notion of how the aristocracy behaves?"

Like he'd ever break up with her. He wagged a finger at her and stood, unwilling to be drawn further into this conversation. When she regained her memory she'd be singing a completely different tune.

"You're fishing again." He gave her a peck on the forehead. "Get some sleep. I'll see you in the morning."

He pointed his feet to the door and got out of there quick, before her tempting eyes and tempting lips could tempt him into having any kind of hope for any kind of future with tempting Lady Zara.

"It's just a title, Walker," came her parting shot.

"Night, sugar."

Good thing all he had was a case of monumental lust for

her, and nothing deeper. What he'd been feeling for Zara was *not* love. How could it possibly be? They'd spent a sum total of forty-eight, okay, now maybe sixty, hours together. A man didn't fall in love in three days. It just didn't happen.

So he'd be fine. As soon as she got her memory back, he'd be out of there. Then he'd be A-okay. He had a good job and plenty of offers for female company. Who needed the complication of keeping a fickle, high-maintenance aristo in his bed?

Not that she seemed all that fickle.

Still, he'd been right not to pursue her all those years ago. He must have known instinctively it could only end badly. For him, anyway.

And now, of course, it would be downright impossible. Not with the scandal of Ramona Burdette's accusations still clinging to him like static-charged laundry.

Unless Zara was only after another quick roll in the feather bed, he was just not destined to be her man. Not now. Not ever.

Cinderella. Yeah, right.

Chapter 5

"Lady Zara." Lord Carrington extended his hands and took hers warmly when she arrived at his private office along with Walker.

"Your Grace." She returned his air kisses with just the right deference for a future king. She couldn't believe the little rascal who'd regularly chased her and her brother around Danehus with water balloons when his parents came to visit had grown up to be this tall, imposing man. And married to a princess, nonetheless. "I hope your beautiful bride is well."

"She's doing fine. The morning sickness has nearly passed."

"Oh! A baby? Congratulations, Russell. That's wonderful news!"

Carrington hesitated, flicking a glance at Walker, who shook his head slightly. She flushed, understanding at once she must have been aware of this before.

"Please tell me I didn't attend the announcement dinner," she said with a groan.

"You were in surgery, I believe," he said smiling, a hint of the mischievous boy she'd known shining through.

"Thank God for small favors. Forgive me. My memory is still a bit murky."

"So I hear." His smile turned more serious. "How are you? You gave us all quite a turn yesterday."

"Leave it to me to get food poisoning along with amnesia. I'm fine, though. And slowly getting the memories back."

A hint of citrus drifted through the room. Russell's cologne? Furniture polish?

"Good." He ushered them to a set of elegant visitor chairs. Taking a seat behind his inlaid mahogany desk, he glanced again at Walker. "The thing is, Zara…"

Suddenly, it dawned on her this was not a social call. She straightened. "What is it Russell?"

"I don't want to alarm you, but…we need to talk."

"About what?"

"There is evidence that seems to indicate…well, that you might be the target of a bit of foul play."

She blinked. "Foul play? Whatever do you mean?"

The duke turned to Walker in appeal.

"What His Grace means," Walker said, clearing his throat, "is that yesterday's poisoning may have been deliberate. And the accident where you lost your memory might not have happened exactly as we—"

Deliberate? Alarm trickled through her limbs. "How can food poisoning be deliberate? And you never told me what kind of accident I had," she added, her concern rising even more. "Did it have something to do with the king? Is that why you took me to see him?"

The two men looked at each other. Walker sighed. "I told you she'd figure it out."

"Always has been too smart for her own good," Russell agreed resignedly.

"What's going on?" She was becoming genuinely anxious.

"We think someone may be trying to kill you," Walker said.

"You mean the king."

"No. You."

An incredulous laugh escaped her. Then another. And another, until she was laughing outright. "Why would anyone want to kill *me*?"

They weren't even smiling. "We rather hoped you could tell us," Russell said. "If that damnable memory of yours would only come back we might have a clue."

"Good lord, you're serious."

"Deadly, I'm afraid." Her old childhood friend folded his hands over his desk and leaned forward. "Zara, Dr. Shaw thinks you're ready to see the scene of your accident. I'm worried you're not strong enough after yesterday."

She looked from one to the other. This was absurd. They had to be wrong. "I feel fine," she said, standing. "Will seeing the accident scene bring my memory back quicker?"

"The shock just might do the trick," Walker said, also getting to his feet.

"Then what are we waiting for?"

Shock was an understatement. When Walker opened the door to the dark, cold suite at the end of the corridor, disbelief slammed Zara square in the chest. She stood and stared at the destruction, her jaw nearly hitting the rubble-strewn floor.

"*Good Lord*. What hap—" Suddenly, lights flashed in her

head, and an explosion sounded in her ears so thunderous she covered them with her hands.

And just like that, the memories were back. All of them. Like they'd never been gone.

She felt Walker's hands on her arms. "Zara?"

"Bloody hell," she whispered, moving her fingers to her mouth as he pulled her to his chest. "A *bomb?*" She felt him nod. "Have they found out who did it?"

"Not yet. Do you remember something, anything, that might help the investigation?"

She searched the newly resurrected memories, probed into the hours, even the minutes, before it had happened. And shook her head. "I can't think of anything even remotely suspicious. I was with the king, holding his hand and talking to him, worried because he still hadn't emerged from his coma, from the surgery. No one went in or out that I noticed."

"Well, keep mulling it over. Something may come to you later."

Her mind reeled. Someone had tried to *kill* the king. What sick mind would want to murder such a sweet old man just to make a political statement?

The king.

Suddenly, all her concern and fear over King Weston's recovery returned, like an avalanche crashing over her.

Oh, God, she needed to get to him.

She straightened out of Walker's arms. "The king! I must go to him. I can't believe I forgot I'm his doctor! His brain tumor—" She jerked away. "Has he regained consciousness yet?"

"No." Walker grasped her arm as she was about to rush out of the room. "Zara, listen. Dr. Landon is taking care of the king now. Until you are cleared to resume your practice, you can't—"

Dr. Landon, the doctor who had also been officially treating her. She knew him. He was brilliant, but—

"I remember everything, Walker." *Including the guilt. Lord, especially the guilt.* "It's been over a week," she said, her voice rising with each word. "I have to run tests. Make sure the king's tumor hasn't—"

"Dr. Landon is doing everything—"

"No! Don't you see? *I* have to do it! If I don't check everything myself, something might—"

She halted at Walker's concerned frown, battling to stop the flood of raw emotion bubbling up from deep within her. Irrational emotion she knew stemmed from the unnecessary death of a child two years ago. When she'd trusted the nurse to administer the correct dosage of—

She squeezed her eyes shut. Used pure willpower to calm herself. As she'd done every time the crippling guilt nearly overwhelmed her, making her second-guess her every move since that awful day. It didn't happen very often any more. Logically she knew it hadn't been her fault. Despite what the child's mother, Mrs. Lloyd, thought. All doctors, including her, lost patients. Nurses sometimes misread charts.

If she'd only checked the dosage personally...

Yes, accidents happened. *But not on her watch.* Not ever again.

All at once, she remembered what Walker had said in Russell's office about the bombing. *Had that been her fault, too?* Sickened by the very thought, she took in the twisted debris of the room. *Because of her?* No, that was insane.

She turned to Walker desperately. "You said earlier that

someone is trying to kill me. But…surely this was an assassination attempt on the king by the Union for Democracy? They've been threatening to disrupt the upcoming coronation for months now. What better way than this?"

Walker's firm hands guided her out into the hall, closing the door after them, then propelled her slowly down the corridor. "I don't think so. Lord Carrington met with Nikolas Donovan yesterday."

"The leader of the UD?"

"Yes. Donovan swears they had nothing to do with the bombing. However, he did warn that a faction is growing stronger within the Union that condones violence."

"There you are, then. It must have been them."

"Zara—" Walker's expression turned grave. "We have Lazlo agents, including a bomb specialist, investigating every angle. We'll soon know the truth. Until then—"

"I need to be with King Weston."

"Naturally you can visit. But until you're given a health clearance and a specialist has extensively tested your medical knowledge to be sure it's completely intact…"

He didn't need to finish. "Of course," she said, contrite. No one more than she wanted to be absolutely certain of her competency. "I wasn't thinking. How quickly can the recertification be done?"

"Under the circumstances probably within a day."

He regarded her oddly. Then stopped to lean his back against the corridor wall. They were nearly to the empty nurses' station. Soft laughter reached them from the lounge behind it.

"Which I guess means my job here is done." He continued to watch her with that strangeness in his eyes. A kind of wary expectancy.

"Just like that?"

It hit her then. *She still didn't remember him.*

He looked at her as though she should.

She licked her lips. Where did she have to be, again? It was singular how when Walker looked at her everything else flew from her mind. Everything but him.

"Unless…there's something else…?"

Why couldn't she remember him?

Perhaps there was nothing to remember?

His eyes said there was.

She took a step toward him. "Does that mean I'm no longer your patient?"

"As soon as I sign off on the job."

She licked her lips again, dropping her gaze to his mouth. Maybe if she kissed him—a real kiss this time—she'd remember….

"Today?" She took another step, bringing her to within touching distance. "Right now?"

"Zara, do you—"

She kissed him. Before he could ask the one question that would make him stop her.

Her lips met his and opened, inviting him in with a soft moan. He hesitated for a split second, then took her mouth fiercely, scooping her up in his arms, pulling her close. He groaned as his tongue swept in, the taste of him bursting through her, the smell of him surrounding her. His mouth covered, took, demanded.

He swung them around, pressing her back against the cool wall. She shivered. Shaking with the sudden need to give him everything he wanted. Everything she wanted.

"Walker," she whispered on a moan.

Her whole life had been ordered and regimented toward

a specific goal. All logic, all reason. But this man made her want to *feel*. For the first time since college she wanted to let herself go, and just fall into the dark velvet sea of the impulsive unknown.

"Ah, sugar," he murmured between kisses. "You have no idea how much I've wanted to do this. It's been torture, ever since I saw you lying in that hospital bed. But…are you sure?"

"Oh, yes." Her bones were slowly dissolving, her blood deliciously thick in her veins. When was the last time she'd felt like this? Maybe never… "It's been a long time since you held me," she whispered, taking a chance.

"A lot has happened in those years."

"You'll have to tell me everything."

Suddenly his tongue and lips stilled. "Zara?" he asked, his voice gravelly. "You don't know? Or you don't remember?" His chest rose and fell against hers as he waited for her answer. One she couldn't give.

"It doesn't matter," she whispered. "Whatever it is, I don't give a flip."

He swore under his breath. "Damn it, Zara! I thought you said you remembered everything!"

"I do! Everything except—" She clung to him when he would set her away.

"Except me?" His brow rose. "Or is your whole love life gone?"

She gave an unladylike snort. "Assuming I had such a thing. Which I don't."

"Great." He pulled free and paced away from her, thrusting his hands in his pockets. "Just damn great," he said disgustedly. "I guess we're not done here after all. And so exactly the damn memories I want to be working with you on."

She pulled the ends of her hair together and twisted them

into a knot at the back of her neck. "There are sod-all memories to work on! I'm telling you, Walker, I haven't a clue why I've blanked you out, but I do remember how I live my life. Men are not a part of it."

He propped a hand on the wall and gazed at her, his expression mildly disbelieving. "You gay, or what?"

She managed, just barely, to rein in her outrage and find a tone of sarcasm. "Lord, no. Here I thought *you* were gay."

He raised a finger and shook it at her.

"I've kissed you twice now. You've yet to return the favor, so I assumed…" She waved a hand. "Whatever. There's no shame in being gay. Some of my—"

He strode right into her face and said, very calmly, "I. Am. Not. Gay. And you know perfectly well why I haven't returned the favor. Now, tell me why the hell there aren't a dozen damn men in your life, dying to return your kisses and a whole lot more."

"Because…" She jerked away from the temptation of his hard-edged stance and quivering muscles and crossed her arms over her soft silk blouse. A reminder to soften her expression.

"I told you yesterday. I have a thing about being the best at what I do. I have goals. All of that takes dedication and commitment. Men in my social circle tend not to like being interrupted by a woman's pager every time they're just getting to the good bits."

He looked away, his jaw working. "The good bits. Cute. I guess that figures. Stupid. I plumb forgot about your whole social circle thing." He blew out a breath. "Johnny Reb at the Court of the Marchioness of Daneby. Whooee," he mimicked, making a mockery of his beautiful accent. "I suppose that explains why I disappeared so resolutely into the quicksand of your mind."

"Walker!" She grabbed his arm when he turned to storm down the hallway. "Don't."

"Sugar, believe you me, you're better off this way."

"No. I don't believe it and you don't, either."

"I'm seriously not the kind of man a woman like you would knowingly get involved with."

"Why do you keep saying that? I know you, and—"

"That's where you're wrong, baby," he interrupted, and eased his arm from her grip. "The damn truth is, you don't know me at all."

Walker swore at himself the whole time he was instructing Nurse Emily to make sure Zara got in bed and stayed there for the rest of the day. The betrayed look on Zara's face as he stalked off was almost enough to crack his resolve. Almost.

"I'm not tired!" she yelled after him.

"You've had a shock," he answered without looking back. "You need rest if you expect to pass your medical re-cert tomorrow."

He had to get out of there. To somewhere quiet where he could regroup. Lifting his cell phone from his pocket, he thought about the Bourbon rose garden the docent had described yesterday. That had sounded real quiet.

But first he called Lord Carrington and let him know the strategy had worked. Lady Zara's memory had returned and she was chomping at the bit to be tested and get back to work.

"You don't think it's too soon?"

"That's for Dr. Landon to decide. If her medical knowledge checks out, I see no reason to hold her back. This kind of amnesia doesn't relapse."

"Excellent. I've arranged for her to take a full board ex-amination so there'll be no doubt."

Next he called Corbett for a progress report on the investigation into the bombing and poisoning.

"The tox screen's not in yet, but the explosives expert has confirmed your suspicions about the placement of the bomb. It was planted in Dr. Smith's office, in an unlocked file drawer. He's flown up to London to take a look at the reconstructed device at New Scotland Yard."

There wasn't a better bomb team than the guys who worked for the Lazlo Group. By the time they were finished, they'd know where every part of the thing had come from, how it had been put together and in what order, what the bomber had eaten for breakfast the day of the blast and the color of the shirt he was wearing.

Instead of being reassured, Walker hung up feeling even more angry.

He definitely needed to find a quiet place and calm down.

But it wouldn't stop eating away at him. The burning question. Who the hell was messing with Zara Smith, and why?

Not that it was his job to find out; that was up to von Kreus. Walker had done his part. He was out of it now. Walker Shaw was not a criminal investigator, he was just a doctor. A psychiatrist.

Correction: a *former* doctor. *Former* psychiatrist. Just a consultant.

And a lover good and gone from Zara's life.

Former lover.

He brooded over that as he exited through a set of French doors and made his way around the outside of the palace. The gardens were as opulent and showy as the rooms inside. A precise riot of bloom in coordinated beds of carefully planned casual disarray. Perfect cozy English gardens within a strict grid of French symmetry.

Not unlike his own life. Outwardly casual and devil-may-care, but inside walking a razor-thin line between a stolen past and a future he resented.

No. He didn't resent his future. He loved working for Corbett. He just resented like hell that the choice of what he could and could not do had been taken from him.

Still and all, the flowers along the brick walkway were pretty and smelled nearly as good as the ones back home. Normally they'd work just fine for a spell of relaxation, but not today. Today he longed for the dissolute splendor of a decaying Southern plantation in which to soothe his righteous frustration.

The abandoned rose garden was more Keats than Tennessee Williams, but it would have to do.

He barely noticed the tangle of creepers, heavy with sweet-smelling blossoms, that covered the crumbling brick walls of the courtyard. He homed in on a small patch of green grass that militantly guarded the center of the crumbling square, surrounded by fragrantly overgrown bushes dotted with white and butter-yellow buds. Dropping onto the grass, he pulled off his shirt and tossed it aside.

It was hard to stay mad surrounded by all this beauty, but somehow he managed it. Damn, he could use a drink.

He propped his arms under his head and gave in to a scowl. For the first time since turning his back on his old home and familiar life, he wondered if he'd made a mistake walking away from the scandal. Should he have ignored the threats, stayed and fought it? Denied the accusations, demanded a fair hearing?

Would anyone have listened?

Probably not. He was only the wonder boy, the handsome but penniless young doctor of psychiatry who'd had the devil's own timing, managing to study just the right thing and meet just the right people and get just the right grants to ensure an early stardom in his chosen field, and what's more, to help a whole lot of folks along the way. There'd been no down side to his life. Everyone admired him. Everyone loved him.

Including, unfortunately, one of his patients.

She was the daughter of the state senator, brought in after a car wreck. She'd lost her memory and her daddy wanted the best his considerable fortune could buy. Daddy's daughter wanted Walker. He did not share her ambitions. She was his patient. She didn't care.

When he refused her advances, she turned ugly and accused him of all sorts of improprieties, none of which were true. Other than, perhaps, that first surprised kiss.

But who did the tabloids and gossip rags believe? A bad-boy head doctor who came from nothing, or the innocent daughter of an illustrious senator? But what the press didn't know, and he soon learned to his everlasting sorrow and fury, was that the woman was unstable. When he said he would set the record straight, she threatened his family—his parents, sister and brothers. When his daddy had found his favorite hunting hound with a slashed throat, Walker had started to take her seriously. He didn't say a word to the press. The woman was genuinely insane. But her father was a senator….

His old employers had known the truth of his innocence, and yet, because he couldn't defend himself, they had shown him the door. Perception was far more important than truth, they'd told him. Everyone knew that. No one would send their daughters or fathers or grandmothers to a medical facility with any whisper of sexual scandal attached to it, not in the conservative South. They were certain Walker understood why they couldn't stand by him…not against the senator who controlled their funding.

Walker understood, all right. When all was said and done, skill, brains, dedication all meant squat. All that mattered in their world was who your people were. If it came down to a choice, there was no contest.

Just as there'd be no contest when Lady Zara found out exactly who he was and what sordid secrets lay pressed between the pages of those forgotten memories. If she'd just been plain Dr. Jane Smith, he might have stood a chance if he laid it all out for her. But an aristocrat, one of a handful of privileged European nobility? No way. There'd be no more kisses for him from that quarter. Oh, no. That little future marchioness would not be trolling in his waters again, not once she knew the truth.

That was for damn sure.

And that was one, pure, damn shame.

His cell phone chirped, rousing him out of his even greater frustration. He wasn't one for a pity party. Normally he took his licks like a man and moved on. But Zara had him twisting in the wind.

He flipped open the phone and checked the name scrolling across the screen. Corbett.

"Yeah, boss?"

"Where's Zara? Is she with you?"

"She's in bed resting. She had a rough—"

"Is there someone guarding her?"

Instantly alert, Walker sat up and reached for his shirt. "Estevez, the agent assigned to shadow us yesterday, is keeping an eye on the medical wing. Why? What's going on?"

"You were right. She was poisoned."

He swore roundly. "You got the tox screen back?"

"Just this minute. The prelim definitely shows digitalis. Garden variety, not pharmaceutical grade."

Walker was already on his feet. "Just like the stuff that killed Prince Reginald."

"Except this time the pasta was spiked, not a line of cocaine. I'm sending von Kreus to question the restaurant staff."

Besides being a top-notch investigator, von Kreus was the group's information extraction specialist. The best interrogator on the planet. "He'll put the fear of God into them if anyone can," Walker said, hurrying toward the medical wing entrance.

"I'll let you know what he comes up with. Meanwhile, get Estevez on Zara's door. You'll have to take the night shift unless I can find a rent-a-cop. The Group is spread pretty thin right now. I've got three other cases going besides this mess in Silvershire."

"Already on it," Walker said, thinking of a thousand problems with that scenario. But he had no choice. "I'm fine with temporary babysitting duty. Unless you've got another job lined up for me…?"

"You signing off on Dr. Smith's recovery, then?"

His boss didn't need to know the only gap left in her memory was Walker himself. Because he didn't signify. "I've done everything I can do. There may be some holes, but as long as Dr. Landon gives her the okay on the medical stuff, I'm officially signing off."

"All right. Relieve Estevez tonight. Until we figure out her role in the crazy palace intrigue playing out in that country, I don't want her left alone for a minute."

"She'll object, you know. She thinks we're barking up the wrong tree."

"Not her call."

"She's not going to like us on her ass."

"Walker?"

"Yeah, boss?"

There was a slight pause. "Then make her like it."

Chapter 6

*P*ounding.

Something was pounding, pounding like a drum. Like a fist. A fist on the door.

Awoken from a deep sleep, she gasped as the door was flung open.

Walker!

The room was dark, black dark, midnight dark, and he was standing in a wedge of dim light shining in from the corridor, the corridor that was always lit, always eye-blindingly bright. But now it was in a dim glow, as if by candlelight. Or the golden dawn of Italy…

Walker's blond hair shimmered as though wet, too long and quiveringly untamed and…caveman-sexy. He wore soft blue jeans and a long-sleeved shirt, open, that billowed out from his skin in a warm gentle breeze. She could see his chest, broad and muscular and coarse-haired, with small flat nipples that beckoned to her tongue.

She shivered.

"What do you want?" she asked, though she knew the answer. She could read it in his eyes. She'd read it there the first time she'd seen him, and in each moment that had passed since.

"You."

She licked her lips. And realized she was completely naked. Lying on a cloud-soft bed that smelled of...roses.

"Scared?"

"I've never done anything like this before," she whispered. "Ever."

Sex with a stranger was dangerous. In every way possible. But she wanted him.

And he wasn't a stranger. He was Walker.

She spread her legs, very slightly. His didn't miss the movement. He stepped into the room and closed the door. Instant blackness. She heard the snick of a lock. Her heartbeat zinged.

"You are a very naughty little girl." His lazy Southern accent was smooth and sinful, reaching out to her from the absolute darkness.

She spread her legs wider. Dizzy with anticipation.

"Yes," she said in a small voice, the tips of her breasts tightening to hard, aching points. Her body so ready for him she would surely die if he didn't come to her soon.

"I do like that in a woman," he purred.

She felt the bed dip. Smelled his cologne. Spicy, rugged, American. So different from what she was used to a man smelling like—refined, elegant...boring. Walker was different from any man she'd ever met.

"You know what I want, Dr. Shaw?" Shy. Demure. Teasing. So unlike her.

The bed dipped again and the edges of his open shirt brushed over her breasts. A cascade of goose bumps. Strong legs in rough denim forced her thighs far apart. The smell of crushed rose petals. The whisper of warm breath.

"What does my lady want?"

Him. *She wanted him so badly her whole body trembled beneath the weight of his erotic appeal.*

She put her mouth to his ear. Told him exactly what she wanted. In words she'd never uttered aloud.

He chuckled. Full and wicked, laden with a rogue's promise. "Whatever you say, sugar. Your wish is my command."

Then his tongue was on her breasts. Her body lifted, bowed. Blinding pleasure. Endlessly blinding pleasure. His tongue…his tongue. Oh, yes. Oh, yes.

"Walker!" she cried.

He tried to stay in the chair. Honest to God, he did.

Three times Walker had risen to his feet, and three times he'd made himself sit back down in the overstuffed armchair by Zara's bedside. She hadn't awoken when he'd slipped into her room, relieving Estevez just before midnight. Estevez had stayed in the corridor. Walker preferred being inside, with visual contact. He hadn't known she'd be naked, tangled in the sheets….

Now she was dreaming. And it was obvious what she was dreaming about. Christ, he felt like a voyeur.

He didn't dare get any closer to her. Hell, he should have marched right out of the room at her first whimpered sigh. Made himself sit in the molded plastic chair outside her door. Like a gentleman.

But he was no gentleman. Ask anyone.

So, in guilty fascination, he watched. And listened. And sweated. And ached.

But at the sound of his name on her lips, cried out with such passion, such surrender, his willpower crumbled. He vaulted to his feet, overcome by the sheer stunning temptation of it.

Sweet holy Jeezus.

How much could a man endure?

Yet he stood there, stock-still as his lover's body quivered with pleasure at the hand of his own incubus, glued to the spot by his perpetually inconvenient sense of honor.

She was gorgeous in her unconscious abandon, a living, moaning portrait of how every man dreams of making his woman feel. The irony of the situation was not lost on him.

He watched until she stilled on the disheveled sheets with one long, final exhale. He exhaled, too. Far less contently.

"Walker?" she whispered, eyes opening at some silent signal, disoriented by the potent morphia of sleep and satiety. Her hand reached for him. "What are you doing out of bed?"

He swallowed heavily. Naturally, he would not be let off so easily.

"Zara. Wake up. You've been dreaming, sugar."

Her slumberous eyes took in his finger-mussed hair, his unbuttoned shirt, his enormous arousal.

"No," she whispered. "I've been remembering." Her hand remained raised, her fingers poised in invitation. "Italy. Rose petals. And the touch of a man who truly wanted me."

His gut clenched. A war raged within. "A man who'll always want you," he quietly admitted.

Her lips curved up, softly sensual, and he knew he'd lost the battle before it had begun.

"Come back to me."

He took her hand. Allowed her to strip him of his clothes

and draw him down on top of her. Sighed with need as he sank into the cradle of her embrace, even as his conscience made one last stab at making sure she was fully aware.

"Zara—"

"Shhh. I remember, Walker. Now, make love to me the way you did in Florence."

He groaned. Unable to resist her. All the while knowing the whole affair was doomed; they were not meant for each other and never would be. She didn't know about him. Couldn't. He didn't care. He wanted her too badly.

He covered her mouth and her body and took what she offered. Took every beautiful inch, every whispered entreaty, every sweet moan. And in return gave her everything he had.

For this night she was his again. And he was hers. Completely. Until morning intruded, there was no outside world. No princes and ladies, no scandals and ruined chances. No perceptions.

Just two minds and bodies intertwining in perfect union.

He would forget everything else and concentrate on that. On tonight. While he still had the fantasy within his grasp. Tonight would have to last a lifetime.

Because tomorrow…

Well, tomorrow was another day.

When Walker awoke, the sun was shining through the mullioned windows, filling the room with the clean, crisp light of morning. Zara was draped across his chest, yawning and starting to stretch muscles that must be as tasked as his own. His arms were around her, loosely, her hip just grazing the evidence of his continued want of her.

He felt the moment she became conscious of his presence under her, of their nakedness, of his arousal, of all they had done the night before. She gave a soft gasp, then glanced up at his face and smiled.

Suddenly, though, it faltered. Her sleepy eyes became questioning, wary. And his heart sank.

So soon, his reprieve was up.

She opened her mouth, but he carefully laid his thumb over her lips.

"Hush, now. I was afraid you hadn't recalled everything last night. But now you do. I understand that you have to take it all back and let me go. But please, sugar, don't think badly of me. I couldn't stand it if you did."

Her head gave a little shake. Uncertain. It broke his heart.

He wanted to spin her under him again, beg her to let him take her one more time. One last time fill her with his length, and know what it was to possess her.

But he didn't have the courage. Her rejection would shatter him. And reject him she surely would. She had to, if there was a hint of doubt in her mind that he had slept with that girl back home. Last night was too soon after Zara had officially ceased being his patient—or whatever she was—to be a convincing argument in his favor. He knew that. He had known that when he'd made the choice in the throes of temptation.

Still, she would believe in him, or she would not. He prayed she would. But in the end it would not matter. It was those ubiquitous perceptions that would prevail if she remained true to her lifelong dream.

She slid off him, eyes cast down, hurrying into the bathroom.

Damn, he thought. Damn, damn, damn.

He rolled out of bed, swiped up his clothes and threw them on, then paced back and forth at the foot of the bed. When he heard the shower turn on and the curtain move, he knocked and opened the door.

Just getting under the water, she turned to him guardedly. He leaned a hip against the door frame and folded his arms across his abdomen, trying not to react when she whipped the opaque plastic across the rod, shutting him out.

"Your medical board with Dr. Landon is set for nine o'clock," he said.

"I'll be there."

Well, at least she was still speaking to him. A good sign?

He glanced at his watch. The second hand advanced slowly. The sound of water hitting flesh was driving him crazy. "Estevez will be back to start his shift in about twenty minutes."

"I don't need a bodyguard, Walker. I don't like it."

He sighed. Stubborn woman. "In case you hadn't noticed, someone may be trying to kill you, Zara."

"I'm not convinced—"

"Doesn't matter." He cut her off. "Lord Carrington's orders."

Long, awkward moments ticked by, filled with hot steam and the scent of floral soap and shampoo. He stuck his hands under his armpits against the urge to pull back the curtain.

"Fine, whatever," she finally said. "Hand me a towel, would you please?"

"No," he said. Perversely petulant. He wanted to see her lush curves again. All of them. She could get her own damn towel.

There was a brief pause, a jetted breath, then the curtain yanked back. She regarded him, doing nothing to hide her nudity. Then she jerked a towel off the rack. "Walker, I don't regret what happened between us, if that's what you think."

"Good. Because Corbett put me on guard duty with Estevez. I've got your back every night until this thing is solved."

Her eyes went wide and she forgot about the towel.

He didn't. He shifted his stance, leaning his back against the jamb, and crossed his ankles, wishing he could do something about it. "Don't worry. I'll stick to a chair in the corridor from now on." Like a proper gentleman.

"No need for you to put yourself out."

"Zara—"

"I'm moving home today."

"What?" He almost fell backwards in his haste to straighten off the door frame. "When was this decided?"

"Just now."

"No. No damn way. Corbett'll have a hissy fit and I—" his gaze slid over her water-slick body, making her pull the towel around herself "—I'm not comfortable with that arrangement."

Her chin rose. "As I said, there's no need. If Russell insists I have a bodyguard, I'll hire someone else."

It was as though she'd slapped him full on the face.

Hurt and fury swirled through him. He stared at her in disbelief.

Hell.

He didn't deserve this. He'd maintained his honor and integrity throughout this whole painful ordeal, succumbing to his true feelings only *after* she was no longer his patient. When *she'd* invited him in. He'd cut it close, true, but he had waited. Unlike her, who'd repeatedly thrown herself at him.

"You don't give a good goddamn about my side of the story, do you?" he growled.

At least she had the grace to look embarrassed. She started to speak but he slashed his hand in a gesture for silence.

"Never mind," he said, spun on his heel and stalked out.

"Walker!" she called after him, but it was too late. He was done.

He slammed the door behind him, the bang echoing off the three-foot-thick stone walls like a gunshot. Juvenile, but gratifying.

He stormed down the hallway, almost running into Estevez. The other man's brows hiked. "Hey, what's up, buddy?"

"Not a damn thing," he gritted out. "She's all yours."

And he was welcome to her.

Oh, God.

What had she done?

Zara groaned out loud.

Walker was right. She'd been brutally unfair to him. Like the imperious Queen of Hearts shouting "Off with his head!" Condemning him without a trial because of her own fear.

She'd been gutted by the brilliant memory of what they'd shared in Italy. Gutted by their incredible night of lovemaking. And even more gutted by the subsequent recollection of his very public fall into professional disgrace—and the reason why.

Because that fall made all the rest impossible.

Just as he'd said all along.

He'd known. And when she'd realized she couldn't have him, she'd resented him for it. For not warning her.

Except he had. Repeatedly. And she hadn't listened. She'd listened only to her own foolish fantasies. Turning a long-ago schoolgirl crush into something it wasn't. Something real. Making a charismatic scoundrel into something he wasn't. An honorable man. The whole academic community involved in neurology had been abuzz with the scandal involving their golden boy. His lack of denial had shocked everyone, condemning him in absentia.

She straightened her spine. But even a scoundrel deserved a fair hearing. She hadn't given him a chance to give his side of things. Maybe there were mitigating circumstances. Lord knew, she herself had thrown professional ethics to the wind easily enough when it came to Dr. Walker Shaw.

She was of the nobility, the daughter of one of the most respected men in the country, and she was supposed to set an example for the people of Silvershire. Use wisdom and reason in all things. Make decisions founded on facts, not rumor. With Walker, she'd acted on pure, base emotion. She of all people should know better.

And she did. She took a deep, cleansing breath. After she was finished with the medical recertification, she'd go to him and apologize. Listen to his side.

Then maybe she could forgive herself this particular guilt. So she could get back to her life. To her work. Because that was all that mattered now. Now that Walker was lost to her.

Meeting with Russell and Dr. Landon in one of the intimate palace salons, Zara was somehow able to push Walker to the back of her mind and concentrate on answering their questions. After the obligatory tea and biscuits had been served, Russell went first, quizzing her gently about friends and family.

"They've been very worried about you," he told her. "It's been hard on your parents to stay away all this time. They'd like to see you, now you've recovered."

She smiled. Her father had probably been a royal pain in Russell's backside with his phone calls. She and the Marquis had their considerable differences, but he took his duties as a father seriously. Despite her heretical opinions about the succession of his title and her ambitions in that direction, he would see her to rights.

"Are they here in Silverton?" she asked.

"They want you home at Danehus."

"Ah." The warm-fuzzies dimmed slightly. "I'll give them a call this afternoon. I don't like leaving King Weston while he's still critical." She gave Dr. Landon an apologetic look. "I know you're doing everything in your power—"

The distinguished doctor waved her off. "It will be a relief having you back on the team. Perhaps together we can figure out what is keeping him in his coma."

With that segue, Russell excused himself, and Dr. Landon settled into his questioning, starting by asking her about her health in general, and if anything at all had changed since the accident, other than her memory.

She stifled a sigh. *What hadn't?*

But she wasn't about to go there.

She picked up the Royal Copenhagen teapot from a silver tray at her elbow and refilled their cups, avoiding his gaze. "I've had some rather bizarre dreams," she admitted, endeavoring not to blush at the one she'd had last night. The one that had directly led to this morning's fiasco. She wasn't going *there,* either. "But I suppose that's to be expected with a head injury."

To be honest, she was a little concerned about the two other, really strange dreams she'd had. They'd been so extraordinary and yet so…lifelike, they almost hadn't seemed like dreams at all. More like hallucinations. No, like *visions.*

"Are you still having them?"

She added milk to their tea. Regardless, she had no intention of letting a couple of silly dreams prevent her from going back to work. "I really only had two or three," she evaded. "I'll let you know if I have any more."

Thank goodness that satisfied him, and he brought out a National Medical Board exam booklet and the real test began. She was able to answer each question to the degree that they actually started debating theory together and comparing notes on the various procedures they'd done in common. Instead of being the chore she had anticipated, it was so exhilarating that several hours later they both looked up in surprise to see Russell walking in followed by two liveried manservants carrying loaded lunch trays.

"I say, is it so late?" Dr. Landon asked with a laugh.

Russell gave him a dry look. "It's after three. I thought you both might have passed out from hunger, so I took the liberty."

Zara grinned. "No sardine sandwiches, I trust." Russell had been an infamous prankster growing up. One of his specialties had been making sardine sandwiches for their picnics—using fish bait instead of the traditional ingredient.

The future king feigned a wounded look. "Certainly not." Then they burst out in laughter.

The country of Silvershire didn't know what it was in for with him as head of state.

As they ate and chatted, she thought about how much he'd changed from that carefree young rapscallion. Though he didn't exactly have the stolid, serious demeanor of most reigning monarchs, he had taken on the heavy responsibility without protest, putting his all into the job, even though he had stated publicly he really didn't want to be king.

On the other hand, she had stayed much the same.... Ever the serious, driven perfectionist. Even as a girl, she'd always been the epitome of propriety and aristocratic decorum. Yet here he was destined to be king, and she...would she ever achieve her goal of becoming the first Marchioness of Daneby...?

Russell supported her quest to change the ancient laws, even going as far as to say he'd bring it up for discussion with the Privy Council when the time came. So there was finally some real hope on the horizon.

But not unless King Weston recovered. If he didn't, no one

would ever speak her name again at court. So it was time to put her whole focus on work.

Which meant she had to clear up one last lingering problem....

"Your Grace," she said after Dr. Landon had taken his leave, "There's something we need to discuss."

Russell glanced up at her use of formal address. His mouth assumed a determined line. "It's not up for discussion."

"But you haven't even heard—"

"I know exactly what you're about to say. Dr. Shaw has informed me of your intention to hire some outside body-guard. I'm afraid it's out of the question."

She opened her mouth to argue.

He raised a finger to stop her. "No. I've appointed the Lazlo Group to take care of this whole painful situation, and I trust Corbett Lazlo's judgment implicitly. If he has assigned Shaw to be your bodyguard, your bodyguard he shall be. Also," Russell continued, taking the wind completely out of her sails, "Shaw mentioned something about you wanting to move back home. That I may consider, though my instincts are against it."

She flopped back in her chair with a scowl. "You've really gotten quite bossy in your old age, Russell," she said peevishly.

He had the nerve to grin. "I do rather like being king of the world." He looked at her sympathetically. "So. What's going on between you two?"

She held her expression perfectly neutral. "Whatever do you mean?"

"Don't even try, Zara. I recognize all the signs. Having been there myself. Very recently." He steepled his fingers. "Dr. Shaw is a good man. However..." He paused. "Be careful. He does come with a certain amount of unpleasant baggage. You'd do well to be discreet, given your position in society."

She had no idea what *signs* he was talking about, but she'd heard enough. She didn't need Lord Russell Carrington's advice. He had been the very height of indiscretion, carrying on with the late crown prince's fiancée practically on the eve of the royal wedding! Their hasty marriage after the prince's untimely demise had been nothing less than a scandal. But Amelia was a princess, so that made everything all right….

Shocked at her uncharitable thoughts, Zara was nevertheless unable to stop a subtle rebuke. Rising from her chair, she used every ounce of aristocratic bearing she could muster, and said, "You know me better than that, Your Grace. What I cannot do openly, I won't do at all."

With a sigh, Russell came to his feet as well. "Yes. I do know. Come, darling. I didn't mean to insult you. I only meant, once in a while you should let yourself do something really reckless. Just be smart about it."

He sounded so sincere, she was unable to stay angry with him. "Like you, you mean?" she softly chided.

There was that grin again, the unrepentantly mischievous one that said he'd do precisely the same things all over again, and more, given the chance. "Yes. Exactly like me."

"Well," she said, allowing him to pull her into a brotherly hug and kiss her on the forehead, "I'll think about it."

And undoubtedly she would. For a long, long time to come. But that was all she'd do. Because anything more would be…reckless.

Chapter 7

"What the hell happened?"

Fearing the worst, Walker rushed into the emergency room at the Royal Medical University Hospital. After running the gamut of reporters and tabloid photographers and a line of cops, he headed straight for the white curtain surrounding the only occupied bed in the ER.

The urgent message he'd gotten from the Lazlo Group secretary had been garbled by bad cell reception, but he'd heard the words *Zara*, *hospital* and *hurt* loud and clear.

He scanned the small enclosure after hurriedly pulling back the curtain. Zara stood by the headboard with her arms wrapped around herself, looking shaken. Estevez was lying in the bed grimacing as a doctor fussed with his arm.

Walker let out a whoosh of relief that their positions weren't reversed. Breaking the speed limits to get here, his only thought had been...too awful to contemplate. He was still mad as hell at Zara, but that didn't mean his heart hadn't almost stopped beating, thinking about her injured, or worse.

"Jeezus, what happened?" he repeated, his pulse lowering a bit.

They both looked up. "Just a broken arm," Estevez said, giving him a pained smile. "Nothing serious."

"Nothing serious! He was sideswiped by a car!" Zara exclaimed, her voice a couple of octaves higher than normal. "The blighter didn't even stop. I'm so angry!"

Walker looked from Zara to Estevez, his pulse kicking right back up. He didn't say a word, but his expression must have asked the question for him. Estevez lifted his shoulders almost imperceptibly, his eyes saying he wished he had a better answer.

"How did it happen?" Walker asked Zara.

She paused for a second, then said, "I spent the afternoon with King Weston and planned to go back this evening, but I wanted to move my things home to my apartment before it got too late. Mr. Estevez and I had done that, and were walking across the street to a deli to grab a bite of dinner." She took a deep breath. "Neither of us saw the car. I think it must have been parked and didn't see us as it came out into traffic."

Estevez remained impassive as he added, "I saw it first and pushed Dr. Smith back onto the sidewalk, but couldn't get out of the way fast enough. He just clipped me, but I landed badly."

"Was it intentional?" Walker asked, deliberately keeping his voice even.

"What do you mean?" Zara asked, frowning. "Of course it—" The words halted as her eyes widened. She glanced at Estevez tentatively. "It was an accident…wasn't it?"

"Under the circumstances I'd definitely treat it as suspicious," he responded, then said to Walker, "Didn't get the plates, but I gave the cops a pretty good description of the car."

"I assume you called Corbett?"

"On the way to the hospital. He said not to let Dr. Smith out of my sight until you got here. Obviously I'm out of commission for guard duty. You're supposed to stay with her until he can find someone to take over for me."

"*Me?*" Walker stiffened, turning to Zara. Now that he knew she was unhurt, all his previous fury with her returned. "I thought you hired someone else."

Her gaze skittered away. "Lord Carrington nixed that idea. He wants you with me."

Oh, wasn't that just peachy. And just what Walker wanted, too—to spend another night in her immediate vicinity. Not. He slashed a hand through his hair and shot Estevez a look. "You going to be okay, buddy?"

The other man nodded. "No sweat."

"Call me tomorrow," Walker said, and started out through the curtain, holding it open for Zara. "Let's go."

She still didn't look at him as she ducked past. "I know a way out that won't take us past the media circus outside."

They didn't talk as she led the way through a series of busy passageways then up a flight of stairs, eventually emerging into the parking structure.

"You've used this escape route before," he said, unlocking the passenger door of his rental car.

"Being the daughter of a marquis has its advantages, but also its downsides. Paparazzi being the worst."

"Tell me about it," he said disgustedly. "A bunch of vultures." The response had been automatic. Visceral. Stupidly revealing.

"Were they very bad to you?"

He didn't need to ask what she was referring to. Not that he wanted to talk about it. She'd had her chance. "Bad enough. Get in, please." She hesitated, then did as she was told. "Where to?" he asked, buckling himself in. She hesitated again.

He made a concerted effort not to snap. "Look. I'm no happier about this situation than you are. But unless I quit my job we're stuck with each other until morning. And I'm not about to quit my job."

"That's not… Walker, I want to apologize," she said, finally meeting his gaze. "For this morning."

"No need," he said, voice gruff. He *so* did not want to have this conversation. "Last night was my fault. I knew better." God, did he ever.

"Oh, and I didn't?" she said dryly.

"No. You didn't have all the facts." He spun the car toward the rear exit, away from the hoopla out front.

"I still don't. Why don't you enlighten me?"

What was the point? It wouldn't make any difference, even if she believed every word. She was trapped by her circumstances, just as he was by his. "Why don't we just drop it, and you tell me where we're going."

She folded her hands in her lap. He figured it was to keep from strangling him. When he was calmer he'd appreciate her efforts. But right now he didn't.

"Fine." She gave him directions to where she lived. It wasn't far. A stylized nineteen-thirties building of about a dozen floors, it was situated on a prime piece of real estate overlooking the River Kairn, with views of the Golden Bridge and the historic district across the water. She obviously had some serious bucks. Or maybe her influential family owned the thing. Maybe both. Must be nice.

When the tires squealed into her assigned spot in the building's underground garage, he looked around, suddenly remembering the reason he was with her. He was supposed to be protecting her.

For the first time in his life Walker wished he owned a gun. Corbett had tried to give him one on several occasions, saying, "Take it. You never know when you'll need a little persuasion," but he had always refused. He was a doctor, not an agent. Sure, he was a Southerner, had hunted deer and ducks with his daddy all through his youth, and could handle a gun better than most—at least a shotgun and hunting rifle—but he didn't like the things. Doctors saved lives; they didn't take them.

"Is something wrong?" Zara asked.

"Just checking the scene."

Something didn't feel right. He backed the car out of the narrow slot and headed for the opposite end of the garage. "I think we'll skip your usual spot for now. Are there any unassigned spaces?"

She frowned. "Is this really necessary?"

"I'm not taking any chances," he said. "But I think you need to know, I'm unarmed and I don't do daring rescues."

"Doesn't matter. I'm used to doing my own rescuing."

For some reason, the firmly stated pronouncement tugged at his gut. That was just plain wrong. His mama would agree with Zara, but his daddy would have a thing or two to say about it. Daddy was from Alabama and believed that a man should take care of his woman. In every way.

But Walker wasn't his daddy, in any way, and Zara sure as hell wasn't his woman. So he didn't comment.

"Here, put this over your shoulders," he ordered after getting her door for her. He slipped out of his suit jacket and held it out. When she stared at him uncomprehendingly, he slid it around her, flipping up the collar. Then he put his arm around her waist, tugged her close and started for the elevator.

"What are you doing?" she demanded, attempting to pull away.

He didn't let her. "If it wasn't an accident this afternoon, someone may be hiding down here, watching for you. They won't be looking for a romantic couple."

Her steps faltered for a split second before she melted into his side. "The garage is gated."

"Yeah. That'll stop them. No, don't look around," he told her when she started to.

He heard her swallow. He followed suit. But for a totally different reason. He hated being this close to her. He could smell her scent, the scent with which he'd reacquainted himself so intimately last night. The warmth of her body as it rubbed against his ribs was the final straw.

He felt himself harden, unable to stop the images of their lovemaking, or his body's reaction to them.

"Walker?"

"Yeah."

"Thank you."

He turned to her, startled. "For what?"

"For doing this. I'm not exactly sure what your job description is with the Lazlo Group, but I'm pretty sure bodyguard isn't it."

"I do a lot of things for Mr. Lazlo," he said as the elevator arrived and they got in. The second the door whooshed closed he let her go and stepped as far away from her as the tiny cubicle allowed.

Holding the lapels of his jacket in her fingers, she pulled it tighter and leaned back against the elegant mirrored wall. "I'd like to hear about them."

He leaned his butt against the opposite wall and regarded her, wanting to hit something when she unconsciously closed her eyes and brushed her nose over his jacket collar, obviously smelling him on it. Her almost imperceptible smile made his already hard arousal lurch.

"No you wouldn't," he growled, and her eyes blinked open. "What floor?" he asked in the same harsh tone.

"Top," she said.

The penthouse. Figured. He punched the button with a little too much vehemence.

The elevator was insufferably slow. It crawled up the twelve floors like an overdressed snail, fluid and silent. She watched him the whole time. He wouldn't give her the satisfaction of looking away, but kept his eyes steadily on hers. As annoying as it was, it impressed him when she didn't look away, either.

As the car crept past the eleventh floor, she said, "Russell thinks I should have an affair with you."

He didn't even move an eyelash for shock. *What was that supposed to mean?* They reached the penthouse and the door opened to a gorgeous marble foyer. They continued to stare at each other until he finally said, "Remind me to tell Carrington to mind his own damn business."

She lowered her eyes and walked out. He followed, acutely uncomfortable on so many levels he lost count. She got her key from her purse and he took it from her.

He pointed off to one side. "Stand there and don't move until I say you can come in."

She opened her mouth. He glowered at her and she closed it again.

Cautiously, he unlocked and cracked the door, sticking his head in before entering. Damn, he was no good at this stuff. What did he know from clearing a scene? Still, he figured it was mostly common sense—turn on all the lights and don't put your nose where you can't see.

Which was exactly how he proceeded—as soon as he recovered from his first glimpse of her apartment.

In keeping with the building, the massive living room was done in high Art-Deco style, with muted colors and graceful curving furniture of burled walnut. Crystal vases, bowls and other arty pieces of frosted pink, clear and sea-green glass dotted the tables and glass bookshelves, some containing dead flower arrangements. A long, low, gray sofa grouping meandered around an incredible inlaid stone Art-Deco fireplace.

Everything in the room oozed of style and class. He was almost afraid to move for fear of breaking something.

Snapping himself out of it, he quickly searched though the rest of the rooms, until he got to one that contained a huge bed with richly carved head and footboards, covered with a pink satin comforter and lace pillows. It smelled of Zara.

He stood paralyzed for a moment on the threshold of his lover's bedroom in a sudden agony of desire, battling against the overwhelming need to go out to the foyer and grab her, throw her onto this seductive bed and thrust himself deep inside her. Fisting his hands at his sides, he counted to ten, twice, and made himself skirt the suitcase sitting by the door and walk in.

He held his breath as he checked the closet.

When he turned to get out of there, she was standing in the doorway. Watching him. Looking like she wanted to say something but was afraid to do so.

He raised a warning palm—*don't*—and swept past her, out of the room. "I thought I told you to stay in the corridor," he gritted out.

"And I told you, I do my own rescuing." She walked after him, the sound of her fashionable high heels on the carpet all but disappearing into the deep pile. "I thought you might need—" she blanched at his expression as he whipped his head around "—a drink. I certainly do." Her voice tried to be resolute but he detected a slight waver.

She went directly to a sleek bar cabinet in the living room. When she lifted the lid it lit up inside, and the front automatically opened down to a flat surface, like a writing desk.

She fetched up a glass from inside, and a bottle with a fancy label. "I'm having a vermouth. If you want something mixed, you'll have to fix it yourself. All I can manage right now is ice." The bottle clinked against her glass and a few drops spilled. "Blast."

He wondered what the chances were of her having a beer in that contraption, and decided slim to none. "Bourbon's fine. No ice."

To his everlasting amazement, she actually pulled an excellent Kentucky brand from deep in the bowels of the cabinet. "It says twelve-year-old, but I imagine it's at least fifteen by now." She tried to smile, but failed miserably. Picking up a squat glass, her hands shook so much he took pity on the bourbon, strode over and relieved her of it.

"Thank you," she murmured, and slid away from him as he poured his drink. She left her heels half way to the sofa, letting them lie where they fell in an artful arrangement.

Damn the woman. She even made taking off her shoes a sensual experience.

He threw back the finger of bourbon he'd poured.

Suddenly, he decided the last thing on earth he should be doing was drinking. After a moment's vacillation and a silent curse, he poured himself another. A double. But made himself walk away from the bottle.

Strolling over to the mantel, he propped himself against it, sipping. She was sitting on the sofa, shapely legs crossed, her head tilted back on the cushions and her eyes closed. In her hand, her glass was empty. He debated filling it for her.

Instead, he decided to let the angry gator out of the pen. "What made you say that? About Russell Carrington?"

Her tongue peeked out from between her lips and swiped over them. An endless moment later, her lashes lifted. "Because every time I see you, all I can think about is taking your clothes off. I wanted you to be as miserable as I am." Her eyes studied him for a moment, then drifted closed again.

He took a long time easing out the breath that had instantly backed up in his lungs at that little tease.

What the goddamn *hell* did she expect him to say to that? "Why don't you, then?" he wanted to shout, but stopped himself. Just.

He tossed back the rest of his drink. "Believe me, sugar, I am," he said.

That little wisp of a smile appeared again at the corner of her mouth, and his balls started to ache.

"Good," she whispered. "Now if you would just accept my apology, I might be able to sleep tonight."

"You're a real piece of work, you know that?"

The smile spread. "Surely, you can do better than that? I've been called much worse."

"I can believe it," he muttered.

She lifted her head and tilted it somberly. "Walker, I am sorry. I had no right to judge you. If you don't want to talk about it, I understand. But I really would like to hear your side of the story."

"Why? So you can assuage your embarrassment over seducing me?"

She grimaced. "Ouch."

He was being unfair and a royal bastard. He knew that. Regardless of who seduced whom, he was the culpable party. He was just so goddamned angry with her because she *had* judged him.

But before he could say anything, she rose, went over and carefully set her glass on the bar, then turned to him.

"I'm not embarrassed. I'm glad. I just wish…" She stopped, sighed and shook her head. "Never mind. The guest room is the first on the right. You should find everything you need. I'll see you in the morning."

Frustration swept through him as he watched her walk down the hall without looking back. Should he go after *her*? Turn the tables and seduce her? Get his piece of revenge by showing the perfect Lady Zara exactly what she'd be missing here in her cool, perfect penthouse without a man to warm her bed? Specifically, him.

Tempting.

But no. He'd never met a woman with a stronger backbone than Zara Smith. She'd kick him out of her bedroom in a hot minute if he went sniffing in there.

Besides, his daddy's words were ringing in his ears…the ones recited as Daddy'd let him borrow the keys to the farm truck on his sixteenth birthday. "Remember, boy, never drive drunk," he'd said with the devil's warning on his usually temperate face, "and don't drive mad. They'll both git you in trouble faster 'n a snake'll bite your ass."

Tonight he was two for two. Drunk—not on bourbon but on lust, egged on by an imagination intoxicated by the bliss they'd shared last night. And definitely mad. Mad enough to know better than to go within fifty feet of the woman while she was sleeping.

Nope, going for a ride tonight would be plumb stupid.

Which left what? Sleep? Not in this lifetime. More bourbon? Not a bad idea, but…he was on duty tonight. He'd already had more than he should.

So he triple-checked the locks on the front door, humored himself by checking under all the furniture and in all the drawers for explosive devices and settled down on the sofa to a long, sleepless night. Trying desperately not to think about how much he wanted to walk to the end of the hall and crawl under that pink satin comforter.

Pounding.

Something was pounding, slowly, like a drum. A timbal. Like a timbal in a funeral procession.

The king's funeral.

She clutched her head, her heart. Massive guilt descended, down, down, pressing her down into the depths of despair.

The king was dead! All her fault.

Suddenly she was in a meadow. A forest meadow, filled with birds and flowers and…no, not flowers, symbols. Strange symbols and letters in gold. Dancing mockingly across the waving grass toward—

Two men. Young men. Fighting. Like two wolves, snapping, tearing, two bears swinging angry fists.

A gun!

The two men stopped, the deadly weapon between them. Pointing. A death knell for…

King Weston! It was the king! Younger, stronger, healthy. But not for long. The other man—who was he?—pulled the trigger. Slowly. Agonizingly. The king's face. Sad. Questioning.

Why?

The sound of the gun exploded in her ears.

No!

* * *

Zara woke up screaming.

"No! Stop! Not the king!"

Two powerful arms came around her. "Zara!"

She had to get away! She fought against him. "*No!*"

"Zara it's me. Walker. Wake up. You're having a nightmare."

She stilled, scraped the cobwebs of terror from her mind and struggled to emerge from the blackness.

"Walker," she whispered. "Oh, God. It was awful. The king. He was trying to kill the king."

A strong hand stroked soothingly down her back. "Who, baby?"

"I—I don't know."

"Tell me what he looked like," Walker's deep, smooth voice urged.

She clung to him, the remnant images of this dream merging with the others she'd had, forming a trio of horrible, frightening visions. *What was wrong with her?*

His warm breath whispered over her temple. *Baby.*

"Tell me. Tell me about it."

She hated weakness. Hated when she felt needy and out of control. But she'd never needed anything in her life more than she needed his arms around her right now.

"Hold me," she murmured. "I'll tell you, but I need—" She didn't finish, ashamed and mortified over her own vulnerability, yet unable to resist the comfort his presence would lend. "Hold me. Please."

Four long heartbeats went by before he moved. Through his clothes she could feel the reluctance in his muscles as he slid into bed beside her and took her into his arms. He froze for a second when he realized she was naked; she was terrified he would vault out of bed again and leave her. She tightened her arms around his waist. It wasn't intended as an invitation, exactly, but if he took it as such, so be it. She needed him there that much.

"Thank you," she whispered, then nestled up against him and told him what he wanted to know. She described the young man with the gun, and at his urging, the rest of the dream as well. Then she told him about the other two. How similar they were. How vivid and lifelike. And frightening.

"What could they mean?" she asked when she'd related everything, down to the tiniest detail. He'd been quiet throughout, except for an occasional probing question.

"They could mean anything. Or nothing," he said after a thoughtful moment. "The mind is an incredible instrument. You don't think you remember anything from the bombing, but maybe you do and the dreams are its way of coming out."

"I suppose…although these really don't feel like memories. They feel more like…visions. Like some kind of a warning. About the king."

"You mean, for the future? I thought you said he was young in the dream."

"Yes, but— Oh, I don't know. The whole thing sounds absurd, even to me."

He was silent a while as his fingers slid unconsciously over her skin. Her body moved instinctively under them, making slow, involuntary undulations as they trailed down her back and over her hip.

"No. Not absurd," he finally said. "I'm sure these dreams are somehow meaningful to you. The question is what they're trying to reveal, what they're all about. You are a highly educated woman and the symbolism could come from anywhere your mind has been. Despite the appearance of the king, they may not be about him at all, but some other man. Or situation."

"Like what?"

"You tell me."

She smiled against the smooth cloth of his shirt. "You're starting to sound like a psychiatrist. Always questions. Shall I get on your couch?"

He made a choking noise and his fingers stopped. "I think you're already quite comfortable enough." His breath shuddered out. "Do you always sleep in the nude, Dr. Smith?"

"My one guilty pleasure, I'm afraid. I love the feel of cool, smooth sheets on my bare skin."

His fingers moved a fraction, and suddenly tension hung in the air as thick as the morning fog over the Kairn.

"Zara?" he whispered.

"Yes?"

"I should go."

Chapter 8

"Stay."

The word slipped out of Zara's mouth before she could stop it.

A soft groan rumbled in Walker's chest. "Baby, this is not going to solve anything."

"I know."

"It'll just make things worse."

"Undoubtedly."

"A glutton for punishment, are you?"

"Only with you."

Pushing his fingers through her hair, he gathered her closer, letting her feel which side of this argument his body was on. "Is this just sex?"

She wasn't sure which answer he wanted. Yes, or no? Most men would prefer the former. But Walker wasn't most men.

"If you want it to be," she whispered.

"And if I don't?"

"Then we're both in trouble."

He swore lightly and canted over her, the weight of him putting a sigh on her lips and a race to her heartbeat. His fingertips glided slowly from her hip to her breast and back. Her breath caught in her throat, along with an ache of desire.

"I'm furious with you, you know that," he said, almost conversationally, as his fingers wreaked havoc over her trembling body.

"Yes," she said. "I noticed. I did try to—" she sucked in air as his knuckles grazed her nipple "—apologize."

He looked down at her, his face barely visible in the dim light of the moon that shone through the window. He was so deadly handsome in his rough-edged, bad-boy way, sexy enough to suck the willpower right out of her. As he had from the first moment she'd seen him, back when she was too young and too filled with blind ambition to appreciate what she had found. Why hadn't she ever answered his calls that final year in the States? What a fool she was.

"I'm not interested in apologies," he said. "I want you to believe me. To believe in me." His fingers caught her nipple. Squeezed. "Do you believe *in* me, Zara?"

She was panting. Squirming. His fingers were slowly, systematically killing her. She started to speak. But his lips came down on hers.

"No. Don't answer," he whispered into her mouth. "I don't want lies. Don't ever lie to me, Zara. Even if it hurts."

"I won't," she promised as his mouth covered hers and he kissed her. Wondering if she had been about to do that very thing…

Pushing away the thought, she opened to him, relished the taste of him, the feel of his cotton shirt scraping over her breasts and the wool of his trousers tickling her thighs, the smell of their desire musky in her nostrils.

When he reached for his buttons, she stopped his hand. "No. I want to."

He let her roll them so she was on top, straddling him. He looked so incongruous—his disreputable hair and two-day stubble jarring against the feminine pink satin and white lace of her bed linens.

He was so wrong for her. So inappropriate. A disaster surely waiting to happen.

But she'd never wanted anyone or anything more. And he was all hers.

For tonight, at any rate.

One by one she undid his buttons, kissing and licking his sweat-spicy skin as she went. He protested mildly when she broke off to peel his shirt from his arms, but the protest ended on a moan when she worked his zipper down and parted his fly. Like everything else about him, his arousal was flagrant and demanding, pulsing hungrily beneath a thin veil of cotton.

"Don't stop now," he murmured, rough and low.

"Not for anything."

She pushed both layers of clothing down his hips, and took him in her mouth.

His reaction was powerful and instantaneous. He bowed up, swore harshly, and held her head still with an iron grip. "Sweet mercy, woman."

She could taste his passion, salty and potent, and smell the earthiness of his fever. She licked around him, circling his iron-hard thickness with her tongue.

A second later she was on her back and he was on top of her. Then he was inside her. Moving. Thrusting. *Pounding.*

She wound her arms around his neck. Giving herself up to

it. To him. And she knew with desperate certainty that if she weren't careful, this man could spell the end to her life as she knew it, to all her dreams.

To have this…this incredible feeling, could she throw it all away?

How could she choose?

He took her without mercy, without quarter, without sweet words or promises. But without questions, either. Which was good, because she wasn't sure she could answer them truthfully.

Except for one. The only question she could think of as he scythed into her over and over, bringing them both to the glittering edge of sanity.

Did she want him, always?

Tumbling over the other side, she called out her answer. "Yes! Oh, Walker, yes!"

The next morning could have been awkward. Should have been awkward. Their differences and impossibilities still lay over them like a shroud, nothing having been solved and everything hopelessly muddled by indulging in another night of lovemaking.

Except that Zara awoke to Walker's formidable length sliding into her from behind.

She smiled, coming awake by delicious degrees. "I could get used to this," she said on a soft moan.

"Definitely." He lifted her hair to kiss the back of her neck. "A surefire way to have a good morning."

He held her and thrusted, making her toes curl. *So good.* How could you push away a man who felt so extraordinarily right inside you?

She couldn't. Closing her eyes, she allowed him to set the pace and bring them both to a leisurely but earth-shaking climax.

After last night's tumult of dream-visions and then the carnal excesses of Walker's lovemaking throughout the intervening hours, she felt spent and boneless. But oh, so wonderful. The imprint of his body was on hers permanently; she could still feel him hot and hard between her legs even when he finally withdrew to slide from the bed.

"What are you planning for the day?" he called from the loo.

She stretched luxuriantly. "Back to work. I need to be with King Weston."

She heard the shower start. "Wow. This bathroom is something else. I thought you said your only sinful indulgence was sleeping in the nude." He appeared in the doorway with a grin. "Four heads? A fireplace?"

She grinned back as she got out of bed. "A woman has to take her pleasure where she can get it."

His brow hiked roguishly. "Yeah? Tell me more."

"You are incorrigible." She gave him a quick kiss that somehow turned into a long one. "Lord, Walker, even you must have a limit."

"Haven't found one yet. There an extra toothbrush in that guest bedroom?" She nodded, and he said, "I'll be right back."

By the time he returned she was in the shower. He joined her without asking, and immediately plastered her against the cold marble wall for a quickie she didn't think she had in her.

Afterward, she laughed, grabbing his shoulders when her knees threatened to dissolve under her. "Darling, when you asked if this was just sex, I thought that proposition included things like breathing and eating in between."

"Can't keep up, eh?"

"I'm shocked you can. We're not teenagers."

He winked. "I've had a bit of a dry spell. Besides, we have a lot of time to make up for. Seven years' worth."

She mock groaned. "I'll need crutches."

He gathered her in his arms. "You complainin', Dr. Smith?"

After another long kiss, she sighed dreamily. "Definitely not, Dr. Shaw."

They finished getting ready, and Walker grimaced at putting the same clothes back on again. "Since I haven't heard from Corbett about Estevez's replacement, when we get to the medical wing I'll arrange for a couple of the palace guards to take over for a while. I need to go to the hotel and collect my things." He glanced up at her. "I assume it's okay if I move in here?"

The question threw her for a loop. She hadn't really considered that aspect of their relationship.

If Walker showed up at her apartment with his luggage in hand, the tabloids would have a field day. She knew Edwards, the doorman, must have an arrangement with the *Quiz* to keep an eye on her comings and goings. They always seemed to know everything she was up to, complete with photos. Even now, she was sure they had a photographer downstairs to catch them as they left the building.

A bodyguard she could explain, after the bombing. But not one with a suitcase and a sated smile on his face. They'd want to know everything about him. And they'd find out, too. The *Quiz* was fickle and relentless.

Her hesitation caused his smile to disappear. "Zara?"

"Walker, I'm not sure that's such a good idea."

As her meaning became clear, his mouth thinned to a flat line and his beautiful blue eyes shuttered to a hard gray. "I see," he drawled. "Forgive me. I seem to have forgotten my place, milady." He made a mocking bow and strode from the bedroom.

"Walker, wait!" She hurried after him, grabbing her jacket on the way. "I didn't mean we can't—" The words congealed in her mouth at the stony look he gave her.

He took a pair of silver reflector sunglasses from his pocket and slid them on, effectively cutting her off. "I'll be waiting in the foyer when you're ready, Lady Zara. As befitting my station as your bodyguard. Even one providing stud service."

She reeled back as he whisked through the door and closed it behind him with a definitive snick.

Stud service?

Oh! Of all the impudent, rude, arrogant—

For the first time since she was a girl she wanted to stomp her foot and growl, then smack the man but good. The bloody *nerve!*

Moving in together after a couple of nights in bed might be what one did in America, but it certainly *wasn't* what one did in Silvershire. Especially if one was a public figure. Everything she did reflected on her family name; not to mention her chances of convincing an old-fashioned public and a hopelessly calcified Privy Council into changing the ancient entailment laws.

Walker would have to understand. Making love to her was like making love to a thousand years of tradition.

Except, of course, they *hadn't* made love. They'd had sex. Complicated sex, but just sex. They'd agreed…hadn't they?

He'd even warned her himself about getting involved with a man like him. Implying that the scandal surrounding him would rub off on her. Did he think because she'd slept with him she was willing to take that risk?

Apparently he did.

Oh, God, she had made a terrible mistake!

As selfish as she was, she *wasn't* willing to take the risk. His reputation *would* rub off on her and she'd be tainted, her childhood dream shattered. And now, of all times, when it was so close to coming true. When Russell had promised…

With a frustrated huff, she finished getting ready and sailed out the front door to join her recalcitrant lover.

"Allow me, milady," he said, and smoothly took the key from her hands to lock up.

"Stop it, Walker," she snapped. "Just bloody stop it."

He turned the deadbolt key belligerently and handed it back to her. "Sorry if my service displeases—"

"Don't be a snot." She closed in toe-to-toe and poked him in the chest. She could be as intimidating as any man she knew, despite her lack of inches. "You know damn well how I feel about you. I couldn't have made it any clearer. I've never been as foolish with any man as I've been with you." Sentiment aside, she was dangerously close to being on a tear. And Dr. Zara Smith on a tear was a force to be reckoned with. "But just because I've been foolish doesn't mean I'm a fool. I have to live in this country long after you've gone. I want to be with you, Walker, but I must use a little discretion."

She refused to back up when he looked down his rebellious nose at her with a raptor's stare. "Is that what Lord Carrington told you?"

"What?"

"To use discretion. When he advised you to have an affair with me."

Her mouth gaped. "This has nothing to do with what Lord Carrington did or didn't say! I have a reputation to maintain. And you—" She halted. Laying it out in black and white was unnecessary. He knew all this already.

"And I," he pronounced carefully in his slow, honeyed drawl, "am a major liability." His mien was flinty and his eyes tried hard to be cold, but the chill disguised the barest shadow of hurt. "Here's the thing, sugar. I don't do boy toy. Which is why I told you all along to keep your hands off me." His mouth thinned. "I have no interest in being Lady Zara's dirty little secret."

With that, he sidestepped her and went to the elevator, holding the door that opened right on cue.

She stared at him for a moment, uncertain whether to feel chastised or insulted. A little of both, she imagined. And more than a little chagrined that he had pinned the situation so unequivocally. Not that she had thought of it in exactly those terms…but the truth of it was undeniable. If they were to continue, she would have to hide him from public view.

She got into the elevator and after he punched the button, she went over to him, again standing toe-to-toe. But this time she lifted her lips to his cheek, brushing them over his skin, absorbing the scent of him, shivering at the prickle of stubble on her chin.

"I'm sorry," she whispered.

And since that said it all, she stepped back and turned away, steeling herself for the long ride to the ground floor, and whatever lay beyond.

Walker kept his mouth shut and was careful to stay a step or two behind Zara, as befitted a hired watchdog. He'd worn his reflector shades and deliberately not shaved since starting this gig, to make himself less recognizable to the *Quiz* paparazzi. He kept his face away from the phalanx of cameras as the car emerged from the parking garage, and again while walking into the Royal Palace.

He was being a prick to Zara, he knew that. But he just couldn't help himself. He didn't like being treated like a servant. He was used to calling the shots, being the head honcho, the star talent on the team and basking in the limelight. Not the rent-a-grunt hidden in the back room. He *hated* that.

For the first time since joining the Lazlo Group, he felt

renewed anger over his lost career and furious frustration at the circumstances under which it had been taken from him.

And for the first time ever, he considered calling Ramona Burdette's bluff. He should have reported her to the police and told the press the truth, even if they didn't believe it. For his honor, if nothing else.

Doing that might not have helped this situation any, but at least he wouldn't feel dirty and ashamed. He could hold his head high when Zara refused to acknowledge him publicly and know she was dead wrong.

But as things stood now, who could blame her? She had no way of knowing about the threats to his family, and he was not about to tell her, or anyone.

Damn, what a mess he'd made of his life.

How had that happened?

All he'd ever wanted was to help people, to do his medical research, making the world a little better for his being in it.

He had definitely hit bottom when the woman he was falling in love with wouldn't even admit to the world they were dating, much less in a relationship. If that's what it was.

Nope. Until he figured things out, it was far better to keep some distance between them. Letting his emotions run wild was the very worst thing he could do. All that would accomplish was landing himself in a world of hurt. And that was something he could live without.

"Sorry, old thing," Corbett said on the phone a few minutes after Walker had delivered Zara to King Weston's bedside. There were already two guards posted at the king's door, so Walker felt safe leaving her there for a few minutes to call Lazlo.

"What do you mean, you can't find anybody?" Walker fumed. "There's got to be someone who can fill in for Estevez!"

"Afraid not. Everyone's on assignment. We're stretched to the limit."

"What about Carrington? Can't he lend you a couple of palace guards, or pull someone from the National Police?"

Corbett cleared his throat. "Lord Carrington seemed to think… That is, he implied that it wouldn't be a problem for you to stay with her 24/7."

"And what the hell gave him that idea?" Walker demanded. Unless Zara had called him in the middle of the night—which he knew for a fact she hadn't—there was no way Carrington could know about them.

"Didn't say. I just assumed you two had taken a stroll down memory lane. As it were." Corbett chuckled at his own joke.

Walker gritted his teeth. "I'd just as soon skip being smeared all over the European tabloids and dragging her along with me. Which you know will happen if they think we're an item and find out who I am."

"Lad," Corbett said more somberly, "Work with the aristocracy long enough over here and it's bound to happen sooner or later. May as well get it over with."

"I won't take Zara down, too."

"Ah." Corbett sighed. "Well, in any case, we've no choice. She needs protection, and you're the only one who can do it right now. I'll call as soon as anyone frees up."

Shutting off the phone, Walker let out a string of curses. Damn, damn, damn. He was so screwed. And he had a sinking feeling Zara was, too. All because of him.

"Lord Carrington has invited us to lunch."

Walker glanced up from the book he'd been pretending to read in a wingback chair across from the nurses' station. Carrington? Just the meddling son of a gun he didn't want to see. "No thanks."

Zara's brows furrowed reprovingly. "One cannot refuse the acting monarch his generous hospitality."

"I can." He lifted his book again and ignored her.

Her pretty flowered pump swung back and kicked him neatly in the shin, almost surprising him into a smile. "Stop acting like a petulant child, Walker. Honestly, you'd think I'd refused your advances instead of practically dragging you into my bed."

He couldn't stop his lip from curling at her description. Yeah, he'd been kicking and screaming, too. He leaned back and regarded her. "Not a petulant child, baby, a wounded lover."

Her little chin went up. "I can't help the world I was born into, Walker. God knows I wish things were different. But they aren't. Can't we at least be friends?"

"Friends?" he asked, incredulous. "Are you insane?"

She huffed. "All right, civilized, then."

He gave a humorless bark of laughter. "You forget, I am an untamed savage from the colonies. A Southern bad boy with manners to match. I don't do civilized."

"Silvershire never had colonies," she said archly, and crossed her arms over her breasts. "And I'm growing a bit weary of all the things you don't 'do.'"

"You didn't have any complaints last night," he said evenly. Goadingly. It infuriated him that even now, after all that had been said between them, he still wanted her. His body pulsed with need just from her nearness and the slight drift of her scent that reached him from where she stood.

"No," she said just as evenly. "Only this morning. Come on. Russell is waiting."

She looked so expectant and imperious that he almost continued to refuse. He was dead sure no one dared refuse her anything when she used that look. She must have studied it for years in front of a mirror to get it just right. He'd love to see her reaction if he really put on his mule and dug in.

But he was her bodyguard and shouldn't let her out of his sight. Life sucked.

"Well, in that case—" he stood resignedly and swept a hand for her to lead on "—it wouldn't do to keep His Grace waiting."

Walking three paces behind her down the ornate hall of mirrors and portraits, he decided the view might be worth the concession. She had on some kind of couture suit the color of a Caribbean sea, very tailored and very flattering to her auburn hair—even stuck up in a confining twist the way it was. The pencil skirt fitted her like a kid glove, showcasing all the right curves in all the right places. Her killer high heels were the perfect height to show off her slim, shapely legs. And the whole package was even better because she knew how to walk like a samba. Hell, she was so sexy she made his mouth water.

What was wrong with the men of this country that they'd let a woman like her remain single for so long?

Then he remembered who she was. There probably weren't a lot of men who measured up to the standards she set for herself. Hadn't she said something about that? About a duke, a prince, an earl, being a suitable match for her? No wait, that had been him talking.

Why didn't he ever listen to himself?

"Darling, you look lovely," Carrington said to Zara as they entered the small salon where the noonday meal was being served. He kissed each cheek, glancing smugly over her shoulder at Walker, who was doing his best not to react to the sight. Or flatten the bastard.

Hell, Carrington was a duke, soon to be a frigging king.

Had she had designs on him before he'd run off and married a princess? A sobering thought.

"Dr. Shaw, so glad you could join us."

Walker politely refrained from pointing out he'd had no choice. You see? He could be a gentleman when he had to.

For the Lazlo Group's sake he continued to exhibit exemplary manners that would make his mama proud, though they were damn difficult to maintain while Carrington oozed continental charm all over Zara and fairly ignored him throughout most of the meal. Especially when the duke turned to him and said, "So, Shaw, I trust you are keeping our Lady Zara safe…and happy?"

"Safe, yes," he replied with a hint of challenge in his tone. "Anything else is none of your business." At Zara's gasp, he added, "Your Grace," with an incline of his head.

Instead of being furious at the affront, Carrington gave a roar of laughter. "I see you've finally met your match, darling," he said to her with a grin. "I had a feeling that might be the case."

"*Really*, Russell," she admonished, an unreadable look on her pinkened face.

The grin stayed firmly in place, but Carrington's eyes were deadly when he turned back to Walker and said, "See that she stays safe, Shaw. I would be very unhappy if she were hurt— in any way."

"As would I," Walker said with equal gravity, and seized his opportunity to get out of this untenable situation. "Which is why I'd like to ask you to find someone else to watch Dr. Smith's back. Someone who actually knows something about security."

Carrington's brows shot into his scalp. "Indeed? You don't feel competent to guard her?"

"I'm a doctor. I've had weapons training, but not much else. I don't even have a gun."

"Well, that is easily rectified. But I'll admit you've taken me by surprise. I hadn't foreseen a request for a replacement."

He glanced at Zara, who was studying her dessert plate with an inscrutable expression. "I'm afraid, though, that I'm inclined to leave the decision to Lady Zara. After all, it's her life we're talking about."

"Dr. Smith is hardly the right person to—"

But Carrington waved off his protest. "Zara? Is that your wish, too? Shall I place your care in someone else's hands? Or...do you still want Dr. Shaw?"

Chapter 9

Walker didn't cotton to having his future decided by others. He liked even less the feeling that the use of his body was being negotiated as though he were some kind of male courtesan. "Do you still want Dr. Shaw," had nothing to do with guarding her safety, and all three of them knew it.

Walker swept to his feet, but before he could spit the protest from his tongue, her eyes met his and she calmly answered, "Yes. I still want him."

His outrage was tempered only by the gratification that she was willing to humble herself to the ruler of the land to keep him in her bed.

Faint recompense for the sting of her not believing in him.

Carrington smiled. "Well, then, it's settled. I'll notify the captain of my guard, Dr. Shaw, and you will be issued your weapon of choice."

His weapon of choice would be dueling pistols at dawn

But that wasn't likely to happen. Besides, he wasn't sure who should be holding the other pistol. As appealing as the thought of Carrington was, the duke was only trying to run his country by protecting a possible witness to treason. By comparison, his own concerns didn't amount to a hill of beans, as an equally cornered man once said.

Walker was plenty Southern enough to know when to stand tough and when to retreat to fight another day.

Loosening his grip on the back of the Louis XV dining chair, he sketched a half bow. "Your Grace." But he wasn't going down without some concession. "I'll need my things," he stated. At Carrington's questioning look, he said, "My luggage. I'll want it delivered to Dr. Smith's apartment."

"I'll see to it at once," the duke said, and signaled to a servant standing by the door. As quickly as that, it was done.

Zara was watching the exchange, those inscrutable eyes still peering at him from above blushed cheeks. He gave her a take-that look and her spine straightened even more than it already was. He didn't know why that subtle gesture made him want to sweep aside the porcelain and crystal from the table, push her onto it and—

Lord have mercy.

Where the *hell* was this coming from? Time to get out of here.

"Thank you, Your Grace. If you'll excuse me, I think I'll go see about a weapon right now, while you two finish up."

With that, he strode toward the door.

But Zara's voice stopped him. "Dr. Shaw, when you're free, would you please join me in the medical wing? I'd like your help with a project this afternoon."

He turned, shocked to feel heat creeping up his neck. But no. Even *she* couldn't be that bold. "A project?"

"I assume you can use the Internet?"

It took a good five seconds for him to drag his mind back north from where it had wandered. "I know what Google is.'

"Good. Then bring your reading glasses. If you need them."

He regarded her for a long moment before wordlessly turning on a toe and striding out the door.

She knew damned well he needed reading glasses.

In Florence they'd spent a highly memorable hour or so putting words into actions from a small volume of nineteenth-century erotic Italian poetry she'd had in her purse from an earlier shopping expedition. She'd made him read as she translated the Italian onto his body until they'd been so distracted they'd forgotten all about the poems—and his wire-framed reading glasses, which he'd found later, bent all out of recognition.

The little witch.

What exactly, he wondered with an unwelcome mix of arousal and aggravation, was she planning?

Zara couldn't miss the amusement on Russell's face after Walker's temperamental exit from the dining room.

"Are you sure you want to play with that fire, darling?" he asked with a grin.

"I'm sure I don't know what you mean," she said, carefully placing her fork back on her plate at just the right angle, tines downward, signaling she was finished with the mouth-watering chocolate dessert.

As the servant swept the plates away, Russell leaned back in his chair, still grinning like a hyena. Sometimes he could be so infuriatingly adolescent. "I mean, anyone can see the man is way out of your league."

"Thank you very much, indeed, Your Grace."

Russell had the nerve to laugh. "Face it, Zara, you may be at the top of your game professionally, but you're still a novice when it comes to the opposite sex."

"Oh, and you're Mr. Experience, I suppose." She cringed at his knowing smile. Of course he was. And he was right about her, too, the wanker.

"He'll have you for breakfast if you're not careful."

"He already has," she informed him primly. "So I may as well enjoy myself. Wasn't it you who recommended that?"

His amused expression turned gentle. "I was being a twit. I never thought my practical, no-nonsense Lady Zara would actually fall for a rogue in wolf's clothing."

"It wasn't exactly his clothing I fell for," she muttered, making his eyes widen.

He choked on a laugh. "Good lord, now you're making me blush."

She snorted. "Unlikely."

"As unlikely as you and Walker Shaw. Am I making a mistake letting this fire burn uncontrolled?"

She pushed out a breath. "Russell, I know you like to think of yourself as emperor of the known universe, but there are some things even you can't control."

She, neither, it seemed. Unfortunately.

She was fairly certain she had just made the biggest mistake of her life, insisting on keeping Walker in it. What was it about the man that had her treading on ice so thin she could see right through it to the treacherous depths below, and still keep right on going?

She could already clearly hear the ice cracking. But she was powerless to stay away from the pond. She just prayed when the plunge came, she remembered how to swim.

* * *

"Where the hell is he?" Zara mumbled to herself, checking her watch for the umpteenth time.

She slammed the book in her lap closed, then glanced up guiltily at King Weston. But seeing his slack face only reminded her how ecstatic she would be if he actually did wake up from the sharp sound. He was still in a coma, and she was growing more desperate for each hour that went by without him regaining consciousness.

Guilt weighed so heavily on her she wanted to scream. Had she done something wrong in surgery when she removed his brain tumor? Or was it the residual effects of the bomb explosion? Either way, it was Zara's fault he wasn't waking up.

With unbidden images of the dead little Lloyd girl doing a macabre dance in the back of her mind and the sound of Mrs. Lloyd's shrill accusations ringing in her ears, this morning Zara had gone over the king's thick chart again and again, searching for something, anything, that would explain the coma. But there was nothing.

It was probably the stress of the past week's events, the threats on her life, the unsettling dream-visions and the out-of-control situation with Walker that had stretched her nerves to the snapping point. But she couldn't shake the growing feeling there was some important bit of information she was missing. Something she could still do to help save the king.

But the only thing she could think to try was to find some meaning in the strange letters and symbols that kept recurring in the nightmare visions in which he had appeared. The ones that felt like warnings.

It seemed woefully inadequate, but anything was better

than sitting and watching King Weston slowly slip away. So she'd sent to the library for a stack of books on Silvershire archaeology. The ruins and artifacts of ancient Silvershire were rich in symbols. Maybe she could find a clue there.

She'd wanted Walker to check the Internet for symbols used in psychology, such Jungian dream symbology, that her subconscious might be drawing on. But Walker was late.

Too late for it not to be deliberate. It shouldn't take three hours to have a gun issued. Had he stopped at the palace guards' shooting range for some target practice? Looking for a reason to delay seeing her again, no doubt.

She definitely shouldn't have mentioned those reading glasses. That had just been asking for trouble. But she'd been so infuriated with him for the way he'd aired their private affair to Lord Carrington that she hadn't been able to help herself. Just to remind the bloody beast what he was so determined to walk away from.

Sighing at her serious lack of judgment, she dropped the richly illustrated hundred-year-old book onto a pile on the floor and reached for another. So far, she'd found exactly nothing in her reading to help her interpret her visions.

"Dr. Smith?" Nurse Emily opened the door, her round face filled with concern. "Someone just brought this in. I thought you should see it right away."

"Yes? What is it?"

The nurse handed her a newspaper. "This morning's issue of the *Quiz*. Center page."

A prickle of foreboding shivered over Zara's arms as she took the newspaper and opened it to the middle page.

Horrified, she stared at the headlines. "Oh, my God," she whispered.

The entire two-page spread was filled with pictures of her

and Walker taken over the past two days, accompanied by text
and headlines blaring out Walker's identity, the scandal from
his past, and a thick, black question regarding the exact nature
of the Marquis of Daneby's daughter's relationship with her
black-sheep bodyguard.

The byline was that of Paul Seacrist, the most tenacious
reporter at the *Quiz*. He must have spotted them on their excursion to the old town. Some of the pictures in the article
were almost intimate, showing them laughing together, or
with Walker's arm around her. There was even one of him
carrying her from the taxi into the emergency room after she
was poisoned, with a look on his face that clearly conveyed
his feelings for the woman in his arms.

"Oh, my God," she repeated. Her dirty little secret was
secret no more.

With every muckraking word she read, the angrier she
became. *How could they get away with this?* The things they
said about Walker, the awful veiled and not-so-veiled accusations, were simply not true! He would never have seduced
that girl! *Never!* She knew firsthand how honorable the man
was. Especially about that sort of thing. Why, just to get him
to kiss her, Zara'd had to—

All at once she jumped to her feet. She had to do something to quell this slander!

Damn it, he was *innocent* of those charges. Every one of
them! She knew that now with every fiber of her being. And
anyone who'd bother to get to know him would, too. Why he
hadn't denied them back then she had no idea, but Walker
Shaw was *not* guilty of professional misconduct. She didn't
need to hear his side of the story to know that much was true.
It was obvious from every action he'd ever taken with her.

Every verbal caution. Every physical stepping away when she'd tried to get closer.

And this article was exactly what he'd been warning her about.

Had he seen it? It would destroy him. Especially if ill-willed reporters caught up to him before he'd had a chance to formulate answers to their nasty, insinuating questions.

She must find him. Warn him.

And tell him she believed him.

That was what he was asking of her last night. The thing she hadn't understood because she was too wrapped up in her own selfish needs to see his.

She realized now she did believe in him. Whatever else stood in the way of their relationship, that wasn't it.

Hurrying from the room, she asked Emily to sit with the king. "Get me on my mobile if there's any change in him," she called over her shoulder as she rushed down the hall for—

For where?

After trying Walker's mobile and getting the answering service, she rang the captain of the palace guard and asked if he was still there. He wasn't, but the captain put out a page and reported back, "He was last seen heading for the old section of the palace, where the abbey is. He asked one of the guards how to find the Bourbon rose garden from inside the palace, so I expect that's where you'll find him."

The Bourbon rose garden. She'd never been there herself, but remembered the docent describing it on their tour the other day. Walker had asked her if she liked roses, knowing all along she adored them.

She smiled, remembering her reaction to the canopy of yellow blossoms hanging over the balcony of his palazzo room in Florence. The first time they'd made love was on a rose-fragrant, petal-strewn feather bed.

It was so romantic she wanted to weep.

What had happened to her since that starry-eyed girl had a crush on Walker so achingly sweet it still filled her with longing? Why had she never felt anything like that before or since? Was her life so empty of emotion?

Or was Walker that special?

She had a sinking feeling she knew the answer.

At the velvet ropes cordoning off the oldest part of the palace, she lifted the soft barrier and ducked under it, hurrying down the increasingly dark and dusty corridors toward the courtyard nestled in the middle of the ancient abbey.

She'd spoken to the same guard Walker had, and received the same directions. It seemed easy enough. Two rights, a left, to the end of the passage, another left, then a short flight of steps down. The thick wooden courtyard door was off the vestibule at the bottom of the stone stairway.

She got as far as the other left, but didn't see any stairs, stone or otherwise. Had she remembered wrong? Was she supposed to take a right? Hopelessly muddled, she tried to retrace her steps, but got turned around and ended up in a maze of interconnected rooms with no hallways at all and very little light.

Despite the stale, chilly air in the uneven, neglected passageways, she felt a trickle of sweat glide down her spine.

No reason to panic.

She was *not* lost. She knew the trick for getting out of mazes—always keep your fingers touching the left wall and simply walk until you wend your way around all the barriers. It might take a while, but eventually you'll get out. Besides, this was the palace. How lost could a person get inside a building?

More minutes later she'd still not found her way out. Her heartbeat started to speed. Memories of the moldy, dark tunnels of Danehus sent goose bumps cascading down her arms. She'd always hated tight spaces, and her brother had mercilessly dared her to go exploring with him, knowing she would do anything to prove she was braver than he. Invariably they'd gotten lost, stuck in the bowels of seemingly miles of "secret" underground passages under the estate, until a footman was finally sent to retrieve them. Her brother had thought their expeditions a great adventure. She could hardly breathe when they'd finally emerge into the light of day.

"Don't be a ninny," she told herself firmly. It was July, the middle of summer. The sun would be up for a good four hours yet, and there wasn't a tunnel in sight. She had nothing to fear.

Nothing at all.

She stopped and closed her eyes to clear her head of nonsense. When she opened them again, she was calmer. There wasn't much light, but there was some. Which meant there had to be windows somewhere. Examining her surroundings, she saw that one doorway was brighter than the others. Pulse pounding, she went through it and kept following the light until at last she emerged into a grand hallway with arched windows along the top. At the other end was the gothic doorway of a chapel entrance.

Easing out her breath that had stalled in her lungs, she sent up a silent prayer of thanks and walked to the tiny chapel. The wooden door had long ago disappeared, leaving the entry open to the pillared hall.

She gave a gasp of delight when she stepped inside. There at the end of the shadowy, narrow chapel was a stained-glass window, a beautiful red rosette centered in another gothic arch of purple. Gorgeous fractal light was thrown in all directions by the sun filtering in through the colored glass. Four dark wooden pews, worn smooth by the silks and satins of bygone worshippers, still stood sentinel before the raised stone altar gracing the sanctuary.

A sudden stab of pain made her grab her temples and cry out. Flashes of red and purple assailed her for a split second, swirling with gold, then disappeared as quickly as they came. Just like her first vision.

Grasping the cool wood of the nearest pew, she sank into it, rubbing her forehead. Catching her breath. Forcing herself to calmness.

She thought of Walker. He must be so close, yet she couldn't find him. *Where was he?* Again the panic started to rise. Just as it had in the vision.

No! Desperately, she looked around, battling the fear that struggled to break through her levee of determination.

Along one wall she saw a wrought-iron stand filled with the remnants of candles. A candle. Yes, she would light a candle. Jumping up, she hurried to the stand and searched between the stubs for matches.

She found none. Inexplicably, her eyes wanted to fill.

She sucked down a hiccup. This was ridiculous. She refused to cry over something this silly. Suddenly, she noticed a sparkling glint of light above the stand of unlit candles. She stumbled backward in stunned surprise.

It was a framed icon. The bronze relief-work shone like gold in the beams of light tunneling through the darkness from the stained-glass rosette. She rubbed her eyes and stared.

Instead of the usual grouping of saints, it depicted a landscape containing an odd building. A series of symbols crowded the outer edge of the relief.

The same gold symbols as in her vision.

It was déjà vu.

Walker wanted to skin someone alive. Slowly. With his dull, rusty Boy Scout knife. Starting with Paul Seacrist, the bastard who had written this newspaper article.

Lying on the grass in the ancient palace courtyard was supposed to be calming his anger. Instead, it was growing with every breath he took.

He tossed the newspaper aside, not caring that it fluttered away in a breeze, catching on the thorns of the old rose vines covering crumbing stone walls. He stacked his hands under his head.

Well. He'd wanted to be reassigned. This great publicity ought to do the trick. He was just sorry Zara had been caught up in the dirt, too. As exasperating as she was, she didn't deserve having her world blown out from under her like this. Because of him.

If he were any kind of gentleman, he would tell the press they were right. She was innocent. He'd deliberately seduced her. And everything else they'd written about him was true.

His curse echoed through the rose-scented courtyard.

If he were a gentleman.

"Walker? Are you all right?"

He didn't bother to open his eyes. He knew who it was. Would have known it if she hadn't said a word. "Just peachy. And you?"

"Been better." There was a pause. "You saw?"

"Oh, yeah."

"I'm sorry."

He slitted his eyes and peered up at her. "What the hell do you have to be sorry about?"

She didn't answer, just sighed, so he closed his eyes again. He didn't want to see her. Didn't want to look at her beautiful, expressive face. Didn't want to see her adoration turn to suspicion, as it had yesterday. Or doubt, like this morning. What variety of knife blade would she use now, after the *Quiz's* meticulous exposé? Simple hatred? He didn't think he could take that one.

He heard the rustle of cloth, two soft thuds, and suddenly she was lying next to him. He lifted his head in surprise. She'd taken off her jacket and shoes and flung them on the grass by the newspaper. Stray auburn hairs tickled the underside of his bent elbow, her body tucked so close to his they were almost touching. Almost. He laced his fingers together under his head to keep himself from lowering his arm to close the gap.

"I'm sorry I got you into this whole sordid mess," she murmured.

She could save her pity for someone who needed it. "You didn't."

"If it weren't for me you wouldn't be here. They'd never have written that story."

"Then it would have happened somewhere else."

"Why didn't you fight it, Walker? When they first accused you?"

He gave a humorless laugh. "Why? What would have been the point?" Even without the threat to his family, it was a losing proposition.

"Because you're innocent."

Her three simple words floated in the air around them like the sound of birdsong so poignant he didn't quite believe it was real. "And how would you know that?"

She rolled to her side, fisted her hand on his chest and rested her chin on it. "Because you've always behaved honorably with me. I don't believe you have it in you to behave any other way. Neither does Corbett Lazlo or he wouldn't have hired you. Neither does Lord Carrington or he wouldn't be trusting you with me. That's a lot of evidence in your favor, Walker."

He let these words settle over him, welcoming them into his soul like a much-needed balm. Wanting to believe them so badly.

"You might be a bit biased," he suggested.

"Maybe. But that doesn't make it any less true."

He felt a great weight lift from his chest. In its place he felt the warmth of her body canted over his, the press of her breasts into his ribs, the slide of her thigh against his leg.

Making what he had to do all that much harder.

"It means a lot to me to hear you say that, sugar. Unfortunately, it makes no difference to what's happening."

"Darling, you have to fight it. Tell them the truth."

"And dredge all that stuff up again? No thanks. I have no desire to see my name dragged through the mud again. And this time they'd drag yours right along with it. What would that do to your chances of having Silvershire's entailment laws changed? Even ol' Russ couldn't help you then."

She was silent for several moments, then she sighed again and rolled off his chest, resuming her place next to him. Not touching. He felt the absence of her warmth like a physical blow.

"It's not fair," she whispered.

"Life's a bitch and then you die," he agreed, feeling the truth of the old cliché down to his bones. In his peripheral vision the newspaper fluttered against the tangle of blossoming rose vines, resurrecting his impotent fury.

She'd said she believed in him.

But there was still no way they could be together. Even though so far the press was casting her as his innocent victim, they'd be dogging her like bloodhounds. And there was no way for him to defend her without putting his family in danger from a crazy woman. No, Corbett would have to find Zara a new bodyguard, and Walker wouldn't even be able to see her from a distance, let alone…

He drove his fingers through his hair, letting out a swear word he seldom used.

She looked up. "What?"

Jetting out a long breath, he did his best to contain the rage in his heart.

He knew what he had to do. It was the hardest thing he'd ever done. Harder than losing the job of his heart, harder than losing his honorable reputation, harder than walking away from the family he loved to start a new life thousands of miles apart from them because of a lie.

"I can't stay," he said. "I have to get out of Silvershire so they won't create a scandal around you."

She would keep her dreams, even if he couldn't. He'd known all along it had to be this way. It would be too selfish to stay, just because he'd found the woman he wanted to share the rest of his life with.

She spun back over him, grasping his arms. "But, Walker—"

He gripped her shoulders, holding her firmly above him. "We have no choice, Zara. I have to leave you."

Chapter 10

Zara's eyes misted over. "Why are you so damned stubborn?"

"Guess I inherited my daddy's 'Bama pride,'" he said, holding her away from his body, though it was killing him to do so.

"If that were true, you wouldn't be letting them kick you while you're down," she said, her pretty mouth in a downward curve.

Walker winced. "Ow, baby. Have a little mercy, here. I'm doing this for your sake."

"The hell you are. If you really wanted me you'd be out there clearing your name so we might have a chance to be together."

"Dammit, it's not that simple—"

"Simple? Do you think it's *simple* to change attitudes and laws that have been in place for over a thousand years? Do you see me giving up just because it would be easier that way?"

His temper spiked. She didn't understand. He had no option. "Zara, listen to me—"

"If I'm going to be a marchioness, I need a man my people can respect. How could they ever respect a coward?"

He jerked back, cut to the quick. "There's a difference between being a coward and being *realistic*. You know, realistic. As opposed to foolishly naive wishful thinking."

She gasped, wide-eyed with outrage. She tried to yank herself out of his grasp.

He didn't let her go.

"Zara, sugar—"

"Don't you sugar me, you bloody—"

Ah, hell. This was not working.

He pulled her down on top of him, drove his fingers into the twist of hair at the back of her head and brought her lips to his. Her quick intake of breath opened her for his taking.

She struggled at first, until his tongue persuaded her to delay her ire for a more convenient time. She made a noise that could have been a protest. Or it could have been a moan. He didn't stop to find out.

Honorable? Not this time.

He rolled her under him. Tipped his head for a better angle and plundered her mouth. She moaned again, opened wider and slid her arms around him.

"That's right, baby. We're no good for each other, except for this part."

He wanted her to deny it, to tell him he was wrong. That they were good in so many other ways.

But all she said was, "I hate you, Walker Shaw," and deepened the kiss.

He stripped her of her aqua skirt and pale yellow blouse, her pantyhose and lacy underwear, then made quick work of his own clothes. When he slid between her thighs, she started to speak again, so he kissed her. Hard.

He didn't want to talk. He only wanted to enjoy her one last time. Feel her body wrapped around his. Feel her sweet response to his loving. Feel the rightness of being one with her.

He buried himself deep inside her. Spread her legs wide and thrust as far into her as he could get. She sobbed out a moan, clinging to him.

They stilled, locked together in love's most ancient puzzle. Around them the courtyard buzzed with life, insects humming, birds twittering and a warm breeze riffling through the trees. The smell of crushed grass filled his nose and the taste of his lover lingered on his tongue as he pulled back and looked into her eyes.

"You know it's impossible. We're impossible," he said softly. Angrily.

"Yes," she said, eyes reflecting his own pain. "I know."

"You deserve better than me."

She gazed up at him wordlessly for a moment. Then, "No. And I shouldn't have to choose."

"But you do."

"It's not fair. I've always had to choose."

He gave her a sad smile. "Keep your eye on the prize, baby."

Under him, her body moved. A tiny undulation, like the last remnant of a wave reaching shore. Pushing him even deeper in. "What if I don't want the prize?"

"But you do."

She licked her lips. "I don't know what I want anymore."

"Yes, you do." He kissed her gently. Swallowed. And lied. "This is just sex, Zara."

"It isn't," she whispered.

He took a deep breath. "It has to be."

She bit her lip, and he kissed it, kissing away the sting of the nip, kissing away the sting of his words. Kissing away the agony of losing her before she was even his.

He pulled out of her and pushed back in again. Pulled out and pushed in. Numbing the hurt and uncertainty in the lush response of her body to his physical possession. At least he could have that much. Until they had to leave this secluded courtyard and face the world apart.

She never wanted to leave.

Zara held Walker close long after they'd floated back to earth from the almost desperate ecstasy they'd shared.

He trailed his fingers down her cheek. "We should go back. They'll wonder where we are."

"They know where we are."

"I need to call Corbett."

"For your replacement?" she asked, trying not to sound snippy. But she felt the waspishness swell within her.

"Yes," he said calmly. "Though I hope he won't replace me in all ways."

"I guess you'll never know." She met his furrowed brow with a tipped-up chin. "Since you insist on slinking away into the sunset."

They were still joined, his relaxed body reposing within hers. She could feel the sticky wetness between her thighs, an apt analogy for the sticky relationship between her and her lover.

"Baby, don't start. I'm the one they're trashing in front of millions," he reminded her. "You wanna trade places?"

She released a petulant breath. "No."

"All right, then." He pulled out and rolled off her, and she had to grit her teeth against screaming in frustration.

Again. The man had a preternatural ability to get her ire going. One minute furious, the next panting with desire. Made even more maddening because usually she was so composed.

"Come on, your ladyship. Better put your clothes back on before they start taking pictures over the wall."

He was joking, but she cast a worried glance around them as she sat up. Her gaze snagged on the large sheet of rolled-up paper she'd brought with her to show him. "Good Lord. I completely forgot!"

Earlier, when she'd found the bronze icon, she'd taken it from the wall and rushed back with it to the temporary office that had been set up for her after the bombing. Using a large sheet of exam paper and a thick, soft pencil, she'd made a meticulous rubbing of the scene and the symbols depicted on it.

"What?" he asked, pulling on his trousers.

"The rubbing!"

His grin told her he'd totally misinterpreted her remark. He started to unzip his fly again. "Well, if you—"

"Oh, be serious," she said, and crawled the few feet to the tube of paper on the grass. "You are not going to believe what I found."

Legs stretched out in front of him, he leaned back on his hands and watched her with interest. Of course, she wasn't exactly sure if it was what she was fetching that interested him, or her on her hands and knees doing so.

She snatched up the tube from the grass and carefully undid the tie around it, unrolling the paper to show him the drawing. "Look."

His face was blank as he examined her handiwork. "Uh…"

"Around the edge, they're the symbols from my visions. And this landscape…it looks familiar. I think it was also in one of the visions."

He frowned. "Where did you get this?"

"I was coming to find you, here, and got lost in the old

abbey. There was a chapel, and this was hanging on its wall. I mean, the bronze icon I took the rubbing from was."

He stood, swatted the grass from his butt and swiped up his shirt. "Where? Show me."

"It's in my office, hidden behind a bookcase. I needed paper and pencils to copy it with, so I took it there. But—"

"Let's go take a look."

"There's more. When I lifted the icon from the hook in the chapel, there was a small niche hidden behind it. Inside was a lever attached to the wall, like a handle of some sort."

"A handle? For what?"

"I think it may unlatch a secret door."

He shot her a skeptical look as he took the paper from her hands. "A secret door."

"It's not as strange as you might think. Not all of Silvershire's history was peaceful. Old castles and manor houses here are riddled with secret doors and underground passages." She shivered involuntarily and told him briefly about her adventures with her brother at Danehus. "I've also heard rumors of tunnels under the Royal Palace, but the docents all insist they don't exist anymore."

He looked over the rubbing, then thoughtfully watched her as she put her clothes back on. When she was slipping into her skirt, he asked, "Have you been in the old abbey before?"

She shook her head. "Never."

"Any idea what the symbols mean? Or this weird building in the landscape?"

"Unfortunately not."

"Maybe you've seen something else by the same artist. In a different castle or a museum."

She put her shoes on. "Perhaps." But she didn't think so.

"I want to go back to the chapel and take another look at that handle. Find out what it opens."

"Not a good idea," he said, shaking his head. "Let's just report it to Lord Carrington and let him decide if he thinks it's worth investigating."

"And say what?"

"Well, exactly my point. I don't really think a handle in some old chapel means anything at all. It has nothing to do with the bombing or the attempts on your life."

"I think it does."

"Such as…?"

"I…I don't know. I just have this…feeling. That it's important to the king's safety. I've had a strong feeling all day that I was missing an important clue, that the visions are a warning. I don't want to leave any stone unturned, no matter how improbable."

He regarded her as he slowly rolled up the rubbing. "You know I've taken you seriously about these strange dreams of yours. But baby, this is starting to sound a little *X-Files*, don't you think?"

She drew herself up. "If you don't want to help, that's fine. I'll go by myself. I'm sure I can find the way—"

"Now, sugar, don't get all prim on me. I'll go anywhere you want."

Seeing him standing there with an indulgent smile on his face, too handsome for his own good in his incongruously tailored trousers, his collarless shirt casually unbuttoned, with shirtsleeves rolled up, she suddenly remembered she was peeved at him. "That's not what you said earlier today, at lunch."

Before she knew what he was doing he had caught her around the waist. "You think this is easy for me? I'm trying to do you a favor."

"By leaving me?"

He pulled her tight to his body, still warm and musky from their lovemaking. "Yes. Zara, I can't keep my hands off you. It was only a matter of time before the press started noticing. I thought I could spare you the scandal. I'm furious with myself for not leaving sooner." He gave her a grim look.

"Well, I'm glad." She slipped her arms around his neck. Wanting him again, desperate that he *would* leave her, regardless of her wishes. "I'm not ready to let you go yet."

His blue eyes softened. "Keep looking at me like that and I won't ever have the strength to leave." He kissed her. "Come on. Let's go see that secret door handle of yours before I land you in an even bigger scandal than I already have."

She clung to him for a second more, then let him go.

Why was this so hard? Because of her lofty goals, she'd sacrificed her personal whims and desires all her life. She'd never had trouble giving up those foolish things before. He was right; even if he was innocent, they were impossible as a couple. The harm to his reputation was done, and would take a miracle to reverse. The press knew it. That's why they smelled blood now. The blood of yet another of her sacrifices. But this one was tearing her heart out.

Banking her depressing feelings, she followed him out of the rose garden into the ancient part of the palace through the side door that had eluded her earlier. With only a few wrong turns she was able to find the chapel again.

"We'd better make it quick," Walker said as she led him through the gargoyled arch into the darkening interior. "There's only about half an hour before the sun sets."

"And I never thought to bring a torch. Darn." The light from the rosette window was muted, but even more beautiful for that. The chapel air sparkled with violet and scarlet dust motes, the shadowed walls painted in the same dusky hues.

They approached the niche in the side wall, a square black hole that whispered to her of secrets and furtive danger. The musty, clammy odor of damp stone filled her nostrils and she held her breath as a tense, mysterious hush fell over them both. She could hear nothing but the beating of her own heart.

Walker reached up and ran his fingers along the handle, which she realized was also made of bronze.

"Shall I try it?" he asked quietly.

"Yes," she whispered, her pulse speeding.

Taking a firm grip, he gave it a tug. His face registered surprise when it easily slid a half turn. He glanced at her, and they both waited in palpable anticipation.

Nothing happened.

They turned away from the wall, searching the nearly dark interior of the chapel for any change—an open panel, a hidden door, a sliding reliquary.

Nothing.

"Well," she said in disappointment. "What do you make of that?"

"The thing it's controlling must be somewhere else."

She glanced at him, brightening. "Of course. The other side of the wall!"

She hurried out and searched the corridor for a door to an adjoining room. It didn't take her long to find it.

She wrestled open the solid wooden door and was about to plunge into the windowless space when she felt a firm grip on her arm. "I'll go first," Walker said. He had his gun in his hand.

Startled, she eyed the weapon warily. "Is that really necessary?"

"I hope not."

He went in. She followed at his back, hooking a finger in his belt loop because she was getting more nervous by the second. It was much darker in here than in the chapel.

"I can't see a thing," she whispered. But she could feel something. A cold, stale breeze.

"There's an opening," he said, going closer to the side that adjoined the chapel. "There."

"Oh!" she said, and stopped abruptly, peering down at the floor in front of where Walker had come to a halt. At his feet lay a gaping black rectangle that discharged a steady draught of cold, dank air smelling of fetid earth and ancient decay. She shivered violently and clung to him. "This is too creepy."

"I'll say."

"It looks like a tunnel."

He nodded. "One of your secret escape tunnels, I imagine."

"Supposedly they dated from the time of the original abbey, but historians insist nearly all of them collapsed yonks ago, and the few remaining were walled up during World War II, according to the docents."

"Obviously, they've been misinformed."

She stood for a moment, staring down into the blackness, her pulse racing, swamped with an overpowering sensation that she must descend into its depths. "I don't think I can," she whispered.

"Can what?" he asked.

"Go down there."

He turned to her and even in the barely existent light she saw the incredulity in his expression. "What, are you nuts? There's no way you're going down in that tunnel. Me, neither, for that matter. Come on. Let's turn the handle back and get out of here. I can hardly see."

She resisted his urging hand. "But—"

"Forget it, Zara. I mean it."

She knew his order was only prudent. It would be madness to set one foot into that horrible abyss without a torch—and a big bag of crumbs to lay down so they could find their way out again. Not that *that* story had ended all that well.

But the compulsion was so strong it nearly overwhelmed her common sense. She felt to the marrow of her bones that this place, this secret passage, was important. A sickening dread filled her at the prospect of even crossing the threshold of the yawning void. The last thing she ever wanted was to feel the confining darkness and close airless space of an underground tunnel again. It was suffocating just to think about. And yet…

"I know you're right. But…maybe we can come back tomorrow, when there's more light. Take a quick peek. Just to see where it leads."

His shadowed expression became indecipherable. "You know damned well I'm not going to be here tomorrow. You've got to swear to me you won't go down there, Zara. I don't care what your damned visions are telling you. *I'm* telling you not to."

She yanked her wrist from his hand. "Why should I listen to you?" she quietly demanded. "Since you won't be here to stop me?"

She marched out of the room and back to the chapel, wrenching the handle back to its original position. She could feel him watching her, could sense the black scowl on his face, hear the frustration in his swift breath. Sod him. What about *her* frustration?

Wordlessly they made their way back to the medical wing.

"Show me the damned icon," Walker growled when they got to the nurses' station.

"I should check on King Weston."

If Walker was going to leave her, she wanted to get it over

with. She hated this. Hated feeling vulnerable and helpless against the emotions roiling inside her. Hated having to choose between the man she was falling in love with and her lifelong dream.

He nodded, but instead of taking the hint he followed her past the guards and into the king's room, leaning moodily against the wall as she went through her routine of checking the old monarch's pulse, blood pressure and other vitals, searching for subtle signs of a difference from last time. She lingered over the task, hoping he'd leave her in peace, at least for a few minutes, so she could collect herself.

Instead, he took her arm and jerked his head toward the door. "You're done. Now," he said in a hushed but firm voice.

Reluctantly, she left the king to Emily's excellent care and let Walker steer her toward her office.

"I don't know why you're bothering," she muttered. "You didn't recognize anything on the drawing, so why would the icon—"

Her words cut off in mid sentence as he opened the door.

They both halted in shock at the sight that greeted them when it swung wide.

The room was in shambles, the bookcase lying broken on the floor.

And the icon was nowhere in sight.

Chapter 11

The room was a wreck.

Walker swore and grabbed Zara, yanking her away from the doorway and shoving her behind his body. From his waistband he whipped out his gun and aimed it into the chaos of her office.

Gingerly, he switched on the overhead light. In the brightness the mess looked even worse. But no one seemed to be lurking in the room.

"Stay here," he ordered, and stepped in to make sure. "Is there a closet or a powder room?" he asked.

"No. Just what you see."

He poked around in the debris for a minute, then stuck the gun back in his waistband. "Okay. It's clear."

Zara rushed to the bookcase and checked behind it. "The icon! It *is* gone." She turned to him in dismay. "Why would someone take it? It had to have been in that chapel for ages, why wait until now?"

Unfortunately, the answer seemed pretty clear to him. "The more pertinent question is, how did they know you had it? And so soon? You only moved it a few hours ago."

For a second she looked spooked. Then she shook her head. "It has to be a coincidence. They must have been after something else, like drugs, and found it instead. It's valuable, so they probably thought—"

"Zara," he interrupted. "Get real. Nobody wanting to steal drugs is going to choose the Royal Palace to break into. They'd never get past the guards. Which leads to the next question. How *did* they get into the medical wing—and then out again, with the icon?"

"Oh, God. You don't think...?"

"It must be someone working inside the palace. No one else can get past security. Especially now, after the bombing."

Her eyes widened. "Oh, yes, they can."

"What are you saying?"

"The tunnel. They could have used the tunnel. Oh! Maybe there's even..." She swallowed and glanced around, her expression fearful.

Ah, hell. "A secret entrance somewhere close, like there is in the chapel..."

He cursed again and went for his cell phone, punching the speed dial for Lord Carrington's direct line. When he came on, Walker quickly ran down the afternoon's developments and requested he send the Lazlo Group forensics team to investigate both the break-in and the tunnel.

"I'll notify them immediately," Carrington said, clearly alarmed by what Walker had told him. "You're absolutely certain it's a tunnel you found?"

"Dr. Smith is pretty sure."

Carrington let loose a very unregal swearword. "I had no

idea any of the ancient tunnels were still viable. God knows who could be using it, and to what purpose. It could even be one of the palace staff…."

Walker was just as worried. He asked the duke about old architectural plans of the palace. Maybe they could find more tunnel openings.

"I'll check to see if the royal archives has anything useful. Meanwhile, I'll put palace security on high alert." Carrington's voice grew even more serious. "I trust you are armed and won't let Lady Zara out of your sight? I want her kept safe." The warning in his tone was clear.

As if Walker needed to be told. "You can count on it."

"I understand you've already seen this morning's *Quiz,*" Carrington said after a short hesitation.

Walker's teeth clenched. *Here it comes.* "Yes, I have. I'm sorry Dr. Smith got dragged into my sordid past." But he felt no need to explain himself to anyone, let alone to an aristocrat who'd never in a million years understand how the world worked for someone who came from the wrong side of the tracks, regardless of his accomplishments. "Naturally, as soon as my replacement arrives I'll be leaving Silvershire."

Again there was a slight pause. "I'm sorry to hear that. Lady Zara knows?"

"She knows."

"Well, it's your decision," Carrington said, voice heavy with disapproval, but to Walker's relief he dropped the subject. "In any case, the forensics team should be there shortly."

Walker hung up feeling agitated and annoyed. Would the man never stop meddling in his life?

"You're still leaving?" Zara demanded from behind him.

He counted to ten before answering. "It's not like I have

a choice, Zara. You know that. We already decided it's best this way."

"That was before. You *can't* go now. You're the only person I trust."

He tried to be pleased by her declaration, but felt only an unbearable frustration. The last thing he wanted was to leave Zara in some other guy's hands. He needed to keep her safe himself. But under the circumstances that would be selfish.

"Baby, I promise, the Lazlo Group people are the best in the world at what they do. They'll take good care of you."

For the first time, real worry broke through her expression. "How do you expect me to trust a stranger if I can't even trust the people I know and work with in the palace?"

"But how can I stay," he countered, "and be the cause of your ruined reputation, and possibly the end of your dreams?"

"It doesn't have to be that way. We could—"

"Stop." He shook his head. He was doing the right thing; he knew he was. He knew all about having one's dreams shredded by the actions of others, and he wasn't about to do it to someone else. Especially Zara. No matter how much it would kill him to leave her.

He opened his cell phone with a frustrated snap. "We'll talk about this later. Right now I have to call Corbett."

"Walker, don't you dare dismiss me like—"

He held up a hand when his boss came on the line. "We have a problem," he said into the phone, ignoring Zara's indignation at being cut off. "There's been a break-in in Zara's office."

"Is she all right?" Corbett asked sharply.

"She's fine. She was with me when it happened."

"Anything taken?"

He told Corbett about the icon, and then explained how they'd discovered the tunnel.

"You think there's a connection?"

"The tunnel to the break-in? Yeah, I do. Maybe even to the bombing. Is Aidan Spaulding checking that possibility?"

Aidan was the Lazlo Group investigator heading up the entire Silvershire case. Corbett said he'd been told the same thing as Zara, any remaining palace tunnels were supposed to have been bricked up during World War II, so the investigators had not considered it.

"Well, this one has obviously been unbricked," Walker said. "The mechanism works smoothly, as though it's been in use lately."

"Did you go inside?"

"At the time it didn't seem important. But better get Spaulding and Forensics here right away. They should go over both Zara's office and this tunnel with a fine-tooth comb."

Corbett clucked his tongue. "Unfortunately, Aidan won't be back until late tomorrow. He's chasing down a lead in Leonia, up on the northern coast. Meanwhile, I want you to take a quick peek in the tunnel. If it looks like a viable lead, I'll call Aidan back here at once."

Him? Whoa! "Corbett, I'm not a criminal investigator. I wouldn't know what to look for."

"You're a trained research scientist, fully capable of a preliminary assessment. Look for footprints and other traces of recent use. Look for anomalies. Hell, look for bad guys," his boss added wryly.

"Funny," Walker muttered. "You don't pay me enough for this, boss. What am I supposed to do with Zara?" He avoided her sharp scowl at the mention of her name. "When's my replacement going to be here?"

Corbett cleared his throat.

Oh, great. "You *are* sending another bodyguard, aren't

you? Do I have to remind you that after that flaming tabloid article I shouldn't be seen within a mile of her?"

"I'm working on it," Corbett said placatingly. "Sit tight for a while longer. The security checks should come through any minute now on the new guy I hired. In the interim, I've arranged for a limo with tinted windows."

Walker made a deprecating noise. "Like that's going to fool the press for a nanosecond. Paul Seacrist is a bloodhound, and he's probably camped out at her apartment."

"Seacrist is the least of your worries, if this break-in is any indication. Under no circumstances should Dr. Smith stay in the palace tonight. What about family? Can't you take her to visit her parents for a while?"

"You're kidding, right? You'd need a crowbar to pry her loose from King Weston's side for more than a few hours."

"Do whatever it takes to get her out of there. I'll have Carrington beef up security at her apartment building. You should be safe there for now—the press might even act as a deterrent."

"Listen, I don't—"

"I know I'm putting you in a tight spot, Walker. But Dr. Smith seems to be a key player in whatever's going on, and my gut tells me you'll watch her better than anyone else I could assign. I'm relying on you, lad."

Before he could protest further, Lazlo hung up.

Walker swore out loud. Things had gone from bad to worse, and he was so far out of his comfort zone on every level it wasn't even funny.

"Well?" Zara asked, her scowl firmly in place.

"Looks like I'll be your bodyguard for a while longer."

"Sorry I'm such an inconvenience."

He wasn't about to play that game. With a grimace, he

pulled her stiff body into his arms. "Baby, don't. What happened in the rose garden should tell you exactly how I feel about leaving."

After a second he felt her resistance melt slightly. But only a little. "What happened in the rose garden was just sex," she retorted, using his own words against him.

"Ah, Zara." He sighed, and kissed her forehead. "I'm going to pretend it was, so we can both get through this." He tipped her face up for a real kiss. When he pulled away, he said, "I need you to sit with King Weston for a while."

"Where will you be?"

This was the part he dreaded. No doubt he'd have to handcuff her to the king's bed. Which might work if he actually owned handcuffs.

"Corbett wants me to take a look in the tunnel tonight."

She blinked. "*You?*"

"Extra guards have been posted to the medical wing. But I don't want you to set foot outside King Weston's room while I'm gone."

Her expression froze as she realized what he was saying. "Oh, no. Not a flipping chance. You are *not* going in that tunnel without me, Walker."

He took her arm and tried to guide her down the hall. "You'll be safer here."

She didn't budge, yanking her arm from his grip. "I don't care. I'm going with you."

He didn't like that idea one bit. His instincts screamed not to let her within a mile of the old tunnels. "Baby, Carrington will skin me alive if I put you in any kind of danger," he reasoned.

She fisted her hands on her hips and glowered. "You aren't hearing me. *I'm going with you.*"

Closing his eyes, he mentally debated the relative merits

of being slowly and painfully filleted by Carrington versus what Zara might do to him if he continued to refuse. There was no contest. If he told her no, she'd just go on her own later and he wouldn't be there to protect her. She'd already stated that intention.

He recognized the determination in her every move and gesture. He could fight her, but he'd lose. Against his better judgment, he decided to take his chances with the duke.

He told himself even if the tunnel had been used by the culprits, they'd be long gone by now. He wouldn't be going in there at all if he thought he'd find anything more menacing than fingerprints...despite the niggling feeling of impending doom.

"You'll stay right with me and do exactly as I say?"

Her eyes narrowed. "I'm just as smart as you are, Walker."

"Yeah, but I've got the gun."

She ground her teeth. "You really are an obnoxious bully, you know that?"

He gave a halfhearted smile. "I knew you'd see it my way."

She answered with a withering glare. "Come on. Let's get some torches from the supply cabinet."

Reluctantly, he followed her down the hall. And prayed his instincts were, for once, dead wrong.

Zara held her breath as Walker turned the handle in the niche. It barely made a sound as it easily rotated the gears behind the wall. The musty smell of dust and beeswax candles coated her throat with a tickle of anxiety. For some reason she'd thought the mechanism might somehow have been disabled, but it worked as well now as it had this afternoon.

Nervously, she trailed Walker around to the adjacent room, stopping at the edge of the gaping hole in the floor.

"We should bring a guard with us," Walker said, shining

his torch down into the darkness. "But I'm worried about destroying evidence with another set of hands and feet. I shouldn't even be bringing you."

The idea of having another strong man with a weapon along held definite appeal, but she saw his point. "I promise to be careful. I'll only touch what you touch."

She didn't want to give him any excuse to leave her behind. As terrifying as the prospect was of descending into the black unknown, the thought of being separated from Walker was even more disturbing. The uncanny resemblance to her dream-visions of the symbols on the icon had unnerved her even before the break-in. But the disappearance of the bronze icon had started a slow drip of fear steadily into her bloodstream. Something was definitely going on.

She had a bad feeling about what they'd find in the tunnel. But if the visions had pointed her here, she must find out why. The king's safety could depend on it.

Walker didn't look happy about her being there. In fact, he looked exceedingly unhappy.

"We have the walkie-talkie," she reminded him. She'd almost kissed the guard who'd insisted on giving them his two-way radio when they'd passed him at the velvet cordon. "If anything happens, we can call for help."

"Yeah," Walker said, but she could hear the extreme reluctance in his voice. "Are you absolutely sure you want to do this?"

She was sure she *didn't* want to challenge this particular childhood phobia. But if he was going down there, so was she. "Yes," she assured him, doing her best to sound far braver than she felt.

She stared down at the crude stone staircase that ended in a yawning black abyss. Oh, God, what was she about t

"All right. Give me your hand."

She grabbed it and held on for dear life. And together they stepped over the threshold.

Zara kept close behind Walker as he slowly descended the stairs.

"Keep to one side," he admonished, "where there aren't any footprints in the dust. And try not to touch the wall."

"No problem." She had no desire to put her fingers on the clammy stone, dark with the grime and mold of disuse.

At the foot of the stairs, they halted and took stock. They'd entered a good-sized room, only a bit smaller than the chapel above. It contained some old wooden crates, a few statues and two crypts. She shivered, wondering if the marble sarcophagi contained bodies. Two thick wooden gothic doors that had probably once graced the chapel entrance lay broken in large bits on the ground, an iron lock still attached to the ancient hammered latch.

There was nothing else to be seen.

Disappointment lurched through her, in spite of her nervousness. "Is this all?" she murmured.

"I doubt it," Walker said, examining the dust-covered stone floor more closely. "These footprints seem to lead—" his torch skimmed over the far side of the room "—hmm. Into a wall."

Her pulse kicked up. "There must be another secret door."

Together they searched for anything that might open it.

"Here!" she said, pointing her torch beam at an iron lever protruding from the floor, mostly hidden behind a squat wooden crate. "This must be it."

They approached, but Walker prevented her from pulling it. "Watch out for fingerprints."

Using the lining of his jacket, he knelt and grasped the lever below the middle, then awkwardly pushed. Gradually it eased over, and a few seconds later a section of the stone wall swung open to reveal a second secret entrance, through which the footprints disappeared. Her pulse sped even faster.

"Another staircase," he said, peering down.

One that went even deeper underground. Even grimier and moldier than the first. The fetid odor of dank earth hit her square in the stomach, nearly making her gag. Sharp, terrifying memories of crawling through tight, cobweb-filled spaces assailed her. She slapped her hand over her mouth to keep from crying out.

Suddenly, she found herself wrapped in Walker's strong arms, her cheek pressed to his shoulder, breathing in his comforting, familiar smell.

"You okay?" he whispered in her ear.

She nodded. "Just give me a minute."

"Remind me to beat your little brother to a pulp someday for doing this to you," he muttered, bringing an unwilling smile to her lips at the image of her excruciatingly respectable and polished younger brother being brought to heel by the wickedly disreputable Walker Shaw.

"He's actually not so little anymore. Over six foot," she whispered, scandalized by the certainty of who she'd be cheering for.

"I can take him." Walker's mouth brushed over her hair. "Just say the word."

Smiling, she tipped her face up and found his lips in the darkness. The reassuring taste of him filled her senses, banishing the fear. At least, mostly.

"Want to go back?" he asked.

She was sorely tempted, but shook her head. "No. Let's go on a little further."

He kept an arm around her as they cautiously went through the new opening and down the stairs. At the bottom, the stone floor stopped abruptly, turning to dirt. Above their heads, the tunnel ceiling narrowed to a vaulted shape, made up of bricks instead of stone. Almost immediately, they came to a fork where the passage split into two branches.

"Which one should we take?" she whispered, her low voice echoing off the brick, sounding loud enough to wake the dead.

"Wherever the footprints go."

They shone their torches at the ground, revealing prints leading in both directions.

"Great," he muttered, bending to take a closer look. "Seems like there might be more traces going this way." He pointed to the right.

"Right." She took his hand again and led on, her heart pounding in her throat. A rat scampered across their path and she let out a squeal.

"Baby," he chided, yet his arm went around her waist and he pulled her closer as they crept along the wall. His warm breath came in calm, steady drafts that tickled her ear in the chilly air of the tunnel. She couldn't believe how undaunted he seemed by their ghoulish surroundings. The man's nerves must be made of cold steel.

Which probably explained how he could remain so unflinchingly indifferent to the false accusations which had ended his brilliant career. Then again, perhaps it wasn't indifference at all, but the fact that nobody had stood up for him except his loyal but powerless family. Perhaps it was disappointment—or disillusion—that had led him to walk away.

As he guided her through the stale, pitch blackness, his warm body serving as a steady anchor against the fear clamoring to take over, she knew she had to take a stand for him. He was willing to leave Silvershire to protect her reputation. Was she willing to put her reputation on the line for him in return?

There was no question.

When they got out of this bloody tunnel, she would call Chase Savage, the Royal Publicist. He'd done such a good job spinning the recent palace scandals. He could always use a good story. And he could be relied upon to be impartial until he had all the facts. He'd investigate Walker's background thoroughly and fairly. If anyone could clear Walker's name, it was Savage. It might not be enough to clear the way for her to have a relationship with Walker, but it could be a start. A start she badly wanted.

She was beginning to realize her growing feelings for Walker were not just residual hearts and flowers from a long-ago affair, or based on their present incredible physical chemistry. They ran much deeper than that. Walker made her feel safe and wanted, and soft and vulnerable. And loved. All the things she'd been unconscious of lacking in her life up until now. Up until Walker.

She didn't want to lose those feelings.

She didn't want to lose him.

They came to a bend in the passage and he halted. The walls narrowed and the ceiling sloped down precipitously, so they'd have to hunch over to continue around the turn.

"Want to go back?" he murmured.

Though her knees were liquid with terror, she shook her head. "No. I want to follow it all the way," she whispered. "I need to know how it ends."

She felt his fingers sift through her hair, lifting it from her neck as he placed a tender kiss above her ear. Almost as though he knew what she was thinking.

"Not a good idea," he murmured.

"Probably not," she said. "But it's what I want."

"You could get hurt. Badly."

"I have you to protect me."

He laid his cheek against her forehead. "To the death," he whispered.

They stood there for a second, holding each other, pretending they were still talking about the tunnel.

Or maybe he was, and she was indulging in the worst kind of romantic self-delusion.

"Ready?" he asked softly.

"As ever," she said, and let him go.

She found his hand in the dark and he laced his fingers through hers. Crouching down, she hammered back the terror and followed him into the narrowing passage and around the bend.

They nudged around the sharp turn, then navigated another one going the other way. After several more feet, they came to a third turn, which opened into a wider area.

Suddenly there was a loud shout. A dark figure lunged out at them from the darkness.

Zara screamed, and Walker yelled an oath as his torch flew from his hand, the light cutting off as it smashed against the wall. A loud crack split the air and he hit the ground with a frightening, groaning "oof."

"Walker!"

She looped her light beam wildly about, desperately trying to find him. Their attacker jumped at her, shoving her mercilessly to the dirt floor. She screamed again as he stomped her torch under his boot, and all went black.

But this time she was still conscious.

Chapter 12

Walker groaned, grabbing the back of his head. It hurt like a fiery bastard. The air around him was black as a witch's cauldron, and stank of foul things.

Zara's terrified voice cut through the black vortex of pain and tingly sightlessness. "Walker? Darling, please say something! Are you hurt?"

A hand bumped into his leg and clutched at it, the other joining in as she groped up to his chest and finally found his face. He blinked his eyes anxiously.

"I can't see," he said with another groan when she accidentally shifted his head on the hard ground. "Ow! Hell."

"Sorry," she whispered, sounding close to tears. "He smashed the torches. Are you hurt?"

With a whoosh, he remembered where he was and what had happened.

"Only when I breathe," Walker said, gingerly sitting up,

clenching his jaw against the explosion in his head. As he sat, his hip sang out in pain, too. "Did you get a look at him?"

Zara's fingers slid tenderly over his face, touching his cheeks and eyebrows and lips. "Not really. It happened too quickly. I think he had on a hood or something. Where did he hit you?"

"Back of the head." He grasped her hands before she could test his battered flesh. "How long was I out? Did he touch you?" he demanded, irrationally fearful of what might have happened while he was unconscious.

"I'm fine," she said, her breath shuddering. "Really. He just pushed me down."

Walker put his arms around her and held her close in the absolute darkness. She was trembling badly. "Shhh. He's gone now."

She hitched out a tiny breath as she returned his embrace almost desperately. "How are we going to get out of here?"

"Same way we got in," he said, not looking forward to the prospect without flashlights.

"You still have the walkie-talkie?" she asked, her voice tinged with renewed hope.

That's when he realized why his hip was bruised.

"Damn. I must have landed on it when I fell." He fumbled in his back pocket for the small radio and came up with a handful of plastic bits. But at least he still felt the gun stuck in his waistband. And he had his cell phone. He pulled it out and flipped it open, waiting pensively as it searched for a signal. And found none. "Check yours," he told her.

She did, and it was useless, too.

"We must be too far underground," he said in disgust.

"Oh, God, we'll never find our way out!" The panic rose in her voice with every word.

"Sure we will. How hard can it be?" He put their phones

away and gave her a kiss for confidence. "There was only one fork in the tunnel, and we know which way we came. Come on." He helped her to her feet, blinking in the darkness and grimacing against the pain still throbbing in his head, made worse by the fact that they couldn't walk upright.

Holding her hand firmly, he put his other hand on the slimy, clammy bricks of the tunnel wall. "All we have to do is reach those three sharp bends and find where the bricks turn back into stone. Piece of cake."

"But how do we know which direction we're going? We might have gotten turned around."

"Well, there is that." He exhaled, closed his eyes and thought. "If it's not one way, it's got to be the other, right? See if you can touch the far wall."

She stepped away from him, and he could feel her stretching her other arm out to find the opposite side of the tunnel. "Oh! It feels like… Oh, God, it's another branch."

It turned out they were standing right in the middle of the intersection between four different tunnels, with no way of telling which way led back to the palace.

This was getting complicated.

Zara's hand in his was nearly as cold and damp as the brick walls around them. Was she going into shock?

"I should never have brought you," he growled, anger rising swiftly over his stupidity and spinelessness at allowing her to talk him into this insanity. He knew better.

He heard her take a deep breath. "Nonsense. They know where we are," she said, surprising him with the evenness of her words, though her voice trembled slightly. "If we're not back soon they'll send down a couple of footmen…I mean guards, after us."

His admiration for her went up another several notches.

Those childhood memories couldn't be easy to overcome. "You're being mighty brave, sugar."

"I'm not as frightened since you're here with me," she said softly.

He wasn't sure about the logic or wisdom of that sentiment, but it pleased him nonetheless. He couldn't resist dropping to his knees, pulling her along with him and giving her a long kiss.

For a time the pain and darkness was forgotten in the warmth and succor of her welcoming mouth. He didn't care about the sting of gravel on his knees or the fact that their clothing would probably be unsalvageable. He needed to feel her. To know she was his, if only for a short time in the dark.

The absence of light made her scent sweeter, the feel of her arms around him and her tongue against his more sensual. The pounding of his heart for her louder in his chest.

"Walker?" she whispered when their lips finally parted.

"Hmm?" he asked, changing angles. Wanting one more taste of her before coming back to reality.

"I feel a breeze."

It took them another half hour of stumbling forward in the total darkness, following the barely discernible draft but at last, Zara felt the warm, sultry night air of the outside world caress her skin. The earthy smells of the River Kairn filled her with a sense of profound relief. They'd made it!

As they cautiously emerged from the tunnel, past a tangle of bushes and vines and out into the open, her pulse still pounded with adrenaline. But oddly, the full-blown terror had long since ebbed. Walker's influence? Probably. With him by her side she could face even her worst fears.

She glanced around the starlit landscape, seeing the stately, glittering waters of the river just before them. Above glowed the shimmery yellow gaslights of the Golden Bridge, and beyond, the twinkle of Silverton city. Behind them lay the well-concealed mouth of the tunnel, disguised by a jumble of piquant vegetation, a rusted storm-drain grate discarded in the shadows next to it. This must be how their attacker had entered.

"Think he's out there?" she whispered with a shiver, imagining someone lurking nearby, lying in wait for them.

"He's long gone," Walker said reassuringly, but pulled the gun from his waistband just the same. "Let's hike up to the bridge and flag down a taxi."

A taxi.

And just like that, reality reared its ugly head.

He started up the slope, but when she hesitated he turned back to her questioningly. Something in her face must have given her away, because his mouth thinned and his eyes shuttered.

"Ah. Nearly forgot. I can't be seen with you in public."

She had to think. "Darling—" What had happened to her resolve to stand by him?

"Now, that could be a problem," he interrupted, "because I'm also responsible for your safety. I really can't let you go anywhere alone."

She'd lived most of her life in the limelight and had always handled the press—even the paparazzi—with manners and patience. They were only doing their jobs, after all. But at this moment she wanted to line them all up and shoot them. Or at least their bloody cameras and computers. God *damn* them for making things so difficult.

Wordlessly, she took out her mobile—which functioned fine now they were above ground—and dialed Russell's number.

Shocked and concerned, he promised to send the Lazlo forensics team immediately.

"Come straight to my study when you get to the palace,"

he ordered. "I'll have the police and the Captain of the Guard here to take your statements and begin an immediate inquiry. This is outrageous!"

When she hung up, Walker was staring out across the river with his arms crossed tightly over his chest. Above the murmur of the water and the faint sounds of traffic she heard the distinct popping of his jaw.

She'd hurt him. Again.

She sighed, and for the first time in her life started to question the validity of the dream she'd held dear since childhood.

Did she really want to be the Marchioness of Daneby? Or was it, rather, the unfairness of being denied the chance that was driving her to seek to change the laws? A strike for female equality?

Was being a marchioness really worth having to hurt those she cared about? Was it even worth all the sacrifice and heart-ache she'd already gone through to see it become a reality? Was the fight for women's equality in something so inherently inequitable simply absurd, and meaningless to society as a whole?

Was her struggle really one of pure, selfish vanity?

Shouldn't her highly satisfying career as a surgeon be enough for her?

She wanted to throw her arms around Walker and tell him it was, that she didn't care about his past or his reputation. That being a marchioness didn't matter. That *he* was what she wanted, more than anything else in her life.

But old habits died hard. She was nothing if not cautious about decisions affecting her life goals. And who said Walker was even interested in anything long-term? Sex with him was astounding, but maybe that was all he wanted. He'd never said he loved her. And despite their silent, possibly one-sided, communication in the tunnel, he'd never spoken of a future together beyond bed.

Though, instinctively, she felt that given half a chance he would.

Which scared the hell out of her.

Enough to keep her mouth shut about the whole subject. Because she just wasn't sure how *she* felt.

"Carrington is sending the limo. It should be here any minute," she said, stepping up to his back and resting her cheek against his stiff shoulder blade. "He wants us at the Palace right away."

Walker nodded. "Tinted windows. I remember."

"Will you spend the night with me, afterward?" She ducked her heated face at her boldness. But she didn't want there to be any doubt in his mind what she wanted. At least for now…

"I don't believe I have a choice."

A sting of hurt lanced through her at his cutting tone. "Would you anyway, if you did?"

He turned, gazed down at her. Golden specks from the lights of the bridge reflected in the deep blue of his eyes. "No," he said. "I'd be on my way out of here. For both our sakes."

She looked away, nodding. But didn't speak. She couldn't, for the huge lump in her throat.

He was really leaving. He didn't want her.

What would she do without him in her life?

And that's when she knew she loved him.

She had to do something. Say something to let him know. Maybe there was a way to keep him and have her dreams, too. Together they might be able to figure something out.

But unfortunately, the police and forensics teams chose precisely that moment to show up.

Forcing down her aching need to talk to him, she let Walker

handle them, showing them the tunnel entrance, explaining the situation and what had happened. After several minutes of questioning, she and Walker were released.

An officer led them up the steep slope of the riverbank to the road where the limo waited. Her heeled pumps slipped in the damp grass and mud, and Walker put his arm around her to keep her from falling. She couldn't resist returning the gesture. A small comfort in the turbulence of her mind.

As soon as they crested the hill, the officer gave a loud shout. "Hey! You there! Don't even—"

But it was too late. Suddenly, she was blinded by a multitude of camera flashes, and Paul Seacrist's familiarly irritating voice shouted, "Lady Zara! What kind of trouble did your womanizing psychiatrist get you into this time?"

What a flaming nightmare.

Zara had barely managed to keep from slapping the smug smile right off the little weasel reporter's face. Walker, on the other hand, had given Seacrist a bloody earful. Zara was thankful he'd forgotten about the gun in his waistband.

But for a brief, blinding moment as Walker had ferociously defended her honor with all the verbal fury of a modern-day St. George, she'd been so in love with him that it actually hurt.

Unfortunately, by defending her he had only dug himself deeper into the tabloid quagmire, focusing the cameras and rapid-fire questions on himself. She'd had literally to drag him into the limo so they could escape to the Palace, where they were now sitting with Carrington and Chase Savage, the royal publicist, who had been called in for some much-needed damage control. Better late than never.

She groaned out loud and in one gulp downed the second

glass of sherry Russell had poured for her. "Really, Carrington. Don't you have anything stronger?"

Russell raised a brow, then strolled to the sideboard and mixed her up a double martini, which she accepted gratefully. Walker shook his head at Russell's silent offer, as did Chase Savage.

"I suggest we take the offensive," Chase said. "After the *Quiz*'s spread this morning, and the pictures and quotes they got tonight, everyone will want to know everything there is to know about the notorious Dr. Walker Shaw."

"I say tell them to mind their own bloody business," Zara muttered, picking at the holes in the knees of her tights.

"A novel approach," Chase said with a half smile, casting a glance at Walker, who was standing with his hands jammed in the pockets of his dirt-stained trousers, pretending to study the fireplace ornaments. "But hardly practical. Before the next issue of the *Quiz* comes out, the Royal Palace needs to make him into a hero."

Walker snorted softly, but didn't comment.

"Play up the angle that he restored Lady Zara's memory and has now taken on the job of guarding her safety, foiling two attempts on her life."

"That could be tricky. The Lazlo Group cannot be mentioned," Russell reminded him. "Otherwise the inquiries into Prince Reginald's death, as well as the other incidents, could be compromised. No one can know a private firm has been brought in to investigate."

"I understand," Chase said, then pursed his lips. "I've heard a rumor that Zara and Dr. Shaw had already met several years ago. Perhaps we could use—"

"How did you find that out?" Walker demanded, coming to attention.

"So it's true." Chase nodded thoughtfully. "Good. Yes, I might be able to salvage the situation."

"I want Walker cleared." At her words, the three men turned as one to her. "He's innocent of those charges of impropriety. That's what you should be writing about."

"No!" Walker's clipped refusal cut through the civilized atmosphere of Carrington's study like a swift sword. "I don't want all that dug up," he growled. "Leave it be."

"But, darling—"

"No. It's not an option. Spin me however you like, but leave ancient history out of it."

"Walker, be reasonable. Why on earth—"

"God *damn* it, Zara!" He stalked to her chair and bent over her, nearly knocking the martini glass from her hand. "I know you aristocrats are used to treating commoners like pawns on a chessboard. But I'm sick to death of you lot trying to run my life for me! This is *my* decision, and I've made it. No discussion!"

She stared at him in shock at his outburst, absolute silence reigning in the room. Good Lord, what was he on about?

Suddenly he straightened and backed up a step. Turning to Carrington, he inclined his head. "I apologize, Your Grace. Mama would tan my hide for displaying such bad manners. If you'll excuse me, I'll just wait outside."

With that, Walker strode out of the room.

"Well." Carrington ambled over and took the martini glass from her hand, which was in imminent danger of tipping its contents onto her lap, and set it on the end table. "That was interesting. Wonder what he's hiding?"

"What makes you say that?" she asked in surprise.

"Doesn't seem natural that a man won't clear his own name."

"Hmmm," Chase said. "He could be protecting someone.

I believe I may just do a little digging and find out. You're absolutely sure he's not guilty?"

"Impossible," she blurted out, then felt herself blush when the two men glanced at her indulgently. "I may be biased, but I know he'd never seduce a patient. He's completely honorable."

"Then I'll see what I can come up with," Chase said, his photogenic smile back in place. "Meanwhile, I'll put out daily press releases touting his previous accomplishments and his unqualified success with your amnesia, as well as his heroics in rescuing you from the attempts on your life."

"Chase is right," Russell said. "If the palace treats him as a hero and ignores his supposed disgrace, people will at least question the dirt the *Quiz* is slinging at him."

"Business as usual, Lady Zara," Chase advised. "Treat him no differently than you would any bodyguard. Put him and his gun out there front and center so everyone knows he's doing his job. Show everyone you don't believe a word of the slanderous gossip."

"That will be easy, since I don't."

A few minutes later, their strategy had been set and Zara took her leave.

It was as if a weight had been lifted from her shoulders. She'd hated the whole dirty-little-secret atmosphere that had surrounded her and Walker's relationship, and now that would be gone. Thank God! At least with Carrington and the Palace behind Walker, her reputation wouldn't suffer from associating with him.

She just wondered why he wouldn't let her defend him the way he'd done her. He was being dead cagey about his reasons, immediately deflecting the subject every time she'd brought it up.

Was he hiding something?

She found Walker outside the salon, pacing the grand hallway. When he spotted her he stopped, hands loose at his sides like an old-time gunslinger, looking as handsome and rebellious as ever, despite the deplorable state of his clothes.

Her heart fluttered. God, he was magnificent.

"So, have y'all decided my fate?" he inquired with a slight edge to his voice, though he no longer appeared angry, as he'd been earlier.

"Don't be an ass, Walker," she said levelly, and swept past him. "We're only trying to help."

"I don't need or want your help. Not with this." It didn't take him more than a second to catch up, matching his stride to hers.

"Yes. You've made that abundantly clear. One can't help but wonder why."

His eyes narrowed as they swung to her. "What is that supposed to mean?"

"It means you're acting like a guilty man, when we both know you're not. Is there anything you'd like to tell me?"

There was that shuttered look again. "No."

She pushed out a breath. She couldn't force him to trust her. But it hurt nonetheless that he wouldn't. "Very well."

"Where are we going?"

She made the turn toward the side porte cochere. "My flat. It's after midnight and I desperately need a bath. We'll take your car."

"No tinted windows," he reminded her dryly.

"Doesn't matter."

"No? Since when?"

She nodded to the footman at the porte's foyer. "Dr. Shaw's vehicle, please." Then turned to look at Walker. "Since I decided I don't care what people think. I want to be with you, and they can go to hell if they don't like it."

For a second he looked gobsmacked, disbelieving, as though she'd just pulled out a gun and shot him. Then a painful longing shadowed his eyes and he turned away from her. "You know that's not possible," he finally said. "For a million reasons."

"I don't agree," she said. "But if tonight is all we have left, I don't want to waste it arguing."

Seacrist was standing at the palace gates when they drove out together, Walker behind the wheel of his compact sports car. Zara took particular delight in giving the open-mouthed reporter a sweet smile and a finger-wave. The pillock had obviously thought he'd had Walker on the run, and she could see she'd shocked him by daring to associate openly with her as-of-this-morning-infamous bodyguard. She didn't even mind the chain lightning of camera flashes.

"I can't believe I let you talk me into this lunacy," Walker muttered as he sped expertly past them.

"Royal command," she said. "Carrington was very clear about following Chase's orders that you be highly visible." She'd had to explain this three times before he'd finally agreed to forgo the anonymous limo in favor of his easily identifiable hired car.

"I hope you know what you're letting yourself in for," Walker muttered. "If you think that mob will swallow me as any kind of hero, you're dead wrong."

"True, it would help if you were a little more forthcoming with your heroic qualities…."

He shifted gears with a lurch. "You are a persistent little thing, I'll give you that."

She turned her sweet smile on him. "You have no idea."

"If I didn't like you so much, I'd be damned worried."

Hope brushed velvet-soft through her heart. "Do you? Like me?"

"Baby, you know I do. But you and I—we're not going to happen. We both have to accept the fact that when my replacement gets here, we say goodbye."

For someone who claimed to like her so much, he seemed stone-set on leaving her.

"Do we?" she asked rhetorically. "Anyway, there isn't going to be a replacement," she added, to vex him as he was vexing her. They'd already discussed it, and his opinion was that Corbett would listen to him, rather than Carrington. Obviously delusional.

He glanced at her, mouth turned down. "We'll see."

Unfortunately, that part was right. She just wished there weren't so much riding on the outcome. Or that, either way it went, she would be the loser.

She wondered just how far he was willing to go to avoid further entanglement.

Would he want to share her bed tonight? Or would he avoid that, too?

Chapter 13

There was a cluster of paparazzi waiting at Zara's apartment building, but Carrington had arranged for a National Police guard at the entrance to the underground garage, so Walker and Zara were safe from being accosted beyond the gate.

Despite the police presence, Walker again slid the car into a spot well away from Zara's assigned slot. He hadn't forgotten why he was there. Twice now she'd come close to dying, and twice more had close calls. He wasn't about to let anything happen again. After parking, he came around and opened her door, helping her from the car as he scanned the silent cement cavern for danger.

Something was bothering him. Something that had occurred to him as he'd paced back and forth along the grand hallway earlier, waiting for her to emerge from the meeting with Carrington and Savage.

If the attempts on her life—the bombing, the poisoning and

possibly the car incident where Estevez was injured—were related to the ransacking of her office and the disappearance of the mysterious icon, then why hadn't the man in the tunnel tonight tried to kill her, too? Their attacker had barely touched her—Walker had been the one injured.

And that made no sense at all.

Wracking his brain, he tried to figure out what it all meant as they rode the private elevator up to the penthouse. He had plenty of time; a glance at the lighted buttons reminded him how excruciatingly slow the damned elevator was.

Zara was watching him, a strange, cheerless look on her face. Dirt streaked her cheek, her pretty designer suit was stained and filthy, and the knees of her hose blown out. But she had never looked so beautiful. So incredibly beautiful.

And sad. Because of him? No doubt. She'd barely batted an eye at the rest of the week's stressful events. She'd been stronger than anyone he knew as she'd dealt with one blow after another with grace and poise.

Until *he* had gone and complicated things.

He hated himself for taking the bright smile from her lips, extinguishing the joyous sparkle from her eyes. He'd come to reclaim the carefree girl from Italy, but instead…he'd added to her burden by turning her world upside down. And his, as well.

"You're a million miles away," she said quietly.

"Not really." He jingled the change in his pockets. "Just thinking what a jerk I am."

The very corners of her mouth curved, but she didn't comment.

He leaned back against the mirrored wall. Tilted his head. *God, how he wanted her*. Even now. Even after everything that had happened. After everything he'd told himself about the impossibility of their situation.

"I suppose sex is out of the question?" he said philosophically. Not wanting to give away how desperately he wanted her in his arms. He might have to do the right thing by her, but that didn't mean he had to like it.

She blinked. Then laughed. "Christ, Walker. You really do skip the foreplay and get right to it, don't you?"

He shrugged. Caught her gaze. "Well?"

They arrived with a soft thud at the top floor, and the elevator whooshed open. She went out without replying. At her door she fished her keys from her purse.

He took them from her and stepped close, into her space, standing over her, silently waiting for an answer.

"Yes," she finally said. "Sex is out of the question." She took the key back, turned away and unlocked the deadbolt. "However, I may let you make love to me, if you'd like to give that a try."

Before she could open the door, he grabbed her around the waist, and said, "No." She stiffened. "No, I mean, don't turn that knob. Let me."

He set her away from the door, shooing her farther across the foyer when she stopped too close, then repeated his ritual from the night before, cautiously entering and checking all the rooms, the closets and under the furniture. By the time he was finished, she had come into the living room and was standing next to his suitcase, which had been left in the middle of the floor.

"Please tell me Carrington doesn't have a key to your apartment," he said, looking at it with a frown. And for a crazy moment he reevaluated the duke's place on the Lazlo Group suspect list for this crazy palace intrigue.

"What? Oh, no, of course not. The building manager must have let them in."

Rationality and jealousy fought within him; rationality

won. He made a mental note to see if the building manager had let anyone else in recently. Though, von Kreus would certainly have covered that base in his investigations of Zara's poisoning.

Zara was still standing there next to his suitcase, looking for all the world like a homeless waif amid the bustle of a train station, wondering where to go. His heart melted.

"You look like you could use a slow, sweet loving," he said, aching with the need to reach for her. Knowing it would only make their parting more difficult.

Not that it wasn't already. Already he'd spend the rest of his life getting over her.

Again.

She gave him a half smile. "Is that an offer, Dr. Shaw?"

"Yes, ma'am, if you'll let me."

Her eyes softened. "I'd like that."

And so, after they'd thrown away their ruined clothes and taken a hot shower to scrub the dank tunnel from their skin, he picked her up, carried her to her bed, and made long, sweet love to her until they both fell to sleep, exhausted by the trials of the day and the blissful joining of their bodies.

And that, he decided as he pulled her close with a sigh, was far better than sex.

Walker should have known when he awoke feeling irrepressibly optimistic and lighthearted that the feeling wouldn't last.

But for the moment he just relaxed and enjoyed it, stroking his hand over Zara's hip and waist as she slumbered in his arms. He was hungry for her—as always—but contented himself with tactile indulgence rather than losing himself inside her. He'd done that last night, enough to satisfy any normal man. But when it came to Zara, he'd long since accepted that his cravings were anything but normal. He wanted to bury himself in her, curl up and stay there forever.

But that was not to be. He didn't even get the chance to make love to her again. The insistent bleat of an intercom blasted the peace of the morning and jarred her to wakefulness before he could reach over and tell the idiot, whoever it was, to shut the hell up—if he could figure out where the damn thing was.

She unfurled her body from his and pushed a button on a pink Art-Deco-style box sitting on the nightstand. "Yes?" she asked, her voice soft and sexy from sleep. "What is it, Edwards?"

"Good God, girl, are you still in bed?" a thunderous voice boomed over the surprisingly clear speaker. "It's after nine. Get yourself up at once! Your mother and I are here to see you."

A host of emotions flashed through Zara's eyes before she closed them and, for the first time in Walker's memory, said a colorful swearword.

He would have grinned, except for the obviously awkward situation he was about to find himself in.

"I'll be in the guest room," he said, and slid from the bed.

She grasped his arm. "Oh, no you don't." Her chin went up in that way that never failed to stir his loins. "I'm thirty-four years old, for God's sake. My brother keeps a robe in the guest loo. Put it on and join me in the living room." She shot him a warning glance. "Or I'll come and get you. I'm not facing my father alone."

Hell of a way to meet the Marquis of Daneby: newly mucked by the *Quiz*, fresh from his daughter's bed and wearing his son's bathrobe.

Lord have mercy.

Good thing Walker had been born a Southerner. If all else failed, at least he still had his sense of humor.

He just hoped he lived long enough to use it again.

He found the robe, a hunter-green silk number with the Daneby heraldic crest embroidered on the breast—*that should go over well*. He donned it and went to do his gentlemanly duty.

Zara seemed to find some kind of perverse comfort from his suitcase, because she was again standing right next to it. When the door buzzed he held up his hand to her and went to answer.

Doing his best imitation of a tough, unsmiling bodyguard, he swung open the door.

A tall, formidable-looking iron-gray man, equally unsmiling, waited on the other side. Beside him was an elegant woman in a stylish dress. They stared at him, the woman in apparent shock. The man's expression altered not a fraction, even as it swept over Walker's state of undress. Walker stared back, feeling himself being measured, weighed, catalogued and dismissed.

The thing about being a Southerner—other than the sense of humor—was that in the South there reigned an aristocracy and class structure every bit as formal and rigid as that in Europe. Walker had grown up with it, struggled under the crushing weight of its politesse, and had eventually learned to turn it to his favor.

He waited. Silently.

"Lord Harald Smith, twelfth Marquis of Daneby, and Lady Daneby," the man finally said, voice rigid with irritated formality, "here to see Lady Zara, *if* you please."

Walker pursed his lips.

He didn't mean to be a prick, he really didn't, but he suddenly understood a whole lot about Zara and her drive. A fierce, visceral need to protect her rose up in him. Not only against the threats to her life, but also against the cold hardheartedness of this unsmiling man who was her father.

"Step back, please," Walker said. Drawing his weapon from where he'd tucked it into his belt, he leaned out into the foyer and made a show of checking the blind spots along the wall for anyone who might be hiding there. Satisfied, he moved aside and allowed them to enter.

"So it's true, then," Lord Daneby clipped out as he came to a parade halt before Zara, treating Walker like the Invisible Man.

"Hullo, Father, Mum," she said, giving her mother a quick hug and air kisses. "Walker, I'd like you to meet my parents, Lord and Lady Daneby. And this is Dr. Walker Shaw."

Walker smiled inwardly. His little fighter was definitely alive and kicking.

"Charmed, to be sure," Walker replied in a thick drawl he reserved for just such occasions. "Well, I'm hardly fit for callers," he said, coming to stand by Zara's side. "Sugar, I think I'll mosey on in and put some clothes on."

If possible, Lord Daneby's stance became even more rigid. A blush colored Lady Daneby's cheeks as her gaze flitted over Walker, robe and all, bending down to pick up his suitcase.

Zara's fingers found his and squeezed, making him pause in his escape long enough to give her a kiss on the forehead. Except her face tilted up and it landed on her lips. He smiled, and kissed her again. Very chaste. But potent as an atomic bomb.

"Come right back," his little fighter whispered for all to hear.

As soon as he closed the bedroom door behind him, he heard Lord Daneby's voice start to boom again. "I hope you're proud of yourself, young lady…."

Walker ignored the words, not wanting to hear any more lest he be forced to stalk out there and flatten the old bugger.

After a speed-shower, he shook out his favorite Helmut Lang suit and put it on. Modern-day armor. Oh, yes, this was definitely a battle to the death.

He walked back into the living room just as the words, "The man will be your ruin!" echoed loudly off the plaster, marble and walnut surfaces of the living room.

"Well, then, I'll just make some coffee, shall I?" he drawled into the sudden hush.

"That would be lovely, darling," Zara said warmly, looking up from the sofa with a surprising sparkle in her eye.

He wanted to sweep her up in his arms and hug her. He wanted to grab her and shake her until her teeth rattled. She *shouldn't* be taking his side. Lord Daneby was family, and Walker would soon be gone. He didn't want to be the cause of a deeper rift between father and daughter.

But it warmed his heart to the furthest reaches that she was willing. How could he not love her to distraction?

He went through to the kitchen and filled the strange bulbous vacuum coffee brewer everyone seemed to use in this country, putting in an extra scoop of the gourmet Costa Rican blend Zara preferred. He needed the caffeine.

When he turned, Zara's mother was standing in the kitchen doorway. "How is she?" she asked.

Walker figured she didn't mean in bed. "Her amnesia is gone," he said, "and there are no residual effects of the bombing. You can rest easy. She's back to her old self."

Lady Daneby regarded him with a shade of what could be skepticism. "Is she?"

The fact that Zara's mother was even talking to him—seeking his opinion nonetheless—and seemed genuinely concerned about her daughter's well-being sent her stock way up in his estimation. Which is why he didn't take offense at the question.

He leaned against the counter, crossing his arms over his waist. "Yes. Her personality and judgment are the same as before her injury, if that's what you are asking." It wasn't, but close enough.

Lady Daneby went to the cupboard and started assembling cups and saucers on an antique silver tray, and therefore wasn't looking at him when she said, "You'll pardon me for observing, it's not like Zara to become involved with…"

"A scoundrel like me?" he helpfully supplied with a dry smile.

Their eyes met and he found himself, much to his surprise, liking Lady Daneby. He admired her self-possession and her willingness to shoot from the hip. Concerning her daughter, at any rate. It was obvious which parent Zara took after.

"I assume you've been told of the attempts on her life?" he asked. Lady Daneby nodded, eyes becoming worried. "Well, now that she has her memory back, my job is to protect her. Nothing more."

Frowning anxiously, Lady Daneby opened the bag of breakfast pastries he and Zara had picked up on the way home last night and arranged them on a delicate plate. "I can't think who would want to hurt Zara. She's always been so dedicated and careful in her work, despite what that child's mother claimed a few years back. Are you sure there's no mistake?"

He shook his head recalling the story nurse Emily had told him about the young patient Zara had lost through no fault of her own. "No mistake."

"Then it must have something to do with the king. Or

the coronation. Lord Carrington is a dear friend of ours. That horrible Union for Democracy is somehow behind this, I'm sure of it. Trying to upset the monarchy any way they can."

"We have top investigators working day and night to find out who's responsible," he assured her. "It'll break soon. In the meantime, I'm not letting Zara out of my sight. No one will get the chance to hurt her again, that I guarantee."

Lady Daneby gave him a considering look, then plucked a long sprig of fragrant purple lavender from a vase in the window and laid it on the tray next to the silver sugar bowl.

"My daughter has always had a very level head on her shoulders," she finally said. "I assume if she's…fond of you, there's more to you than meets the eye—or the headlines."

That was as big a compliment as he would likely ever get.

"Thanks," he said. "I'd like to think that's true. But—" he took the full coffee carafe from the brewer and poured the contents into the sterling-silver pot she had set out "—however much I wish things were different, and believe me I do, I understand the difficulties in this situation. I won't be staying in Silvershire beyond the end of the case. So you needn't worry on that account, either."

She didn't say anything, so he picked up the tray and carried it into the living room.

He knew better than to think Lady Daneby was remotely on his side, but he was glad they'd cleared the air. She was one classy lady.

Zara gave him a nervous look when he set the tray down on the coffee table in front of her. He winked, and the tension left her face. She patted the sofa next to her so he took a seat there as she poured coffee all around. Lord Daneby glowered from his place propping up the mantle, but Zara's mother took the chair across from Walker as though it were just another in a long succession of Saturday breakfasts together.

He had to admit, the whole morning had a kind of surreal quality to it.

"Looks lovely, darling," Zara said. She didn't kiss him, or even touch him other than on the fingers passing him a cup. She didn't have to. The way she looked at him said it all. His heart squeezed.

She'd dressed while he and her mom had had their conversation, and was now wearing a silky jade-colored top with a light skirt that rode sexily up her thighs.

"So do you, sugar," he said. "But Lady Daneby put the tray together, so she should get the credit."

Before anyone could respond to that, the phone rang. Not his cell phone, but the phone tucked into Zara's bookcase.

Walker managed as politely as possible to down three cups of coffee—Lady Daneby's brow rose fractionally as she filled the third for him—while Zara talked on the phone for a few minutes, and then spun back to them, her eyes alight with excitement.

"He's awake!" She practically jumped up and down, hanging up the receiver with a clatter. "Thank God, King Weston has regained consciousness!"

"Don't fuss over me, girl! You know how I hate that."

Zara was trying not to hover over the king as the nurses attended to him, but with little success. She was too ecstatic to see his eyes open and a smile on his face not to stick like glue to his bedside, holding his hand. And she checked every single thing the nurses did.

Nothing was going to mar this moment.

"How are you feeling?" she asked, bursting to question

him about everything at once. "Do you hurt anywhere? Your head?"

She would have gone on asking about every place on his body, but for the deep chuckle that the king let out at her worried inquisition.

"Dr. Smith, I am tired, but immensely happy to find I'm still alive. Thanks to you." He squeezed her hand.

Her eyes brimmed with tears. She wouldn't tell him about the bombing yet, not until he was stronger. But guilt over it nearly gutted her. "No, Your Majesty, I'm the one who's immensely happy to see you awake." More than he would ever know. "We all are."

The nurses murmured their agreement as they worked, broad smiles lighting their faces as they busily took his vitals and washed his face and changed his gown.

"How long have I been unconscious?" he asked, letting his eyes drift closed.

"I'm afraid you've been in a coma for quite some time," she said gently. "Around two months."

His eyes popped open. "Two bloody months? Good Lord!" Immediately, grief suffused his expression. "My son, Reginald. He was buried, then?"

Her eyes filled again. She hadn't particularly liked the crown prince, but she knew King Weston had doted on him. It was impossible not to share his pain. "Yes, Your Majesty. The ceremony was beautiful."

"Have they caught the bastards who killed him?"

She glanced over at Walker, who was standing by the door quietly observing. He shook his head. "Not yet, sire," she said, turning back. "But I'm sure they're getting close. The inquiry is everyone's top priority."

"And the other?" he asked, his voice dipping low.

She frowned, unsure. "The other…what, Your Majesty?"

"The one they told me about just before I collapsed," he whispered so she had to bend close to hear. "Have they found the true prince? My other son?"

Chapter 14

Zara nearly fell over, stunned. She had to have heard wrong. *The true prince?* King Weston had another son?

She shot a frantic look at Walker but he was too far away to have heard. "I—I—I don't know," she stammered.

Suddenly her ears were filled with the piercing sound of babies crying. Two babies. *The babies from her first vision.* Slamming her hands over her ears, she ground her jaw and glanced around. It was obvious no one heard them but her.

Walker came to attention. "Zara, what is it?" He started toward her, but she waved him back, taking a cleansing breath. The crying had stopped as suddenly as it began. He frowned, but stayed where he was.

The king had closed his eyes again, his whole face showing his fatigue and emotional upset. The nurses had finished their tasks, so Zara dismissed them for now with a thank you. When she and Walker were alone with the king, she went to fetch her purse and pulled from it the folded rubbing she'd taken of the icon yesterday.

She knew she shouldn't be pressing him in his present condition, but she was more certain than ever that her visions were meant as a warning. King Weston's life could depend on whatever they were trying to tell her. Especially if what he'd said about another son was true. Perhaps it was even his son's life that was in danger….

Now, the assassination attempt on the king made much more sense. Another crown prince! The events of the past weeks were coming together in a frightening way.

She smoothed the rubbing open and held it up before him. "Your Majesty, I wonder if you could look at this drawing and tell me…" She waited for his eyes to flutter open and focus on the rubbing. "Do you recognize it? Or any of the symbols on it?"

He looked at the paper for a long moment, his brows drawn together, then glanced at her. "I think I— What is it?"

She explained briefly where she'd found it, but didn't mention her visions. "Does it mean anything to you, anything at all?"

"Perhaps…seen something like it, somewhere. But…can't recall where."

Disappointed, she refolded the paper.

"There's someone who would know," he said, his voice fading. "Take it to Merlin. He can tell you."

"Merlin. You're kidding me." Walker made a face.

"That's what he said." Zara also thought the old king might be losing it. But it was the only lead she had, so she was determined to run it down. Unfortunately, he'd fallen asleep before she could question him further. "I suppose we could try the phone book."

Walker chortled. "Yeah. Why the hell not?"

After sending one of the nurses back to sit with the king, checking the guards and calling Carrington to give an update on Weston's progress, she and Walker went to the staff lounge and grabbed a phone book.

"Yellow pages?" Walker asked with a grin.

She rolled her eyes. "What do we look under? Fifth-century magicians?"

"Right. White it is. Business or residential?"

"Oh, do be serious." She swiped the book from him and looked up Merlin in the business section. "Good grief. There's a listing! Merlin, Argott, Professor of History."

"How about that," Walker said, peering over her shoulder. "Give him a call."

It turned out Professor Argott Merlin was one of King Weston's good friends, and an expert on all things Silvershirean. After a short conversation, Zara arranged that they should go right over and show him the rubbing. His office was in Silverton-upon-Kairn, in the oldest section of the historic district.

"Hmm, very interesting," Merlin said, clearing a spot for the paper on an acre-sized wooden desk cluttered with ancient books, artifacts, writing instruments and manuscript pages. He got out a loupe and examined the symbols first. "They remind me of the writings of an old, secret, mystical society from years ago. Along the order of the Freemasons. Very hush-hush and ritualistic. I'm afraid I can't help you with the meaning, if there is any. But sometimes these things are just for show."

"More of a decoration, you mean?"

"It's possible. However, I *can* tell you about this landscape," he said with a triumphant smile, examining the center relief. "Why, that's easy. It's the old Oriental Pavilion at Castle Perth."

"Where's that?" Walker asked.

Zara's mind was suddenly in a whirl. "On Perthegon Estate, the ancestral lands of Lord Benton Vladimir, Duke of Perthegon. Thirty years ago he was the heir apparent to the throne, until suddenly, old King Dunford chose Weston, Duke of Chamberlain, to become king instead."

Walker gave a whistle. "A succession intrigue? Dunford had no children of his own?"

She shook her head.

"There was quite an uproar at the time," Professor Merlin said. "The country was very divided over who was better suited to rule. Perthegon was the elder by a few months, and thus was entitled to the throne. No one really found out why he was passed over in Weston's favor."

Walker gave a low curse. "Where is this Lord Perthegon now?"

"That's just the thing," Zara said, a bad feeling growing in the pit of her stomach. "No one knows. He disappeared, and hasn't been heard from since."

"We have to go to Castle Perth," Zara stated firmly as Walker followed her down the narrow alley in old town where they'd parked his car.

"Watch out!" he yelled, grabbing her from behind and slamming her into a recessed doorway as a blue compact car barely scraped by them going way too fast. "That driver's going to get the surprise of his life," he growled, scribbling down the plate number on a receipt from his pocket, "when he gets a two-hundred-quid speeding ticket."

Suddenly, he whipped his gaze to Zara, whose eyes were wide as saucers, watching the car race away. "*My God.* Was that the same car that hit Estevan?"

Zara just nodded.

He speed-dialed Corbett Lazlo. "A car just tried to mow us down. Yeah, same one as Estevan. This time I got the plate." He hung up a minute later, adrenaline surging through his veins. "Corbett's sending von Kreus with the SWAT team to pay the driver a little visit."

Zara licked her lips. "You think he was really trying to…?"

He pulled her into his arms. "Von Kreus will find out the truth. Let's hope getting that plate is the break we've been waiting for. Come on. Let's get you back to the palace."

She pulled away. "Walker, no! We *must* go to Perthegon."

"Baby, that's crazy. Let someone else—"

"No. It has to be me. Why else would I be having these visions?"

Exasperated to the max, he slashed a hand through his hair and counted to ten. He was as open-minded as the next guy about this woo-woo stuff, but Zara's whole vision obsession was beginning to be a severe pain in the butt.

"I'm supposed to be *protecting* you," he said, striving desperately for calm. "Not letting you gallivant all over the country chasing down imaginary clues to imaginary threats of imaginary dangers! God, Zara, this is insane!"

So much for calm. He'd practically shouted that last part.

Predictably, Zara's chin reached for the sky. Without a word, she launched herself out of the recess that had possibly saved their lives, and stalked toward his rental car.

He cursed again, and followed.

"At least let me phone for police backup!" he called after her.

Tapping her foot, she waited for him at the car. "We can call the local plod when we get there, if we find anything. Come on, we're wasting time."

He touched the gun in his jacket pocket, debating whether

he should use it on the bad guys or on Dr. Zara Smith. She had that look again. The one that said he was destined to lose this argument, and if he refused to take her to Perthegon she'd just escape custody and go on her own.

He *really* wished he'd checked out a pair of handcuffs along with the gun.

"All right, fine," he ground out. "But at the first sign of anything suspicious, we're out of there. And I do mean *anything*."

"Fair enough," she said reasonably. Now that she'd won.

Even with two wrong turns, it took just half an hour to reach Perthegon Estate, which lay east and north of the capital city. Silvershire really was tiny, only one hundred eighty-two miles long and fifty-eight miles at its widest point. There were counties back home bigger than this whole country.

County Perthegon was quaintly bucolic compared to the capital city. Farms and hedgerows dotted the rolling hills, cozy cottages and small, quaint villages huddled in the valleys. Occasional patches of woodlands canted lazy streams amid the steeper slopes, becoming more plentiful as they drove north. By the time they reached the estate boundary, the trees were tall and ancient, the forest looming dark and mysterious above them.

Driving up the overgrown road to Castle Perth, Walker's unease increased exponentially. An air of acute neglect hung over the place like a pall.

"Doesn't anyone live here?" he asked.

"No. The duke had no heir, but King Weston refused to confiscate the lands for the crown. He kept hoping Perthegon would turn up. The estate has been abandoned since he disappeared thirty years ago."

The dense, claustrophobic forest canopy nearly blocked out the morning sun. Long fingernails of branches scraped at the roof of the car and tall weeds clogged the dirt road, making it difficult to follow.

"It's like something out of the Brothers Grimm," Walker muttered.

Zara shivered. "Where's the white rabbit when you need him?"

They drove on through the lightless forest at a snail's pace for another fifteen minutes until, suddenly, the trees abruptly stopped at the edge of acres and acres of green meadow filled with dollops of bright red poppies. On a slight rise in the center of it all stood a castle.

"Wow," Walker said, bringing the car to a halt. "Not exactly what I was expecting."

Built of sparkling white stone, ornamented with round turrets and Palladian windows, the tall, cheery edifice looked more like a fairy castle than the Dracula's estate he'd assumed they'd find lurking at the end of the driveway.

"I've seen pictures, but it's so much prettier in reality," Zara agreed, smiling with admiration. "I can't imagine anyone abandoning a gorgeous place like this."

"Tells me the man is guilty of something, that's for damn sure."

Walker let out the clutch and eased the car forward until their path was blocked by a huge set of black iron gates.

"I'll see if I can open them," Zara said.

She jumped out of the car and waded through the weeds to the gate. Walker joined her. The design of the iron lace was delicate and intricate, the ground beneath their feet littered with large flecks of gold paint that had peeled off the black iron.

"Must have been really something in its day," he said admiringly.

"A shame it's all been left to ruin," she agreed.

He yanked on the fist-sized iron lock holding the gates closed. "Locked. Now what?"

A low brick wall connected with the outer edges of the gates, topped by twisting iron spikes, preventing them from climbing over that way. Before he could stop her, she'd slipped through the narrow bars of the gate.

"Come on," she urged. "Suck it in and you can make it."

He did, just barely, but was left with a nasty tear in his favorite Helmut Lang shirt. "You're getting me a new one," he grumbled.

"I'll pick one up while I'm buying myself new shoes," she said, making a face at her mud-covered pumps.

"Which way?"

"Professor Merlin said the pavilion should be in a small grove of pear trees somewhere at the edge of the lawns."

"Lawns?" He looked around. After thirty years any lawns were now indistinguishable from the surrounding meadows, and small clumps of trees had sprung up all over the place; at a distance it was impossible to tell if they were pear or persimmon.

"This could take a while."

Two hours later they'd still not found anything that remotely resembled the strange structure on the rubbing. A barn, a gazebo, a hunting blind, a bandstand, a gardener's cottage, a greenhouse and a pump house, but no pavilion.

"We've circled the bloody castle twice," Zara muttered, rubbing her feet. They were sitting on a huge fallen log taking a break from the search to regroup.

Walker grimaced at the blisters on her heels. He'd tried to talk her into abandoning the search an hour ago when he'd noticed her starting to limp in those ridiculous heels, but she'd have none of it.

They'd even called Professor Merlin on Walker's cell

phone to ask if he knew what direction from the castle the pavilion stood. He didn't recall.

The only place they hadn't thoroughly searched was an area of meadow close to the river which had over the years turned into soggy wetlands.

"We have to check the marsh," Zara said. "It's the only place left."

"You stay here," he said. He was loathe to leave her, but the area was like a swamp and he didn't want her sinking into mud up to her knees. He'd been brought up in the swamplands and was used to it. "I'll go in and check it out."

"Fat chance," she said, springing to her feet with a wince. "I'm going, too."

Suddenly, there was a loud crack, like a heavy branch splitting from a tree. It took Walker the amount of time for another crack to ring out to realize it was a gunshot.

"Jeezus, get down!" he hissed, launching himself at Zara and tackling her onto the ground. They both hit the mud with a spatter, and he rolled her under him, covering her body with his.

"What the bloody hell—"

"*Shhh!*"

He cocked his head and listened. Another shot exploded.

Her eyes widened. She whispered, "*Gun*shots?"

He swore, and nodded. "Now would be a good time to call in the local plod."

A fourth shot echoed across the meadow. He heard a tiny thwack as it hit about twenty feet away.

He swore and scanned the area again. "That was too damn close. You roll as tight into that log over there as you can get, and call the police. I'll work myself around and try to surprise him from behind."

"Walker, no! It's too dangerous."

He drew his weapon. "Baby, I'm getting a little sick of this shitbag messing with my woman. Where I come from that's license to kill."

Her mouth dropped open in shock.

He sent her a grin and a wink. "Jus' kidding. I only mean to shoot off the bastard's kneecaps."

He gave her a push and waited until she'd tucked herself under the log and fished her cell phone from her pocket. Then he started crawling.

"Walker!"

He turned his head back at her urgent whisper.

"Please be careful." The terrified look on her face as she said those words fueled his determination as nothing else could have. She was scared to death. *For him.*

She wasn't the only one.

He'd never been quite so thankful for his redneck upbringing as he was in the next few tense minutes. Growing up, he, his brothers and their friends had played stalking games all the time in the woods behind their neighborhood. He knew all about sneaking up on things. What it took was patience and a willingness to get dirty and bitten by anything that was down there crawling with you.

He heard a soft thump in the opposite direction from him, which was quickly followed by a shot. He listened anxiously. Had Zara moved against his orders?

There was another thud, and another shot.

Suddenly, he realized she must be throwing rocks to divert attention from him. He swore under his breath, his feelings waffling between gratitude and fury. The shooter would see through that ploy in about five seconds, and Zara's cover would be blown.

Galvanized, he scooted on his belly through the tall weeds, making no sound, slowly closing in on the enemy.

After what seemed like hours, he'd circled around far enough to reach the edge of the woods. Now came the tricky part.

Using the trunk of a tree to shield himself, he rose to his feet. Closing his eyes, he just stood there and listened. For several long moments he hugged the trunk with his backside, paying close attention to the sounds of the forest. The birds, the insects, the light rustle of leaves and undergrowth. Slowly, a pattern emerged. And a hole formed in the sounds.

That was where he would find his quarry.

He caught the very tail end of a scent. At first he couldn't place it, just sensed a note that wasn't quite right in the piney, boggy, wild-flowery mix of the smells of the marsh. Something…artificial.

Cologne? Perfume?

His eyes flew open.

It smelled like…citrus. Not his or Zara's scent.

But then it was gone. Could he have imagined it?

Crouching low, he darted through the brush, heading for the target area, hoping to catch another drift of the smell that had seemed out of place.

All at once he came upon a small clearing near the edge of the wood. The grass was trampled, and the jarring scent of sweet citrus lingered in the air.

This was where the shooter had stood.

Walker swung around, gun poised in front of him. Searching frantically. But whoever had been there had fled.

Scanning the forest floor, he saw half footprints leading into the trees, spaced far apart as though the shooter had been running away, just touching down with his toes. Running shoes, by the look of it.

He took off at a jog, following the trail. It appeared the guy was heading for the road.

Gotcha.

Walker knew it was stupid to pursue. He should just stop and call the cops. But he was so damned angry he sped up instead of slowing down.

He was so going to get this guy.

Bursting from the forest, he sprinted onto the road, hurriedly checking in both directions.

There!

About a hundred yards away, a dark-clad figure was diving into the front seat of a blue compact. *The same car.*

"Stop right there, you bastard!" he yelled, fury spiking.

Using every bit of strength he had, he took off running after the car.

But he was too far away. Still sprinting, he watched as it careened away, jouncing over the rutted road.

"Sonofabitch!" he yelled after it.

Raising his gun, he aimed at the tires and squeezed off four or five rounds, missing wildly except for one that pierced the back end.

"Sonofafreakingbitch!"

He couldn't believe it. The bastard had gotten away *again.*

By the time Walker had hiked back and fetched Zara, the local police arrived at the gate with lights flashing.

"Thank God," she said when the two officers emerged from their radio car. "Did you arrest him?"

"Who?" they asked, looking clueless.

Walker's heart sank. This guy was almost supernatural in his ability to elude capture.

"The dispatch call was a bit garbled," the younger of the constables said. "What exactly happened?"

Walker let Zara explain, then answered their questions about his role, particularly the shooting part. Handguns were illegal in Silvershire, except for certain law enforcement officers, so he produced his special permit from the Captain of the Palace Guard. The constables were impressed. Even *they* didn't carry guns.

They were also pretty impressed with Lady Zara. Since Castle Perth was unoccupied, County Perthegon had few genuine aristocrats living within its borders.

"What on earth were you two doing here?" they asked her, glancing skeptically around at the sadly neglected property. "Planning t'buy the place?"

She laughed, also looking around. "It could be a lovely estate with a little work. But no. We were searching for an old pavilion that is supposed to be on the property somewhere." She fished the rubbing from her purse and showed them. "You don't, by any chance, know where this strange structure is?"

The older of the two men lit up. "Why, that's t'old pleasure house. The Oriental Pavilion, they called it. Saw't once when I were a nipper. T'young duke's twenty-first birthday party. Aye, now, *that* were a feast if ever there was one."

Walker interrupted before he could go off down memory lane. "Where is this pavilion?" he asked.

"Oh, well, now…" the constable tugged off his hat and scratched his head, glancing around again. "I believe…aye, t'were over yonder. Spot in t'middle of that little wood there." He pointed in the direction of the marshland which they hadn't gotten a chance to properly search.

"I knew it!" Zara said. "Well, if we're finished here, we'll just—"

"Ack, I'm sorry, your ladyship, but we have to ask you two t'come down to the nick with us," the older constable said.

"There'll be paperwork," the younger confirmed.

Walker's cell phone rang. It was Corbett.

"What the hell's going on?" his boss demanded. "I'm getting reports of you out in the geography and shots being fired."

"We're fine," Walker said, and quickly rattled off the morning's events.

"Damn. I'll send von Kreus with one of the forensics guys to recover the bullets and footprints. Meanwhile get yourselves back to the Palace and report to Lord Carrington. There's something he needs to discuss with you and Zara."

"What about the pavilion?"

"This is more important. Besides, you've been used as target practice enough for one day, don't you think?"

Walker and Zara filed their report, in triplicate, at the local police station, where von Kreus also stopped in on his way to Castle Perth to interrogate them politely regarding the shooting. He took sample shoe and tire prints from them, as well. By that time they'd missed lunch by a couple of hours so they stopped in at a local pub for a bite, then headed back to the capital.

"I'm afraid Lord Carrington just went into a meeting," his secretary told them when they arrived at the palace, taking only time for a quick shower and change first. "Perhaps you can come back in an hour?"

"Well, pish, if we'd known that we could have checked out the pavilion," Zara grumbled as they headed back to the medical wing.

"We can do it tomorrow," Walker said.

She glanced over at him and smiled. She didn't ask, but he could almost read her mind. He was staying another night?

To be honest, Walker was finding it harder and harder even to think about leaving Silvershire. *But he had to*. Didn't he?

Yes. He'd promised Zara's mother, and her father would blow a gasket if Walker hung around his daughter one minute longer than necessary. This morning's phone call about the king had come in the very nick of time. Their precipitous departure from the awkward breakfast at Zara's apartment had saved everyone one hell of a nasty conversation, he was dead certain.

Anyway, they weren't the only reason Walker had to leave. He was still a commoner, and still in professional disgrace. None of that had changed, nor was it likely to, despite Royal Publicist Chase Savages's best intentions. Neither had Walker's reason for refusing to clear his name. And Zara was still an aristocrat with a lofty goal, which would not survive her being personally associated with him unless he did so. For her sake, he couldn't stay. The most he could hope for was to be her bodyguard until her life was no longer in danger, sharing what precious few moments were left to them. And then go.

Which was so depressing he refused to think about it.

When they got to the medical wing, they went straight to the king's room.

"Hello, my dear!" King Weston's face lit up when Zara entered. Then he noticed Walker. "I don't believe I've been introduced to your young man yet," he said with a friendly smile.

"Your Majesty," Walker said with a formal bow, and stepped forward. "I'm Walker Shaw, Dr. Smith's bodyguard."

The king blinked. "Bodyguard? What the devil for? Has someone been threatening Lady Zara?" he demanded.

"I'm afraid so, Your Highness." Walker knew Zara hadn't

told Weston about the bombing yet, or her amnesia, so he was limited in what he could say about why he was there.

"Some madman has taken it into his head to kill me," Zara said, bailing him out. "Walker saved my life. Several times now."

The king's face grew angry. "First my son and now my doctor," he growled. "Do these Union for Democracy fanatics not see they are harming their cause rather than helping it? What's being done to stop them?"

"We're not sure it is the UD," Walker said. "Lord Carrington has spoken with their leader, Nikolas Donovan, who has assured him they aren't behind any of the recent incidents. Every resource is being used to locate who really is responsible."

"I want you to keep her safe, Mr. Shaw. She means a great deal to me, for she saved *my* life."

"I plan to, Your Majesty."

"*Dr.* Shaw," Zara corrected, turning to fuss with some kind of monitor beeping behind the king's bed. "Walker is really a doctor of psychiatry. Bodyguarding is just a recent sideline."

The king's eyes went from him to Zara and back. "I see."

The hall door opened and a nurse appeared, holding a tray with a covered plate on it. "Tea time," she said cheerily, and sailed in. Walker didn't recognize her. His nose twitched. *Citrus...*?

Standing next to him, Zara turned back from the monitor and froze. "Mrs. Lloyd! What on earth are you—"

Her words cut off in a gasp when the nurse lifted the lid from the plate and threw it onto the floor. And grabbed a gun under it.

She aimed the gun right at Zara.

"You there!" one of the corridor guards shouted.

The nurse's finger started to squeeze the trigger.

Walker's world went into slow motion as the trigger eased

home. He shouldered Zara forcefully aside. And realized the king was right in the path of the bullet meant for her.

He swore fiercely and dove onto Weston, spreading his body over him like a shield.

And gritted his teeth as the bullet slammed into his back.

Chapter 15

Zara screamed, paralyzed with terror as everything around her erupted in chaos. All she saw was Walker sprawled across the king, blood blooming from a gaping wound in his back.

She thudded against the wall with an *oof,* then the two corridor guards threw themselves at Mrs. Lloyd, wrestling the gun from her. The woman cursed and clawed. Everyone else was yelling. Except Walker. He didn't move.

The king was trying to tell her something, beckoning her, but Zara couldn't get her legs to work. Couldn't get her mind to stop screaming, *My God, he's dead. My God, he's dead….*

Emily rushed in with another nurse and the lab tech, took one look at Zara and began issuing orders. They lifted Walker off King Weston and onto a gurney that had suddenly appeared. He grimaced in pain at being moved, and Zara almost wept with relief.

He was alive!

Her gaze darted to the king, who was waving them away from him and back to Walker.

"Are you hurt, Your Majesty?" Zara managed to croak, the lead weights in her limbs easing enough to take a step toward him.

"I'm fine. Go at once and tend to Dr. Shaw," he ordered brusquely. "I want him *alive* when I reward him for saving my life!"

An hour later, Zara peeled off her surgical gown, grabbed her purse and hurried after Emily, who was wheeling Walker out of the basement emergency room to the covered ambulance bay. Although the operation to remove the bullet lodged between Walker's ribs had been successful, Zara had decided to transfer him to the Royal Medical University Hospital. The palace medical wing was top-notch, but their first priority was King Weston, now that he was awake.

"Sugar?" Walker whispered from the gurney, sounding groggy and disoriented as they loaded him onto the ambulance.

"I'm here, darling," she said, climbing in after him and reaching to take his hand. "You're okay. I got the bullet out. No complications." He'd been extremely lucky. The bullet hadn't pierced any major organs and had only broken one rib—the one that had stopped it.

The siren blared and red lights flashed.

"You?"

She swallowed around the lump that had been lodged in her throat for the past hour, and blinked back the tears she'd been holding at bay the whole time she was operating. She leaned over and kissed his cheek, his temple. "You don't think I'd let anyone else touch you, do you?"

Was that a smile?

"King?"

"Unhurt." She stroked her fingers down the curve of his neck. "Thanks to you."

"Thank God," he whispered, and his face went slack as he slipped back into unconsciousness.

She put a knuckle to her mouth and pressed hard.

"We're almost there," the ambulance tech said gently, nodding at the large modern building they were fast approaching.

She sucked in a breath and blew it out again, struggling to get her emotions under control. *Everything was all right.* Walker would soon be good as new, the king was unharmed, and they'd finally caught the person trying to kill her.

Mrs. Lloyd. She couldn't believe it. The mother of the child who'd died two years ago. As the guards had dragged her away, she'd been screaming all sorts of awful, ugly things at her.

Zara's feelings of guilt must have been obvious because during Walker's surgery Emily had told her, "It's not your fault. None of this is your fault. That girl's death, either. You have to know that."

Zara wanted to believe it with all her heart. Maybe in time she would.

They checked Walker in as her personal patient, and settled him into a private room overlooking the River Kairn and the Golden Bridge.

She was sitting in an easy chair pulled up right next to his bedside when he awoke a few hours later.

"I suppose sex is out of the question," he said in a raspy voice, drawing her gaze from the window to where he was lying, stomach down on the narrow hospital bed, cheek resting on the fluffy pillow.

She smiled, her heart leaping at the loving way his eyes

caressed her. "As your physician I'd advise against any vigorous exercise until that rib has healed."

"Hmm. Then can I turn over?" he asked with a wink. "Maybe you could…"

"No," she stated with mock sternness. "Not until at least tomorrow. Wouldn't want to pull your stitches."

"Spoilsport," he said, but his lips curved up.

"Sorry," she said, and suddenly felt her own smile fade. She leaned forward and threaded her fingers tenderly through his long hair, touched his dear face. *Almost taken from her.* "Oh, Walker, I'm so sorry. That bullet was meant for me, not you."

He reached for her hand. "*Baby, don't.* It's a damn good thing it hit me, because if it had hit you or the king, I'd have had to kill that crazy woman and I'd be in jail right now instead of kissing you." He brushed his lips over her knuckles. "Who was she, anyway?"

Zara sighed and recounted the whole depressing story of which he'd heard bits and pieces. "I knew Mrs. Lloyd had gone a bit over the edge at the loss of her child, but I never suspected just how far."

"But why now? Why not back then?"

"Agent von Kreus came by earlier to check on you. He told me it was a newspaper article that had set her off. She saw a picture in the *Quiz* of me caring for the king and she snapped. Was certain I would kill him, too. In her mind, she was helping the king by getting rid of me."

"My God. That's nuts!"

Zara had to agree. She shivered, and Walker rubbed the goose bumps from her arms.

"She confessed to everything," she continued. "The bombing, hitting Estevez, the poisoning at the restaurant, trying to run us down. When none of that worked, she followed us to Perthegon. By that time she'd lost it completely."

"So she didn't care if she was caught."

"She probably wanted to be. She's not a bad person at heart. Grief can do terrible things."

He grimaced as he changed positions, turning slightly onto his good side. Zara went and got an extra pillow from the closet, tucking it under his arm to help prop him up those few inches. Then she held his hand again. She needed to touch him, to know for certain he was alive and safe.

"What I want to know is how the hell she found out about the tunnel," he said.

She traced her finger up his thumb. "Well, that's the strange thing. She says the tunnel's not how she got in."

He frowned. "Then how?"

"Apparently she worked at the Medical University Hospital for a while and still had her ID. She dressed in a nurse's uniform and told the palace guards she'd been sent to help because one of the regular nurses in the medical wing was ill. They let her through."

He briefly squeezed his eyes shut. "Idiots. So you're telling me our attacker in the tunnel *wasn't* this Lloyd woman?"

Zara shook her head. "Probably just some kid exploring who we scared to death."

He was silent for a moment, then said, "Well, I guess that would explain why he didn't try to hurt you. What about the icon?"

She shook her head again. "She claims she didn't steal it."

He swore softly. "Then who the hell did?"

"I still think it was someone after drugs. There's no other reasonable explanation."

"What does von Kreus think?"

"He didn't say."

Walker tugged her closer. "Zara. Can you get me a room with a bigger bed? I want you to stay with me tonight."

She smiled. "Darling, this is a hospital. There are no bigger beds. Besides, I warned you about that sex thing…."

His little-boy smile broke through for a second, then vanished. "As nice as that sounds, it's not why I want you to stay. I'm still your bodyguard." He made a frustrated face. "I need you where I can see you."

Her heart melted at the concern in his voice. "Walker, they caught the maniac trying to kill me, remember? I'll be fine. Honestly."

"Still—"

"However," she soothed, "I'm not going anywhere. I plan to sleep right here." She patted the easy chair. "Because I need to be where I can see you, too."

He squeezed her hand and closed his eyes with a tired smile. "Promise?" he asked.

"Promise," she said, and wished to the depths of her soul she could always be where she could see him. Forever and always, for the rest of their lives.

It took Walker two damned uncomfortable days to get out of the damned uncomfortable hospital. He could walk, slowly and at an even pace, without his rib or the bullet wound in his back hurting too much. The painkillers helped a lot.

Which was why, when Zara announced she was going back to Perthegon to find the Oriental Pavilion, he insisted on going with her.

He thought she was out of her mind.

But she had that look on her face again. He didn't even argue.

He had to be out of *his* mind.

Either that or the painkillers were affecting his judgment.

In any case, he found himself in the passenger seat, gritting his teeth as they jolted over the endless pitted dirt road to Castle Perth.

"Sex would be easier on my aching rib than this," he groused.

She gave him a dry glance. "You *had* sex. Not two hours ago."

He smiled at the blissful memory of just lying back and letting her have her wicked way with him. "Yeah, but you made us stop. To come here and torture me."

"I told you, you shouldn't have come."

"As if."

They finally made it to the gate, and suddenly it occurred to him there was no way he'd ever be able to squeeze through the iron bars with his bandaged wound.

She wiggled her eyebrows, producing a small box that rattled when she shook it.

"What's that?"

"Keys. I called the guy at the antique shop where we bought the painting, and he let me borrow his whole stock of historic gate keys. He said one of them is bound to fit because they were all of about the same design, just different sizes."

Walker smiled. It was just like Zara to remember about the gate and solve the problem before it had even occurred to him. "You know what? You're pretty amazing."

She smiled back. "I am, aren't I?"

She jumped out, and by the time he'd made it to the gate she had it unlocked. "Open sesame!" she said and shoved the gate open. Well, sort of. One of the sides wouldn't budge at all and the other squealed like a banshee, grudgingly creaking open only a foot or two before sticking fast.

But it was enough. Together they slid through and slowly

made their way to the marshy area. Today they'd come prepared, wearing shorts, T-shirts and sneakers that had seen better days. So they waded into the muck. It wasn't too bad. Once you got used to the sucking sounds coming from the soles of your feet. And then there was the view.

"This is truly disgusting," Zara said, but Walker was too engrossed in watching her backside in those sexy shorts to notice.

As the cop had promised, they found the Oriental Pavilion tucked away in a small grove in the middle of the marsh.

"It looks like a Bedouin tent," he said, tearing his attention from her legs to examine the rusting, creaking structure. Shaped like a fancy tent some sheikh would live in, the walls were wavy like cloth and bore traces of paint that had once been bright purple-and-red stripes. "I was thinking Chinese or Japanese."

"In the eighteen-hundreds Oriental meant from the Middle East. Must have been built back then."

"It definitely looks rickety enough to be a hundred and fifty years old," he said.

A gentle breeze wafted through the trees, rustling leaves and branches. A lone grasshopper fiddled a tune behind the pavilion.

Suddenly Walker felt uneasy. He glanced around nervously, without knowing exactly why. Something was giving him the creeps.

"Why…it's made of metal!" Zara said in surprise.

"Yeah. Is that significant?" He scanned the outer edges of the grove, but nothing seemed out of place. Except he could no longer hear the grasshopper.

She peered up at him and bit her lip. "It's just…in my visions…I remember something about big sheets of metal."

He really wished she hadn't mentioned her damned visions. Thinking about them only increased his growing sense of…being watched.

"All right," he said briskly. "Now we've seen it. Let's get the hell out of here."

She resisted his urging hand and turned back to the pavilion with a strange expression. "Not yet. We have to go inside."

He grabbed her before she could move, wincing at the pull to his rib. "Oh no. I don't think so. The freaking thing looks like it could fall down any second."

"We *have* to go in. Whatever these visions have been leading me to, it's here…inside."

He drove his fingers through his hair in frustration. If the thing started crashing down around their ears, he was in no condition to hold it up long enough for them to get out. "Baby, please. Can we just open the door and look in from the outside?"

She hesitated, glancing at his torso, which she herself had wrapped in tight swaths of bandages to keep his cracked rib in place. "Okay," she conceded, to his immense relief. "We can start by just looking in, and go from there."

Naturally, she forgot all about her promise when they gingerly teased open the wobbly, broken-hinged door and she caught sight of the inside.

"Oh, my God," she breathed, and darted in before he could stop her.

"God *damn* it, Zara!"

He had no choice but to follow. Which, after one more thorough scan of the surrounding woods, he did.

"Do you see that border?"

She pointed up to where the walls met the undulating peaked roof. Inside, the paint had been protected from the elements and was still fairly crisp, the pattern easy to see despite the dimly lit interior. The border was purple, about a foot wide, filled with gold squiggly symbols and indecipherable writing.

"The same symbols and writing as on the icon."

"And in my visions."

He muttered a curse. "So, what is it all supposed to mean?"

Her gaze met his and held. She looked as spooked as he felt. "I have no idea."

All at once the pavilion started to sway, creaking and groaning as the roof threatened to split apart above them. The back wall *did* split apart. Blinding sunshine poured through the gash into the dimness. Walker shaded his eyes against the glare, but could swear he saw…a man pushing against it!

"Hey you! *Stop!*"

Just then, with a huge squealing crash, the whole pavilion started to collapse on top of them. "Zara, get out!" he yelled above the sickening screech of metal, giving her a firm push toward the door. *"Now!"*

A giant section of the roof fell, catching an edge in his T-shirt. "Damn it!" He struggled to free himself, but couldn't.

"Walker! Watch out!" Zara screamed as a piece of wall collapsed inward, coming straight at him.

He had just enough time to drop to the ground and cover his head before a heavy slab of metal crashed over him. He bit back a cry when it landed on his wound. But miraculously, it stopped short of crushing him flat, giving him enough room to breathe, but not much more.

"Walker!" Zara screamed as another wall came down.

"Zara! Are you okay? Get the hell out of here!"

"Where are you?" Her voice was high with panic.

The rest of the walls and roof landed around him with a metallic thunder Walker would never forget as long as he lived. But somehow his cocoon of air had survived intact, and him along with it.

"Baby, talk to me! Are you hurt?" he called.

"It knocked me over, but I'm fine," she finally said, voice wobbly. "I can see the outside. Oh, my God! There's someone out there! He's running away!"

Thank God, was all Walker could think.

Chapter 16

The fact that the structure had been made of large sheets of wavy moulded metal worked in their favor; big gaps of space had been left between the fallen bits. It took a bit of doing, but Walker was able to wriggle his way out from under the roof section that had pinned him down.

"You doing okay, baby?" he called. Zara had been silent for a while now, though he could hear a constant scraping noise coming from where she was stuck. "I'm almost to you I think."

"Walker…"

"Yeah, sugar?" He grunted in pain as he struggled to move one last wall section. The painkiller was wearing off and his rib hurt like a bastard.

"You aren't going to believe this."

He paused. He really hated when she said stuff like that. It was never good news. "What?"

"I found something."

"Yeah?"

"Buried."

Ah, hell. He prayed it wasn't a body. "What is it?"

"A chest of some sort."

He sent up a quick thank you to the powers that be. "Like a box?"

"I think this is *it*," she said excitedly. "What I was sent to find."

He was about to object to the term *sent,* but figured he didn't have a lot to argue with. It really was as though she'd been guided here by some unseen hand.

With a heave, he shoved the wall section a few feet aside and he could finally see her. Legs sticking out from under the rubble, she lay on her stomach digging with her hands, a pile of soggy earth growing by her side. She glanced up.

"Look!"

In the center of the hole she'd dug was the vaulted top of a wooden chest. It looked old.

"Pirate's treasure?" he asked with a hopeful smile to mask his uncertainty over how to react. This was so weird.

She broke out in a grin. "Gold, you mean? Or pieces of eight? Wouldn't that be cool." But she didn't sound like she believed it.

"What do *you* think it is?"

She shook her head, scraping a stray lock from her eyes with grubby fingers, leaving a streak of mud through her eyebrow. "I don't know. But whatever it is, it must be important. That guy out there…"

"Crashed this thing on purpose," Walker finished.

"Trying to prevent us from finding it."

A charitable interpretation. "I just hope he's not still hanging around." *With a gun,* he amended silently. His own gun was tucked into his waistband, but he didn't relish another shootout.

"I'm sorry I doubted your instincts about the gun," she said contritely.

She'd argued against the need to bring it, repeating they'd already caught the person trying to kill her. But Walker couldn't dismiss the icon and the tunnel incident as easily as she did. It just didn't fit.

"Ditto, sugar." But he had to admit, her visions had been eerily on target. "Let's dig this thing up and get back to the palace with it as fast as we can."

Walker stood next to Zara, who was waiting anxiously for Lord Carrington to say something. They were in Carrington's private study, the odd vaulted chest shedding dirt on a newspaper on his desk. Zara looked as though she was ready to burst from curiosity.

"Well. It's certainly not heavy enough to be gold," Carrington observed, taking hold of the side handles and shaking it. Something inside rattled around.

"Sounds like there are several things in there. Maybe in smaller containers," Walker said. He'd shaken it a couple of times himself on the way back from Perthegon.

"Can we open it?" Zara asked. "Please? I just know it's important."

"Because of the visions?"

She'd just told Carrington about them, how he and Zara had traced the icon symbols and found the pavilion. And how a man had tried to stop them.

"Yes, and…" She hesitated, seeming undecided for a moment. Then said, "And because of something the king said yesterday."

Carrington looked up sharply. "What was that?"

Zara took a deep breath. "Something about having another son."

Carrington froze. "He *told* you?"

"Excuse me?" Walker was sure he'd heard incorrectly. "What the hell are you talking about?"

She glanced at him apologetically.

Walker turned to Carrington in pure disbelief. "Are you saying King Weston has *another son out there somewhere?* That there's another crown prince of Silvershire? Still alive?"

The duke cleared his throat. "We aren't exactly sure. It came as much of a surprise to King Weston as it was to everyone else. It appears that—" His mouth turned down. "—and I assume I don't have to say this information is not to leave this room…?" Zara and Walker both nodded. "It appears that Prince Reginald was not the king and queen's natural child. That somehow the babies were switched and the true prince was, as incredible as it sounds, given to someone else. Naturally, we have every resource possible trying to trace the child…well, man, really, since he would be thirty years old by now."

"Including the Lazlo Group?" Walker asked. Was he the *only* one who didn't know?

Carrington nodded. "Yes. Your assignment was Zara, and this information was strictly need-to-know. We had no idea it could involve you, or Zara." He still looked unconvinced that it did.

"How long have you known?" she asked the duke.

"Since April."

"And it's now July. Well, Carrington, that certainly explains your sangfroid about becoming king. You never expected to be crowned!"

"Guilty, I'm afraid."

"And here I'd been so admiring your sudden maturity," she said, making a face at him.

Carrington laughed and put his hand on the vaulted lid of the chest. Under the liberal coating of dirt, Walker thought it was quite beautiful. Some type of hardwood, probably cedar, had been hand-hewn and keyed together like a Chinese cabinet, bound with strips of brass at the joints, and held together with brass pins. The lock was also brass, of an elaborate design he'd never seen before.

"I wonder what secrets you hold," the duke murmured.

"Russell," Zara said seriously, "I think whatever is in here has to do with the true prince. I have no evidence whatsoever of that, just a strong…feeling."

Walker could see him evaluate her words, as he himself was. He was weighing the obvious outlandishness of the idea of visions leading her to this important discovery versus cold hard facts: the icon had been stolen and someone had tried to scare them away from finding the chest.

"What do you think, Shaw?"

Walker shrugged. "I think whatever has been going on in Zara's head this past week has been pretty damn strange, but it can't be denied she was right at every turn."

"I'm inclined to agree," Carrington said at last. "So, instead of breaking the lock right now, I'm going to turn the chest over to the forensics team to examine the whole thing very carefully before opening. I hope either that or what's inside will provide us with a clue as to the true crown prince's whereabouts, if not his identity."

Suddenly Zara gave a small gasp. "That woman, Mrs. Lloyd, did she also confess to poisoning Prince Reginald? It was the same kind of poison as she used on me, wasn't it?"

Carrington clasped his hands behind his back. "Digitalis was used both times. But she denies killing the prince. And the tox report confirms her story. The compound in your stomach was of a different type and strength than that which killed the prince."

"I knew it," Walker said, gratified at last to hear support for his own conclusions. "I'd be willing to bet whoever stole that icon and pushed over the pavilion today was responsible for Reginald's death."

"You're no doubt right," Russell said. "Lazlo Group investigator Aidan Spaulding has just uncovered evidence that an international female assassin known as the Sparrow was hired to kill the prince. If this chest you found has anything to do with the true prince's identity, the man you saw today was probably the man who hired the Sparrow."

"Which makes it more important than ever to open it very carefully," Zara said, eyeing the chest with regret. "You will tell us what's in it?" she asked the duke. "I'm dying of curiosity."

Walker choked. "Baby, please don't use that word."

Carrington regarded them both. "Well, the good news is, you should be safe now, Zara. There's no reason anyone should want to harm you now that the chest has been discovered and is out of your hands." He cleared his throat. "Which I guess means…"

Walker's job here was done.

He suddenly couldn't move. He wanted to shout, *No! Wait! That guy could still be after Zara! I'm still needed here!* But he knew it wasn't true. Carrington was right.

"It means I'll be leaving Silvershire," he managed to say fairly evenly.

Zara's gaze sought his, looking wounded and stunned. "But—"

Then her mouth shut and thinned, and she turned her head away.

He had no desire to discuss their personal business in front of Carrington, and assumed she didn't, either.

"No need to hurry off," the duke said with an affable smile. "I'd be delighted to have you stay as my guest. In fact, I could use a right-hand man to help keep track of all these infernal investigations. I'm afraid my royal duties have been sadly neglected over the past weeks because my attention has been spread so thin. And now with the king awake again… What do you say?"

Slightly taken aback at the other man's offer, which actually seemed sincere, Walker didn't know quite how to answer. He desperately wanted to stay. But would it simply be delaying the inevitable? Unfortunately, yes.

He gave a slight bow. "Thank you very much, Your Grace. I appreciate all you've done for me, but it would probably be best for everyone if I left."

Zara gave a small, unladylike snort, but didn't speak.

Frustrated anger welled up inside him. "Zara, the press are still hounding you over me. Dragging your name—"

"Don't you *dare* use the press as an excuse," she snapped. Then gave a huff and marched out of the room.

"Zara!"

He appealed to Carrington, who gave him a commiserating look. "Better go after her. Seemed a bit peeved to me."

Clenching his teeth, he said, "Yeah," then headed after her.

"Walker!" Carrington said as he reached the door. "The king would like a word with you. Be sure to stop by and see him."

With a nod, he hurried out into the grand hall to catch up with Zara, who was walking at the speed of light toward the medical wing, high heels clicking angrily on the marble tiles.

"Now who's running away?" he called after her.

She stopped on a dime and spun an about-face, hands on her hips.

God, she was sexy.

It was all he could do to keep himself from grabbing her and kissing her madly, falling to his knees and begging her to come with him. Somewhere. Anywhere. To a place where no one knew his name and they could live together in peaceful anonymity. Somewhere his background wouldn't catch up to him and he wouldn't have to worry about Ramona Burdette's threats.

He'd trade everything he had for that chance. Every penny and every single dream, for the chance to be with Zara, to love her and have a family together and spend their days growing old together.

But that wasn't going to happen. There was no such place.

And even if there were, Zara had her own dreams, dreams she'd spent her whole life working to make into reality. Who was he to ask her to give them up?

"No, Walker," she said. "You're the one leaving, not me."

"And what do you suggest I do?" he shot back, coming up to her, grasping her arms.

"Stay!"

"And do what? Work for Carrington, where I'd be tortured every damned day, seeing you and knowing I can never really have you? That I can never live with you openly, never ask you to marry me?"

She stared at him with glistening eyes. "Try me."

He let out a long breath, fighting like mad not to give in to the plea. Fighting like mad to resist the overwhelming need to take her in his arms. "I'm a commoner. I can't work in my profession, and I can never clear my name. *Never*, Zara. You said it yourself. You need a husband your people will look up to. I'm the furthest thing from that."

"Why?" she demanded as she had once before. "Why can't you clear your name?"

He ground his jaw, wavering only a moment. He trusted her and she deserved to know. "Because if I'm cleared, the woman who made those accusations against me will be branded a liar. If that happens, she has sworn retribution. She has threatened my family. The lives of my parents, brothers and sister depend on my silence. She's rich *and* crazy, Zara. Crazier than Mrs. Lloyd. I'm terrified she'll hurt them. I'm certain she will if I say one word against her."

Zara looked horrified. "There must be something you can do! The police—"

"Have their hands tied unless she actually does something illegal. I'm not willing to take the chance."

"That's so unfair."

"Yeah. Life truly does suck. Especially today." He took a deep breath, brushed his palms down her arms, taking her hands in his, lacing their fingers. "I can't stay in Silvershire and not have you. I wouldn't survive that. But if I stay, the press will continue to crucify you."

"I don't care. Walker, please—"

"Jeezus, Zara. I know what it's like to have your dreams taken away. Everything you've worked for ripped out from under you. Don't you understand? I could *never* do that to you."

A couple of guards strolled by, glancing at them curiously as they stood there with fingers twined and hearts breaking. The bright gilded chandeliers glittered in Zara's liquid eyes, then a tear spilled over her lashes.

"Oh, baby," he whispered, and enfolded her in his arms, holding her tight. The pain in his rib was nothing compared to that in his heart and his soul.

He tilted her stubborn little chin up with his fingers and gently kissed her lips. "I love you, Zara Smith," he said softly. "I'll always love you, as long as I live. But I have to go."

* * *

Zara had thought the moment Walker would first say those precious words to her would be the happiest in her life.

Tears spilled down her cheeks, but instead of tears of joy, they were tears of sadness.

How could he love her, and still leave?

She clung to him fiercely, unwilling to let him go. She *wouldn't* let him go.

"Darling, you have to listen to me," she said between hitched breaths. "I'm telling you I don't *want* to be the Marchioness of Daneby any more. It's just an empty title. It would mean nothing at all without the man I love to share it."

He squeezed his eyes shut. "Oh, hell, Zara," he whispered. "Don't do this."

"It's you I want, Walker. I don't care about your past or what the press says, or what anyone else thinks. If they have any kind of brains they'll love you as much as I do."

His beautiful blue eyes opened and he gazed down at her. The depth of feeling she saw in them took her breath away.

"Yeah?" he whispered.

"Yeah."

"You're willing to give all that up for me?" Quiet wonder filled his voice.

"It's you I love."

He searched her face. "You're sure?"

"Absolutely certain."

His mouth curved up in a smile and he studied her for a long, long time, as though waiting for her to change her mind. She didn't.

"Well, in that case, I've been wanting to do this for seven years…."

She covered her mouth as he dropped to one knee, and took her right hand in his.

"Lady Zara Smith, would you do me the very great honor of becoming my wife?"

She blinked, a sudden rush of joy sweeping through her heart, into her whole body. She felt her fingers tremble on her lips. "Marry you? Really?"

"If you'll have me."

"Of course I— Oh, Walker! Yes! Yes, I'll marry you!" She dropped to her own knees and threw her arms around him, hugging him, rocking with him, laughing and crying with happiness.

All around them applause erupted. The guards, the footman, the maids were scattered about with silly grins on their faces, clapping.

"Ow, baby, have mercy, I'm a wounded man," Walker said, kissing her over and over between laughs and winces.

"Oh!" She dropped her arms contritely, but he put them right back.

"Don't stop. I'll live."

The crowd cheered.

"I assume you have the king's permission?" Carrington said, leaning negligently against his study door with a big smile and that mischievous glint in his gaze.

Walker stopped in mid kiss. "King's permission?" His eyes widened and sought hers. "He's kidding, right?"

She resisted a grin. "I'm afraid not. Daughter of a marquis, and all. A somewhat antiquated law, admittedly, but…" She lifted a shoulder.

Walker actually looked worried. "He can't say no, can he?"

"Well, theoretically…"

He muttered a curse. "Great. I'm s—" she shot him a warning look "—uh, sure he'll say yes."

"Why don't you find out right now?" Carrington suggested, far too keenly, she thought.

So they did.

On the way to the medical wing to see King Weston, suddenly Zara got worried. What did Russell know that she didn't? Even now he was tagging along behind her and Walker, looking cagey and mysterious beneath his pleasant smile.

"Ah, there you are!" King Weston said as they knocked and entered the luxurious private suite he'd been moved to since coming out of his coma. He was making excellent progress, his recovery nearly complete. "Come in! Come in!"

"Your Majesty," they said together, Walker making the obligatory bow. Zara even curtsied, though in her official capacity as his doctor it wasn't strictly required. Russell had knocked her so off-kilter she was running on automatic.

The king was sitting in a chair by the window, wearing an elegant, thick silk dressing gown and slippers. He beckoned. "Come over here, Dr. Shaw. I have something I must say to you."

Zara sensed more than saw Walker hesitate, but he went forward. "Your Highness, I also have something I'd like to say. Or, rather, ask."

Weston held up a finger. "I'm king, I get to go first." He chuckled, and Zara smiled. He really was feeling his old self again.

She could see Walker's shoulders notch down a fraction. "Of course."

"Help me up, lad," Weston said, reaching up to grab Walker's hand.

Zara rushed forward to help, too, but the old man was surprisingly steady on his feet and barely needed it. Still, he kept hold of her hand as he regarded Walker, his expression turning solemn. To her shock, he bowed to Walker. Not just an inclined head, but an honest-to-goodness bow. Walker shot her a panicked what-do-I-do-now? look. She had no clue. Behind her, Carrington leaned against his ubiquitous door frame and looked inscrutable.

The king drew himself up formally. "I thank you, Dr. Shaw, for saving my life. You took a bullet that surely would have killed Dr. Smith if it had hit her, and most probably would have been the end of me or some of my favorite bits, had it hit me." He bowed again.

"Thanks are not necessary, Your Majesty," Walker said graciously, his face flushed with embarrassment. "Really. Anyone would have done the same in my position."

"I'm not so sure," the king responded. "But in any case, I shall reward you generously for your selfless service to the crown."

Walker brightened. "Well, sire, if that is your intention, there is something I was hoping to ask you for."

Weston's brows rose at Walker's charming American brashness. "Indeed?"

"Yes." Walker reached for her. "I'd like to ask your permission to wed Lady Zara."

Weston's brows went even further up. *"Indeed?"*

Walker smiled at her and she beamed back. "We'd very much like to marry."

The king looked from one to the other. "I see." He pursed his lips. "I did have a different sort of reward in mind. Perhaps you'd care to hear it?"

"Not necessary, Your Majesty. Lady Zara is all I want."

"I think I'll tell you, anyway. You can choose which you'd rather have, is that fair?"

Walker nodded, giving her hand a squeeze.

"The reward I'd planned was to make you a Knight of the Realm of Silvershire." He pronounced every word distinctly.

Zara gasped. "Oh, Your Majesty!"

Being made a Knight of the Realm was the highest honor a person could achieve in her country. It happened rarely, maybe once a generation, given only for the most extraordinary service. She grabbed Walker's shoulders. "You can't turn this down. You mustn't!"

The king continued, "It carries the title of Baron, of course. You would be Lord Shaw."

Utterly gobsmacked, Walker swallowed a few times. "I, uh, I'm—I…" He threw a glance for aid at Carrington, who winked, the rat. "I thank you, profoundly, Your Majesty. But as I said, Lady Zara is all I really want."

Weston indicated he wanted to sit down again, so they helped him. As they did, a war raged within her. She desperately wanted to marry Walker, but if it meant he must turn down this incredible honor—and the chance for him to redeem his good name, in Silvershire, at least—she had to change his mind. Somehow.

"Sire, you don't really mean he must choose between being a baron and being my husband?" she pleaded. He couldn't be serious. She knew that the King had a mischievous streak, but still…

Weston waved a hand. "That would be up to the new king," he said with a little smile at Carrington. "He could still grant you permission to marry. If he were so inclined."

She whirled to Russell. "You wouldn't dare refuse! Would you?"

He shrugged expansively. "It might not be up to me, Zara, remember? The true crown prince may be found soon, and he would make that decision if he were king."

Oh, God, she'd completely forgotten about that! It could take ages....

Walker was shaking his head. "Not necessary. My choice stands."

Weston tilted his head slyly. "Perhaps you'll change your mind when I tell you there's more? A baron needs a castle to live in. So I've attached a lifetime entailment of Castle Perth to the barony. It's a beautiful piece of architecture, and it should be lived in."

"But not by me," Walker said firmly, bringing tears to Zara's eyes.

"Oh, darling," she sighed, and wrapped her arms around him. "I do love you so much."

"I love you, too, baby." He kissed her then, long and warm, and only stopped when the king cleared his throat.

"Well, then. If that's your final word, your marriage has my blessing," he said, smiling. Then he frowned and poked the air with his finger. "I don't see a ring."

Again, Walker turned red. "No, uh, this all happened a bit suddenly. I haven't had a chance—"

"Perhaps you'd like to use this?" The king drew an elaborate signet ring from his finger and beckoned Walker for his right hand. When he reached out, Weston took it and slid the ring onto his finger, holding him fast. "I had a feeling you'd choose Lady Zara. But I'm an ornery old man and don't like taking no for an answer...*Baron* Shaw."

Zara pressed her hands to her mouth to keep from crying out. The carved ruby signet that crowned the glittering gold ring was unmistakable—the official seal of a Knight of the Realm.

"Oh! Your Highness! Oh, my lord, I can't believe it!" She was babbling, but she didn't care. She was so happy for

Walker she didn't know what to do with herself. She was actually jumping up and down.

Walker stared at the ring, obviously overcome.

"Better put it on her finger, lad. Before she gets away."

"No! No, seriously." She warded off Walker, making him keep the ring on his own hand. "That's yours. Only yours."

He smiled, his eyes going soft. "And what about you, sugar?"

Sliding her arms around his neck, she said, "I'm yours, too, my lord," and her heart overflowed with love for this incredible man, the man who had stolen her heart seven years ago and had finally come to claim the rest of her. Her own knight in shining armor. "Only yours, for the rest of time."

Epilogue

The proclamation read: "By the King—A Proclamation," but everyone knew it had been the queen's doing. Her idea, her effort, her success. Not that the king disagreed, mind you, because he was as fair-minded and…well, if you really wanted to put a fine point on it, democratic…as she.

Still, it caused quite a stir, regardless of who was behind it. But after the dust settled, the decree was viewed by the common folk as a positive sign of what was to come from their new king, recently installed on the throne. It read:

Declaring His Majesty's Pleasure concerning the Succession of Titles of Nobility and the Dispensation of Land Entailments:

WHEREAS We have taken note of an inequity of gender in the matter of historical Land and Title Entailments in Our Nation, as it was the practice in times past.

We do hereby, by and with the advice of Our Privy Council, change and declare that the traditional practice of male primogeniture in the inheritance of Titles of Nobility and the Entailment of Estates, such as exist now or in the future in the Country of Silvershire, shall cease immediately, and furthermore a new tradition which does not take account of an heir's gender shall henceforth be used.

Given at Our Court at Silverton Royal Palace, this twenty-first day of October, in the year of Our Lord, two thousand and six, and in the first year of Our Reign.

God Save the King and the People

A wide smile came to Zara's lips as she read the heavy, engraved parchment announcement that had arrived at Castle Perth by special liveried messenger directly from the Royal Palace.

She'd done it! Zara could scarcely believe it, but the new queen had kept her word and talked her husband into changing one of the most ancient laws of the land. Actually, she could believe it. Their new queen was an amazing woman.

The young messenger still stood at attention amid the chaos of renovation debris that currently littered the castle's main salon, feathered hat in hand, along with another large scroll. He'd insisted on staying until everyone in the household had read and understood the proclamation.

"Shaw!" Zara called to her husband, who was busy with dinner in the kitchen. "You must come and see this, my lord!"

Walker strolled in, wiping his hands on a towel. "You've

really got to stop calling me that," he said, rolling his eyes. "At least when we're not in bed."

She winked at the messenger. Walker hadn't quite gotten used to his new title yet, but he had found some interesting uses for it. "Now, darling, behave," she said, handing him the parchment scroll. "And read."

The messenger bowed. "Lord Shaw. The king and queen send their greetings."

"What's this all about?" He scanned the thick parchment in his hand, said, "Wow," and read it again, more carefully. Then he broke out in a grin and gave Zara a big hug, lifting her off her feet. "Way to go, baby. You did it! Congratulations."

She hugged him back and laughed, thinking what a difference a few months made. "I'd better call father at once and tell him I plan to abdicate in favor of remaining a baron's wife."

"Can you do that?" She sent him a wry look, which he mirrored back at her. "Never mind. You can do anything you set your mind to."

"Thank you, darling." She accepted a kiss.

"Lady Zara, Lord Shaw," the messenger said, offering her the other scroll he'd been holding. "This was also sent to you by the king and queen." Then he bowed again. "My lady, my lord, I'll take my leave."

"Now I am curious," she said, and unrolled the parchment eagerly. As she began to read, her jaw dropped.

"Good God."

Declaring His Majesty's Pleasure concerning the Dispensation of the Duchy of Perthegon and its Entailments

We do hereby, by and with the advice of Our Privy Council, declare that Lady Zara, daughter of the Marquis and Marchioness of Daneby and wife of Lord

Shaw, for special service to her King and the people of Silvershire, shall inherit the Duchy of Perthegon along with all its properties and privileges, including such leases and entailments as exist upon it, which she shall immediately exercise authority over.

Our Will and Pleasure further is that Lady Zara, renouncing any other Titles of Nobility, shall henceforth be known to all as Zara, Duchess of Perthegon.

Given at Our Court at Silverton Royal Palace, this twenty-first day of October, in the year of Our Lord, two thousand and six, and in the first year of Our Reign.

God Save the King and the People

Zara was speechless. Unable to utter a single word.

"What the hell…" Walker took the scroll and read it three times, looking as astonished as she felt.

Just two months ago, they'd gone through an incredible ceremony where Walker's knighthood had been bestowed, complete with sword taps on the shoulder and all the pomp befitting the honor. Then there'd been their wedding, held in the palace gardens with King Weston presiding in his final formal act as king. Finally, there'd been the coronation itself, where they'd been among the honored guests of the crown.

Her life had been a literal fairy tale for the past three months.

Even the fickle press had changed their tune and done a complete turnaround on Walker. The *Quiz* had dubbed Walker "Lord Shaw, the Cinderella Knight," making him into the darling of all of Silvershire because of his bravery in saving the king's life. And also for his decision to turn a whole wing of Castle Perth into a state-of-the-art facility for treating Alzheimers and dementia in the elderly, with the financial support of the retired king.

And now this! Duchess of Perthegon!

Walker beamed at her, his gaze full of love and his lips curved in an adoring smile. "I'm so proud of you, Zara. No one deserves this honor more than you."

She shook her head and launched herself into his arms. "My God, Walker, It's all a dream, isn't it? I know I'm going to wake up tomorrow and it'll all be a dream. Like Alice in Wonderland."

He laughed with her, stroking his fingers through her hair. "Now you know how *I've* been feeling for the past three months. Like I've fallen down some incredible rabbit hole into a crazy land where all your dreams come true."

"Just promise me one thing," she said, brushing his darling face with her fingertips…his cheek, his mouth, his square jaw. Amazed that he was real. Amazed that he was really hers.

"What's that, sugar?"

She kissed him tenderly on his smiling lips. "When I wake up from this extraordinary dream, please be there with me."

His smile turned gentle, his eyes shining with more love than she'd ever known possible. "Count on it, baby," he said, kissing her back. "Who needs dreams when we have each other?"

* * * * *

She's to be taken alive, Aidan Spaulding reminded himself as he walked the streets of Leonia, trying to become familiar with the lay of the land before heading to his latest assignment—identifying the killer of Prince Reginald.

The Lazlo Group had received information that a world-renowned female assassin was behind the killing. The Sparrow, as she was known, was believed to have poisoned the prince. Aidan was to confirm that and try to capture the elusive gun-for-hire.

Aidan had personal reasons for wanting the Sparrow caught. Two years earlier, he and his best friend, Mitchell Lama, had been on the trail of a suspected terrorist. They had been about to close in on their suspect, unaware that the man they were seeking was also being sought by the Sparrow.

Mitch and he had split up in the narrow, twisting alleyways

of Rome's Trastevere section, communicating via walkie-talkie as they attempted to corner their man.

When the walkie-talkie in his hand had gone dead, Aidan had realized his friend was in trouble. The nature of the mission had changed suddenly as he raced through the alley-ways trying to locate him. He had finally found the friend, who was almost like a brother, sprawled on the ancient cobblestones of a back alley.

Mitch had been nearly gutted and was barely alive. Aidan had held him as he called for medical assistance, but knew he might not survive long enough for it to arrive. Somehow, though, his friend had managed one last word before he died in Aidan's arms: Sparrow.

He had been looking for her ever since, intent on avenging Mitch's death. Now here she was, being handed to him on a silver platter. The only problem was, he could do nothing about it until after the Lazlo Group had all the answers it needed regarding Prince Reginald's murder.

But after that nothing would keep him from giving the Sparrow just what she deserved.

The young woman that they suspected of being the Sparrow—Elizabeth Moore, alias Elizabeth Cavanaugh—ran a restaurant in this modest seaside town. The restaurant, apparently a cover for her real occupation, had become quite well-known for its seafood and Silvershire-inspired cuisine.

He had seen the Help Wanted sign go up late yesterday morning in her restaurant's front window, so it was the perfect time to see about applying for the bartending position.

Pulling his PDA off his belt as he approached the Sparrow's restaurant, he used the walkie-talkie adapter he had built into the unit to cue the Lazlo Group's computer specialist to see if she was picking up the signal from the earpiece he was wearing.

"Mix Master to Red Rover. Come in Red Rover."

A chuckle crackled across the airwaves. "Very command-ery of you, Mix Master. Are you at the location, over?"

"About to go in. Let's get this show on the road."

The sun was warm on her back as she tended the border of flowers in the garden at the front of the restaurant. Wildly spreading nasturtiums lapped over onto the large granite slabs that made up the patio where guests often enjoyed drinks or appetizers while they waited for a table inside.

Elizabeth had rescued the centuries-old slabs from the reconstruction of a dilapidated private wharf on the oppo-site side of town. The gray was somber against the perky yellows and oranges of the nasturtiums, but a perfect foil to the ivy-covered stone building that housed her restaurant and the crisply manicured lawns scattered throughout the grounds.

Carefully she deadheaded older blossoms and picked others for inclusion in one of the seasonal salads she was offering on this week's menu. She was just about finished when she heard a footfall behind her. A man walked through the opening of the low stone wall that separated her property from the main road. A very attractive man.

Slipping the basket holding her garden gatherings onto her arm, she strolled toward him, easing off her gardening gloves as she did so.

"May I help you?" Elizabeth asked as she met him by the path leading to the door of the restaurant. Once she was before him, she realized she had to look up slightly to meet his gaze. He was about half a foot taller than her, with a lean athletic build that accentuated the long lines of his body.

He motioned to her front window with one hand and

replied, "I noticed the sign as I was walking earlier. I'm here to apply for the bartender's position."

She examined him more carefully, from the faded and sinfully tight jeans to his logo T-shirt and black leather jacket. He looked more like a tourist on vacation than someone interested in permanent employment. "I'm sorry. I didn't quite catch your name."

He held out his hand with a brisk, almost military snap. "Aidan Rawlings. Are you the owner?"

With a quick glance at her hand to make sure it wasn't too dirty from her gardening, she shook his hand and said, "Elizabeth Moore. Chief cook and bottle washer. Literally."

He smiled with teeth too white and too perfect for normal humans, apropos with his shaggy and sunstreaked blond hair and eyes so blue, she couldn't believe they weren't contact lenses. His smile broadened as he noticed her perusal of him and that she was still busily shaking his hand.

Yanking her hand away, she wiped it down on the gardening apron she wore, realizing her palm had gotten sweaty from the brief contact. "I'm sorry. You said you were here about the bartender's job."

He nodded and tucked his hands into his jeans pockets. Or maybe it was better to say, tucked the tips of his fingers into those pockets since the jeans were so tight, they didn't really leave a lot of room for anything else besides his long lean legs and…

She stopped herself from proceeding with the perusal.

"Is the job still available?" He rocked back and forth on his heels as he asked, apparently growing uncomfortable, but then again, so was she. Not much of a surprise considering she generally avoided strangers and in particular, men like this one.

Handsome, danger-to-your-common-sense kind of men.

"Do you have experience?" After she asked, she began to

walk toward the door of the restaurant and he followed beside her, keeping his paces small to accommodate her shorter legs.

"I've worked in a number of bars," he replied with a careless shrug.

She supposed that he had, but not as a bartender. There was something about him. Something in the way he moved and in the slight swagger that screamed Bad Boy. She could picture him as either a bouncer, since he had an air that said he could talk care of himself, or an exotic dancer, but not as a bartender.

When she reached the door, she faced him. "I'm sorry Mr.…Rawlings was it?"

"How about you just call me Aidan?" he said with a practiced smile that had probably swept more than one woman off her feet. Aidan, however, was going to get a swift lesson in the art of Just Say No!

"I appreciate you coming by, but the position—"

"Is still available, right?"

She acknowledged his statement with a subtle drop of her head, as if she didn't want to acknowledge it. "Quite frankly, my restaurant isn't the kind of place for a Tom Cruise *Cocktail* redux."

He actually jerked back as if slapped and a stain of color came to his sharply defined cheeks. "Excuse me?"

"I just don't think you're the right type." And he definitely was not used to being turned down by a woman.

Surprise came once more on his face, followed by what she might possibly call admiration, until he carefully schooled his expression.

"And what type are you looking for exactly?" he asked and placed his hands on his hips.

"Someone more…professional. This is a four-star restaurant and my patrons expect—"

"Uptight and pompous? Fair enough." With that, he turned and walked away, but as he did so, she couldn't help but notice just how nice a derriere he had. Not that it would change her mind.

She needed someone who wouldn't cause trouble, and although pleasant to look at, Aidan Rawlings was trouble with a capital T.

**Hidden in the secrets of antiquity,
lies the unimagined truth...**

Introducing

a brand-new line filled with mystery
and suspense, action and adventure,
and a fascinating look into history.
And it all begins with DESTINY.

In a sealed crypt in
France, where the
terrifying legend of
the beast of Gevaudan
begins to unravel,
Annja Creed discovers
a stunning artifact
that will seal her destiny.

*Available every other
month starting
July 2006, wherever
you buy books.*

GRA1

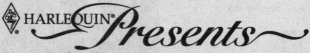

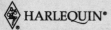

HARLEQUIN®

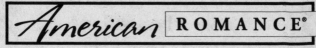

American Beauties

SORORITY SISTERS, FRIENDS FOR LIFE

Michele Dunaway

THE MARRIAGE CAMPAIGN

Campaign fund-raiser Lisa Meyer has worked hard to be her own boss and will let nothing—especially romance—interfere with her success. To Mark Smith, Lisa is the perfect candidate for him to spend his life with. But if she lets herself fall for Mark, will she lose all she's worked for? Or will she have a future that's more than she's ever dreamed of?

On sale August 2006

Also watch for:

THE WEDDING SECRET
On sale December 2006

NINE MONTHS NOTICE
On sale April 2007

Available wherever Harlequin books are sold.

If you enjoyed what you just read,
then we've got an offer you can't resist!

Take 2 bestselling love stories FREE!

Plus get a FREE surprise gift!

Clip this page and mail it to Silhouette Reader Service™

IN U.S.A.
3010 Walden Ave.
P.O. Box 1867
Buffalo, N.Y. 14240-1867

IN CANADA
P.O. Box 609
Fort Erie, Ontario
L2A 5X3

YES! Please send me 2 free Silhouette Intimate Moments® novels and my free surprise gift. After receiving them, if I don't wish to receive anymore, I can return the shipping statement marked cancel. If I don't cancel, I will receive 6 brand-new novels every month, before they're available in stores! In the U.S.A., bill me at the bargain price of $4.24 plus 25¢ shipping and handling per book and applicable sales tax, if any*. In Canada, bill me at the bargain price of $4.99 plus 25¢ shipping and handling per book and applicable taxes**. That's the complete price and a savings of at least 10% off the cover prices—what a great deal! I understand that accepting the 2 free books and gift places me under no obligation ever to buy any books. I can always return a shipment and cancel at any time. Even if I never buy another book from Silhouette, the 2 free books and gift are mine to keep forever.

245 SDN DZ9A
345 SDN DZ9C

Name	(PLEASE PRINT)	
Address	Apt.#	
City	State/Prov.	Zip/Postal Code

Not valid to current Silhouette Intimate Moments® subscribers.

**Want to try two free books from another series?
Call 1-800-873-8635 or visit www.morefreebooks.com.**

* Terms and prices subject to change without notice. Sales tax applicable in N.Y.
** Canadian residents will be charged applicable provincial taxes and GST.
All orders subject to approval. Offer limited to one per household].
® are registered trademarks owned and used by the trademark owner and or its licensee.

INMOM04R   ©2004 Harlequin Enterprises Limited

Silhouette
Desire.

Join Sheri WhiteFeather in The Trueno Brides!

Don't miss the first book in the trilogy:

EXPECTING THUNDER'S BABY

Sheri WhiteFeather

(SD #1742)

Carrie Lipton had given Thunder Trueno her heart. But their marriage fell apart. Years later Thunder was back. A reckless night of passion gave them a second chance for a family, but would their past stand in the way of their future?

On sale August 2006 from Silhouette Desire!

Make sure to read the next installments in this captivating trilogy by Sheri WhiteFeather:

MARRIAGE OF REVENGE,
on sale September 2006

THE MORNING-AFTER PROPOSAL,
on sale October 2006!

*Available wherever books are sold,
including most bookstores, supermarkets,
discount stores and drugstores.*

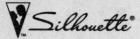

COMING NEXT MONTH

#1427 SOMEBODY'S HERO—Marilyn Pappano
Recently divorced Jayne Miller moves to the small town of Sweetwater, where she plans to revive her career as a romance author…and it doesn't hurt to have a handsome, brooding neighbor for inspiration. Tyler Lewis isn't happy to have neighbors, but no matter how much he refutes his desires, Jayne makes him want what he can't have…not with the secrets in his past.

#1428 MORE THAN A MISSION—Caridad Piñeiro
Capturing the Crown
When undercover agent Aidan Spaulding is asked to investigate the murder of Prince Reginald, he is given the chance to identify the Sparrow—the infamous female assassin who killed his best friend. All signs point to Elizabeth Moore, a local restaurant owner, but as Aidan gets to know the refreshingly kind woman, he realizes there is no way she is the assassin. But if Elizabeth isn't the Sparrow, who is?

#1429 BAPTISM IN FIRE—Elizabeth Sinclair
Two years ago, arson investigator Rachel Sutherland's home went up in flames, followed by her marriage to Detective Luke Sutherland when they were unable to find either their daughter or the fire starter. Now divorced, they must join forces against a serial arsonist—the same one who destroyed their dreams. Could they rebuild in time to find the firebug—and possibly their child?

#1430 DEADLY MEMORIES—Susan Vaughan
Sophie Rinaldi is researching her ancestors in Italy when she overhears plans of a terrorist attack in her host's mansion. Barely escaping death, she turns to U.S. Marshal Jack Thorne for help and finds comfort in his steady gaze. They get swept up in a dangerous attraction, which Jack tries to temper during his investigation. Can Jack keep his vow to capture his enemy without jeopardizing the life of the only woman he will ever love?

SIMCNM0706